Candle Sparks

Adventures and Trials in an Eccentric Alaska Bush Town

Lilly Goodman

Publication Consultants

PO Box 221974 Anchorage, Alaska 99522-1974

ISBN 1-888125-13-6

Library of Congress Catalog Card Number: 97-65868

Candle Sparks

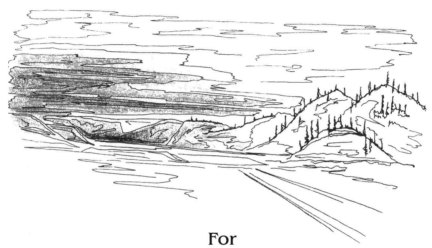

For
all those who care,
and for
all those who thought they didn't.

The front cover, "Goat Hair Ridge," is from an original tapestry woven and designed by Mark A. Vail. The scene depicted on the cover was inspired by the views surrounding Mark's home. Much of the wool used in the tapestry was hand combed, spun, and dyed using natural dyes such as forest lichens. Mark works on his art from his home at Fireweed Mountain, Alaska, where he has lived for 14 years.

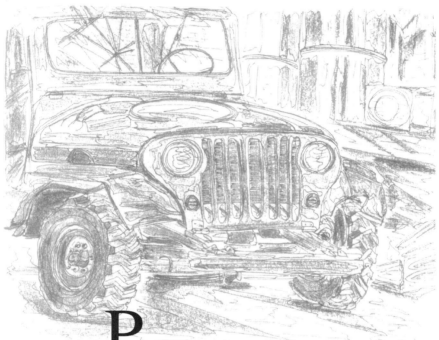

P encil sketches were drawn by German artist, Max Cott, who has lived, on and off, in Alaska since 1993. Cott enjoys capturing his Alaska environment using pencil sketches. Most of the art used in *Candle Sparks* was created during Cott's two-year residence in a 10 foot by 12 foot cabin at Swift Creek, Alaska.

Introduction

I can still clearly remember that fateful day in July of 1992 when my good friend and fellow guide Anne Vick pulled me outside our office to show me the Alaska map on the wall. Without saying anything, she pointed to a small dot in the Seward Peninsula naming the real town of Candle, Alaska. I was down trodden. Candle Sparks was six months in the making. I had already become attached to the characters and their lives. I had already become fond of taking imaginary evening walks along the stony beach of Candle Tarn. There was no way I could simply change the name of my fictional town. I would just have to accept the phenomenon of coincidences and continue on. With all due respect to the real Candle, Alaska (I am sure that it is a lovely place), I have never been there, nor do I know a thing about it.

My Candle, Alaska, is a completely fictional town, as is Hemle, Alaska, and any rivers, mountains, or any other land regions described in this story. Likewise, all the characters are made up, and none of them are meant in any way to resemble any true-life persona. Any similarities are, as with the name of the town itself—a coincidence.

Many of the experiences described in this story such as the moose encounter and the plane wreck however, are based upon my own real adventures or those of my friends. Using my own experiences, I have tried to paint an accurate and vivid portrayal of life in bush Alaska. The story itself is a complete work of fiction although the heartbreaks that are associated with it are not beyond the realm of possibility in real life.

There are also many real people who have made the writing and publishing of this novel attainable. I am very grateful to my publisher, Evan Swensen, who took me under his wing and guided me through the process. My father, Richard Goodman, was instrumental in formatting and presenting my manuscript, and providing endless support. Michael Allwright, Sue Goodman, Paula Goodman, Thea Agnew, and Bill Sherwonit all contributed valuable insight and editorial advice. Both Dave Thorp and Christopher Wright deserve 20 thank yous for their technical help in getting my reams of hand scrawlings onto a computer disk. I am very grateful to Max Cott and Mark Vail for their artwork, and Kris Rueter for her cover idea. Without Ken and Carly Kritchen who gave me their old lap top, and for which I still owe them some hole digging, I would never have completed the editing of my manuscript.

I am eternally grateful to Cynthia Alldredge Shidner who gave me years of support and excellent comments on many different drafts. Finally, I would not have been able to complete this novel without the aid and ideas of my dear friend, Richard Villa, who listened to each chapter word by word as it was created and found solutions for every bout of writers block.

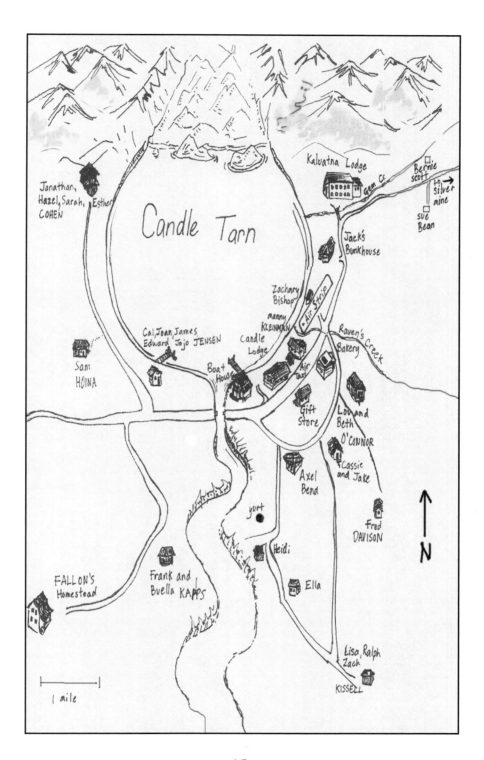

Candle Tarn

Jonathan, Hazel, Sarah, Esther COHEN

Kaluatna Lodge

Glen Cr.

Bernie scott

to silver mine

sue Bean

Jack's Bunkhouse

Zachary Bishop

Air Strip

manny KLEINMAN

Raven's Creek

Cal, Joan, James, Edward, Jojo JENSEN

Candle Lodge

Bakery

Sam HOINA

Boat House

Air Taxi

Gift Store

Lou and Beth O'CONNOR

Axel Bend

Cassie and Jake

yurt

Fred DAVISON

N

FALLON'S Homestead

Frank and Buella KAPPS

Heidi

Ella

Lisa, Ralph Zach

KISSELL

1 mile

15

Chapter 1

At first, I tried to describe Candle, Alaska as a ghost town, but soon realized the only ghouls were in our hearts, and the town itself was alive with warmth and adventure. There were plenty of tumble-down rickety buildings made out of heavy, wide fir timbers, but the buildings certainly were not abandoned. Most of them had a purpose—be it housing a person as rickety and rambly as the building itself, or storing artifacts for the neighbors. I thought, for my letters home, I could call it an old "mining town." But that did not make sense either. Candle did not really have much to do with mining. Any mining had been done way up in the hills, and the miners had lived like moles in tunnels and caverns. Food and hardware had even been brought directly to the mine areas. Candle did, I suppose, develop out of a need for a large number of brothels and bars—due to the fact that there had been a disproportionate number of bored single men with ready cash in the area—especially on holidays. But I could not tell my friends and family I was living in a rundown old red light district. My folks were not religious, but they did have morals. No, it became clear early in the game, way before everything happened, that Candle was not an easy place to describe.

One could always send home pictures of the surroundings. But photos (at least the ones I take) never truly capture nature's charms. Candle sits in a small valley surrounded by the high Ilkita Mountains (pronounced ilKEETah). Blue glaciers drip down from every corner of the mountains, and gather together in one spectacular and beautiful body — the Kaluatna Glacier. All of blue, black, and white, she is both graceful and ruthless as she winds her way down the valley with waters roaring and tinkling in the summer, and as silent as deep secrets in winter. She ends with a crash into a large tarn which is the focal point of Candle. Bluer than a clear sky viewed from high altitude, and usually sporting a few good-sized icebergs in the summer, Candle Tarn enables one to distinguish the eccentrics from the eccentric wannabees by whoever of the old-time residents is crazy enough to strip to his birthday suit in July and get "clean" in the frigid waters. I do not know how clean one gets by merely jumping in, screaming like a chicken, and scrambling out with great speed all blue and purple, for this is all a human being is capable of in waters barely 32°. But I am sure it manages to wash off at least one of the layers of dirt the typical Candle resident might acquire during summer.

In fall, Candle Tarn is a lovely skating rink before its blue visage becomes covered with snow. Cal Jensen joked that when his son James finally hit puberty, the tarn would be the only place James would be able to take Molly (the only girl his age around) out on a date. Cal was ready to build an ice cream parlor by the tarn and wait in it for the occasion.

Of course Cal Jensen is also one of the characters one needs to meet in order to understand Candle. Having witnessed him show his tattoos and plunge into the frigid waters of Candle Tarn one summer, I would list him as one of the town eccentrics. Actually, such a judgement is barely fair, because Cal had a wife and four kids and to be able to keep that many people around, a person must store a tinge of sanity in his soul somewhere. Cal owned a small boat rental service on the south end of the tarn. He had four canoes which he would rent out by the hour to willing tourists with large pocket books. The tourists would venture happily out on the lake, take a few photos, and then, soon enough, paddle madly back toward shore, afraid of either house-sized pieces of drifting ice, or white caps raised by cold winds that blew down the glacier. Tourists would stumble back into Cal's office, made from the splintering remains of an abandoned building, and he would quickly cheer them up with a $4.50 beer or a $3.25 hot chocolate, and show them pictures of the place in 1916 while frightening their wide-eyed children with tales of the giant green monster that lived in the bottom of Candle Tarn.

The town residents were what gave Candle its great flavor. Simply, it was void of wimps. Joan Jensen, Cal's wife, is a prime example of the hearty souls the Candle environment naturally selected. In summers, while Cal stayed at the boathouse frightening innocent youngsters and repairing his endlessly leaky boats, Joan would work in their garden at their home on the other side of the tarn, teach the children, feed the pigs, ward off tourists, unscramble the paper work and bills Cal acquired, and chat with other locals who came to visit. Among them was Sue Bean, who made carvings out of the alder that grew like weeds all over the area and sold them at Lou and Beth O'Connor's gift store in Candle. Originally from Tennessee, Sue Bean had an accent that would charm any tourist, but a fiery nature that somehow kept her beaus taking the mail planes out of town often enough.

There was also Bernie Scott, who occupied a rundown shack way up the mountain on the trail toward the mine and offered tours into the area. Colorful tales of the miners' lives and recent hauntings by prankster ghosts were always a part of Bernie's tours. One could never be certain when the stories were fiction, and when they were fact, but they were always entertaining enough to earn Bernie a few bucks from any tourist who made it that far up the hill.

Then there was Manny Kleinman, who parked his rocking chair in the sun next to the only uninhabited aging building, not counting the ones that were too dangerous to stand near, and played his accordion all day long. He would offer to sell "precious pieces of history," as he called his collection of building artifacts (I called them "trash collected from rotting buildings"), to the same tourists that sucked down Cal Jensen's pricey beer. Usually Manny had enough of his own alcohol on hand also though he did not sell that to tourists. He always kept an "orange juice" glass on one side of him while he played the accordion (the music was actually pretty good if he was not smashed), and on the other side, a double barreled shotgun all loaded and ready to go.

Tourists would approach Manny rather timidly, especially if they had heard Bernie's stories about how Manny occasionally liked to load up on Scotch and then sit back in his rocking chair and shoot off his own fireworks, or should I say firearms-works. Actually, I think Manny has used "Ol' Griz" as he called his trusty shotgun, in place of the more colorful works maybe once or twice, but he was more likely tanked on Jim Beam (not Scotch), and would never, never hit a passing tourist. Even so, mothers usually kept a close grip on their toddler's hands when approaching the old man. Fellow sourdoughs from other parts of the state would of course never be frightened away by such tales. Rather, they would accept a few glasses of Manny's "orange juice," pull up an old dynamite box, and sit down and chat with him for a few hours. Manny was known to even bring out his special Jack Daniel's if his visitor pulled out a harmonica or a banjo.

There are a couple of stories explaining how Candle got its name — all of which I think are pretty poor excuses to change the perfectly beautiful native name: Kaluatna. But, as white prospectors had to put their own names to everything — so be it. Some say Candle is so named because the tarn it surrounds is shaped like a candle. Well, I think you would need a pretty good imagination to see that vision. Maybe they are talking about the flame of a candle — in which case I can sort of understand, for the tarn is a bit pointed on the South end, and maybe in the prospecting days, the point was even more prominent.

The story Bernie favors is the classic mining district type of legend. One dark fall night, two prospectors made camp in the high hills above the tarn. One man, struggling in the milky darkness to see his bed roll, finally lit a candle. And what luck! The flickering flame was enough to create a shimmering reflection on one of the nearby outcrops. Excited, the prospector then woke up his partner crying: "The candle light! The candle light! Look at the reflection!" And the shimmering light was shining from a hunk of silver. So of course, grateful for the illuminating candle, the prospectors pull out a tobacco can and appropriate paper right then and there in the customary fashion, and stake out the claim. A pretty hokey story if you ask me. But tourists like the silver story, and so it is the one everybody tells.

Personally, I think some Joseph E. Candle was the first to build a brothel in the area and was arrogant enough to name the town after himself. Then, when his brother ran back to Pennsylvania and told Joseph's parents that old Joe's business was not the quaint old hotel he said it was, Joe got embarrassed, moved to Homer, and refuted any connection with the town.

Candle, and the surrounding area, had a population of about 25 to 35 people. But about one-quarter of the residents fished commercially in another part of the state during summer and just enjoyed Candle's quiet and moonlit winters. Another quarter figured those moonlit winters and their -50° temperatures should be exchanged for a sun-intense respite in Arizona, Costa Rica, or elsewhere, and resided in Candle only during the fireweed rich and mild summers of Candle. The rest of the population (they knew the true secrets of Candle) persevered all year. Of course the heliophiles who came only for summer had to deal with tougher logistics in terms of getting into Candle. The warmth of summer would cause enough glacial melting to turn the trickle of water leaking from Candle Tarn into a large blue-green river separating the main part of town from the road's end on the west side. In the mining days, a bridge across the Kaluatna river eliminated such access difficulties, but three or four had already washed out, and nobody felt like building a new one.

Year-round residents especially, were happy to support the institution of Candle's "best filtering mechanism" as they called Cal's ferry. He had built a flat, barge-like raft on which tourists would bravely clamber sporting bright orange life vests. The ferry was attached to a thin cable running across the river. Although the two-minute ride required no fuel or motor because it used the current of the river to cross, Cal still squeezed $1 out of every tourist who stepped aboard. If you were a local, and on his good side, he would tell his hired help, in charge of passing out life jackets and explaining operation of the vessel, to permit free passage. Otherwise, you could threaten to build your own ferry, or fly over and land on the airstrip in East Candle.

In addition to the access limitations brought on by the river crossing, the road itself is a pretty darned good filtering mechanism. It is 78 miles of unimproved dirt: dusty in summer, and treacherous in winter and spring because of runoff which freezes and refreezes, eventually piling up as horrendous road glaciers. The road's beginning—the town of Hemle (pronounced HEMlee)—is not altogether encouraging either. The most Hemle has to offer a passing tourist is an expensive gas station whose owner, Hal, might rent you an extra can of gas too if you are real nervous about the long road. There is a little cafe where you can grab a greasy buritto while Hal fixes your suspension, which self destructed on your way out, and a public phone. The most popular of the three was the phone. Candle had no phone service. The only communications were between residents via the CB radio which everyone owned, or from the outside world via the Bush Messenger on the public radio station. But besides that, communications to the rest of the world remained dependent on the U.S. Postal Service, or upon a road trip to Hemle. Thus Candle residents were sometimes known to jump in their junker trucks and tear down the washboard ridden road for 78 miles just to get their dimes in that phone and talk to a lost sweetie, the bank seizing their accounts, their prospective employer in Florida, or occasionally — a 900 number.

Not everybody needed to stop at Hemle however, for a clanky disguised school bus run by the state parks, or the Department of Natural Resources or something like that would clank down the road from Fairbanks four times a week in the summer. Patrons, drugged on Dramamine, were rewarded for their gas saving adventure — free rides on Cal's ferry.

My first journey to Candle did not allow me any of these interesting tours, for it was early fall when my friend in Cantwell told me that Ernie Kitskell was looking for someone to take over his dogs and kennel business. I did not know Ernie, who owned a team of seven beautiful Alaska huskies, and also ran a kennel in Candle on which many residents relied during the fall and summers. Apparently Ernie had suddenly been overcome with an intense desire to change his lifestyle and travel to Indonesia. (It probably had something to do with being 44 and divorced). Ernie was willing to draw up a contract that allowed me to take over his business and his dogs for nothing, except the promise that if he did not return in three years, I would buy the dogs and the business. It sounded like a good deal to me. Time was due for me to get out of the Cantwell Cafe, and anyway, the arrangement allowed me to stay in Ernie's cabin. What was there to lose? True, I had never actually been to Candle, but I had heard many stories about the area's great beauty. And, friends told me I would fit in perfectly with the crazy people who lived there.

It did not take me too long to pack all of my toys in either boxes to mail, or in my trusty old pack held together with more duct tape than thread, and get on the road with my just slightly crooked but mostly perfect thumb. I have used it enough to enable me to pass on a few hitchhiking tips, and one of them is that if you are a female, getting rides around Alaska is as easy as counting to five. But catching a lift to Candle in the fall is another story. When autumn winds start blowing orange and yellow leaves over the red bearberries and red fireweed stalks, there are about as many cars heading to Candle as there are polar bears in Phoenix. I got to know that beginning stretch of the Candle road well. The aspen and poplar trees, splattering the road with their golden gifts, made a canopy of white and yellow arches. In the lowering angle of the sun, they cast long striped shadows across the road, and water droplets on the leaves gleamed like small diamonds. A fine introduction to my destination. Yet— it was not my destination, and at the rate I was going (about 2.8 miles per hour) it was going to take me a long time to get there.

Chapter 2

After I had experienced a cold, wet night on the side of the road, and about 25 miles of walking, a not-too-rusted and overloaded Ford pickup truck came into view. My heart started to get excited: maybe I was going to make it to Candle this month after all! I quickly checked up and down my 69 inches. My tawny brown hair dripping one-third of the way down my back was still held mostly together in a single braid that I had made three and a half days before; my army surplus pants only partially covered my long, lanky legs: they were ripped in odd places; and my holey boots and lower legs were covered with the thick mud I encountered when I had become bored with the road and tried to take a short cut through a swamp. The truck slowed down, almost stopped, and then passed me. All sorts of horrible names spilled from my brain. I had not realized how desperate I had become. Then the vehicle stopped again and waited.

"You son of a mutt" I muttered, and ran to the truck with my too heavy pack and my guitar slapping against my legs. The driver had the door open when I arrived, and I could hear him laughing. For one with an odd sense of humor, he was not a bad looking guy — had curly dark hair which clung to his head just slightly teasing the nape of his neck, a light mustache, and about six days stubble on the chin and side burns. He could have been anywhere from 32 to 44 years old, I thought. I threw my pack in the back of the truck and started to kick the mud off my boots.

"You get mud on my carpet and you're paying for it" he said seriously. I must have given him a look of dismay, or disgust, or something, because then he started laughing again, and said, "Hop on in, I've got glacier silt and sunflower seeds all over the floor."

I pushed aside a clutter of cassette tapes and did not even have my door shut before he started cruising again. I thought maybe he would say something like, "Well gee, that's a long way you've walked," or, "You're quite a trooper;" but nothing of the sort.

Instead, "Where ya going?"

I thought, "Now isn't that fairly obvious?" but answered, "Candle. I'm taking over Ernie Kitskell's dog kennel while he's gone."

"Oh, so you'll be shovelling shit eh?"

"Well yeah, but running them too" I said slightly annoyed.

"Oh, so you've mushed before huh?"

"Yeah." Pause. "For about four winters." This conversation was not going so well, and he had not even told me who he was yet. He was quiet for a while, staring blankly at the autumn speckled road. Then he smiled and looked at me.

"Say, do you know why men in Candle don't eat mosquitoes?"

"Why?" I asked, not really wanting to hear the answer.

"Because, its too hard to spread their tiny little legs apart! HAH!" He laughed again boisterously, and stared once again at the road. I was not quite sure how to respond. Was he trying really hard to make me feel uncomfortable, or was he just socially a moron? Maybe a new direction to the conversation was needed.

I asked, "So, I suppose you live in Candle?"

"I run Candle Lodge, and the Candle Flame Bar."

"My name is Heidi."

"Herbert Kramer." He took a hand off the wheel and shook my hand and then asked imploringly, "Would you name your child Herbert?" I had no idea how to answer this possibly incriminating question, but there was no need to, for then he added, "You can call me Herbie. It goes real well with Bernie and Ernie" and then he started laughing again.

"Who is Bernie?" I asked.

"Oh, another crazy guy who lives in Candle" he responded. "So, you've never been there before? To Candle?"

"Nope." My restless night and long walk, not to mention the previous day of hitchhiking was taking effect, and all I wanted to do was shut my eyes.

"Oh! You're going to live somewhere you've never been to before eh? I like that. You gotta boyfriend out there or something?"

I was starting to wonder if all Candle residents were like this guy, and if so, should I try to become good friends with him?

"No, uh uh" I answered, thinking to myself about the situation I had left behind and wondering about the new one for which I was heading.

"Ah well," Herbert smiled wryly, "You will before real soon. At least you'll have people trying."

"Great," I answered, "Well at least I'll have a couple of dog teams to help me ward them off."

Herbert laughed. "You'll like Candle. You'll probably learn a lot too."

"I'm sure I will" I answered.

The speckled road wound its way through the white barked trees in the dimming light, and occasionally I could see blue mountains turning pink as the sun slowly set. I learned from Herb that he and his wife Louise had moved to Candle from Kodiak in 1979. They bought the lodge on a whim. When they arrived in Candle, broke and frozen, on a late November evening, they found smoke coming from the lodge's chimney, and the windows glowing yellow with warm light. Bernie Scott was inside making hot chocolate and hoping to meet their alleged 18-year-old daughter they had been rumored to have.

I strained my eyes to stay open as my companion entertained me with stories of how he and Bernie had explored the old mine shafts and made discoveries such as skeletons still sitting at old tables, or how he and Bernie had flown their kites from the top of Coco's Mountain and the Coast Guard flying around that day had seen it and thought it was an unlicensed plane and reported it to the FAA. I tried staying awake by propping my elbow on the arm rest and positioning my right hand in such a manner that it was prying my eyelids open, and occasionally stuck a "hmm" or an "ahh" in what I hoped were appropriate spots in the conversation. At last the rear wheels made it over the final washboard and Herbert's truck splashed through the muddy waters that still managed to trickle out of Candle Tarn during the frosty temperatures of fall. It seemed like he drove around in a few circles, and finally stopped. It was too dark to see much but a medium-sized building, but propane lights shining through the windows made it look cheery in the darkness.

"Come on in" said Herbert. "We'll unload this mess in the morning. Maybe Louise will get you a cup-o-something." He knocked mud off of his boots and pushed open the door. "Yoo hoo Louise!"

I found myself standing in a large room—elegant with a touch of rusticity. My muddy boots were about to pollute an oriental-type rug warming a wood floor—the kind that creaks friendly when you walk on it and smells of fond memories of grandparent houses. My reddening eyes wandered from an antique wooden table decorated with cloth doilies to a cedar desk, to a silver watch mounted on the wall, and finally rested on two very comfy looking sofas facing each other.

"Whoo ooh, Herb! We're in the kitchen!"

Herbert led me past the couches to my dismay, and into the kitchen in the back. A head of red fire shot out from behind a large mixing machine. It belonged to a grinning face steaming with energy.

"Oh, Hi Sue Bean" said Herbert. "A bit of late night mixing?"

"Well ya know" she sparked back, "Louise was so nice to let me use your kitchen—I just need to get these cranberries out of my hair."

No doubt, I thought taking in her locks of berry red which casually unfolded themselves to her shoulders. I smiled and made some effort to look as alive as she.

"Hi, I'm Heidi Ravison. I'm taking over the dog kennel for a bit."

"Oh," she continued to grin. "You'll be exercising the poop scoop muscles huh?"

I wondered: did everybody in this town have merely dog doo on their minds? A thin woman with a long dark braid which wagged as she walked came out of a back room.

"Hi Herb" she said. "I was wondering when you'd get back. You didn't send me any radio messages."

Herb gave her a peck on the cheek. "Things got too exciting Lou. I picked up a vagrant off the streets."

Louise gave him a scowl and looking at me said, "I'm sorry your first impression of Candle had to involve Herb." She proceeded to warm up some left over chili for me and Herb, and provide me with the miracle drug of caffeine which she suggested might help when she noticed me using the doorway as a support.

Two cups of coffee, a bowl of very spicy chili, and a few tastes of Sue Bean's cranberry jelly later, I found myself able to answer an overwhelming barrage of questions from both Sue Bean and Louise: How long had I lived in Alaska? Did I have a boyfriend? Did I know how to shoot a gun? Had I ever tried lynx meat? Was I into baking, and if so, did I need some eggs? Was Ernie paying me and did I think he was coming back? Meanwhile Herb planted himself with his chili deep within the billowy sofas that had earlier looked so utterly inviting, and sat quiet—his red eyes staring blankly at the oil lamp on the cedar desk. After I had sufficiently answered their onslaught of questions, had learned to be wary of the Candle bachelors, been blessed with a jar of Sue Bean's jam, and invited up to her place anytime for a cup of yarrow tea or some cranberry brandy, Herbert stood up from his trance, yawned, and stated that perhaps a little shut-eye was in order.

"Well Herb" Louise started, "Maybe you can help Heidi over to Ernie's with her backpack?"

"She don't need any help" he said. "You should've seen her running down the road with that thing."

"Yes, thanks" I said. The chili was starting to brew in my stomach, and a walk by myself sounded like a good idea. "I'm fine. I've barely any luggage."

"See?" Herbert yawned again. "She's a liberated gal."

"Well," said Louise, starting to catch the yawns herself, "You know where you're going?"

"I think so." Now Sue Bean and I were yawning too. We all had tears running from our eyes as if our meeting warranted a sad departure.

"Walk down this road, turn right at the yurt, and follow the sound of a lot of dogs barking, right?"

"Sounds about right" said Sue Bean, "And follow your nose too." We all four interrupted our yawns with a laugh, but as I walked up the narrow road, I hoped the smell of dog doo was not going to be that strong.

The night, free of moonlight was dark, but the sky clear, and as the chili in my stomach rumbled, I searched for the rumbling of Draco the dragon among the stars. I stared at Delphinius the dolphin, and thought about how comforting it was to always have friends in the sky. Delphinius winked at me, and my eyes searched for Saturn. This peacefulness was fantastically calming, and so far, I had only been met with genuine warmth from the folks there.

I walked further up the road looking for the yurt, and the soft lapping of the waters of Candle Tarn became fainter. Ah hah, a solitary frame of a round structure was my signal to turn right. In the dim light of my fading head lamp, I could see that this road was merely a path. Poplars and alder had grown over it only recently. And sure enough, no mistaking where the kennel was: howls and barks greeted me before I was 100 yards from the cabin.

"Hi doggies!" I would introduce myself in the morning. Right then, I deserved a good rest.

The cabin had a good heavy door, I was happy to note, as I tugged it open—no need to lock anything around Candle. I fumbled for matches in my pack, and found a dirty kerosene lamp to light up my new home. Not bad—in fact, mighty cozy for a bachelor's cabin. It was a log structure about 12 feet by 16 feet, with a high roof leaving room for a comfortable sleeping loft. A propane burner sat on a counter, and a sink next to it with a slop bucket underneath. In the corner stood a small, but solid looking wood stove. The temperature inside the cabin was not more than 40°, but I would deal with firewood in the morning. As it was, it was all I could do to climb up the ladder to the loft. I curled up in my sleeping bag. I hoped I had made the right decision by dropping everything and coming out to Candle. No one said it was going to be easy.

I had not expected the grand view that greeted me in the morning through the little bedside window. The terrace bench on which Ernie's house sat, gave a wonderful vantage point. Through the poplars, dropping their golden leaves by the minute, I could see the brilliant blue water of Candle Tarn. Mountains were everywhere— danger appearing to loom out of their every corners in the form of blue broken ice. I expected Candle to be beautiful—but had not anticipated the beauty to be so exciting! I could not wait to go out and explore. But first things first—it was freezing in the cabin. I threw on my clothes and went outside to see if Ernie had left me any wood. The air felt crisp and super clear, typical only of autumn. The new frost on the weeds and grass caught the gleam of the sun's low angle, so that the ground shimmered like precious gems. Before I had a chance to look for the woodshed, I was stirred back into reality by sudden yelps, howls, and barks. Oh yes, I was here to run a dog kennel. I went into the dog yard as all the dogs jumped up and down yanking on their chains, offering me their paws as I walked by petting each one. A woman named Ella was supposedly taking care of them until I arrived. Noticing that a few days of dog doo had already accumulated in the yard, I figured I had better go and tell her that she was relieved of dog care pronto. Not caring to watch the dogs "recycle" their last night's dinner any further, I returned to the cabin to warm it up.

Having already become accustomed to the sight of old refrigerators and 55-gallon drums occupying the yards of most Alaskans, I thought nothing of it when I walked by several 55-gallon drums, a couple of trucks that looked as if they had not moved too far from their present position during the past 15 years, and an old porcelain toilet in Ella's yard. There was smoke coming from the chimney, but I did not see anyone, so I gave my best dog whistle.

"Whoop—down here!"

I looked down following the direction of the voice, and saw a small person standing in a very deep and rocky hole. She had a thin face with a sharp small nose, brown hair which hung completely straight down a little past her shoulders, and a wonderful smile.

"It's good you came by." She wiped some dirt off of her nose. "I wasn't quite sure how to get out of this hole, so I figured I'd just keep on digging until either someone rescued me, or I got to China. Here, help me out."

I braced myself and reached down with my hand. She yanked on it and somehow used the rocks in the dirt for her feet or something— I'm not quite sure what she did, but she was out fast and on her feet— contrary to me who had somehow gotten my legs all tangled up and my pants pretty dirty.

"An outhouse hole, I presume?" I asked managing to get back to my feet and wiping the dirt off the seat off my pants.

"Yeah." She said happily. "Happiness is a brand new privy at the beginning of winter."

"Ah hah!" I said, getting an idea, "So that's what you're doing with the toilet."

31

"Well actually, I thought I'd turn that into a barbecue. Wouldn't that be neat? I could put the grill between the bowl and the seat. I could call it John's Bowl and Grill!" She looked at the confused twitch of my mouth and started laughing.

"Nah, that's a mean thing to do to a newcomer. Yeah, I scrounged this toilet up by the silver mine. I'm going to be the only resident of Candle besides the lodge who has a real porcelain toilet."

I laughed. So far, there was nothing plain about anybody I met in Candle. "Well I'm Heidi" I said, and thinking I would beat someone to the punch line this time added, "I'll be shoveling poop for old Ernie over there."

Her dark eyebrows gathered into a frown. "Don't sell yourself short" she said. "Running the kennel is a tough job, and I'm sure Ernie wouldn't give his dogs to anybody who didn't have years of mushing experience. Come on in, let's have some coffee."

I followed her past the toilet into her small house. I liked this woman.

"I heard the dogs barking at you last night," she said reaching in her cupboard for her hand coffee grinder, "so I didn't bother to water the dogs this morning and—" she stopped and laughed at me.

Overwhelmed, I was staring at all her gear. She had ropes, pulleys, snow pickets, ice screws, and a multitude of climbing equipment strewn all over her house. I had never seen so much gear in such a small place before.

"Sorry for the mess." She began clearing some of it out of the way. "I was just trying to figure out what gear I needed to bring for this course I'm teaching at the Matanuska Glacier next week." She dug out a business card for me. Turns out, she was not only an expert out house hole digger, but a professional alpine guide as well.

"Yeah," she said pouring the water through the coffee filter, "Candle is a great base camp. I'm not around that much though. I try to stay pretty busy with trips."

We drank her coffee and ate smoked fish. I felt wonderfully comfortable talking to her. I did not know her very well, but had a heck of a lot of respect for her already. After coffee, she grabbed her chainsaw in case Ernie did not have a working one for me to use, and we walked back over to the dogs to get acquainted with the friendly canines. There was Popik the lead dog, Willow, Tuska, Larkspur, Nali, Kahtna, and Crocodile. Fortunately their names were already written on their harnesses.

I could tell that the dogs were dying to run. The summer had been long and boring for them, and it was about cold enough now to do some training runs with a wagon or some sort of non-motorized contraption. We watered the dogs, watched them tip over their bowls with a "clang!" then a whimper, gave them more water, and then Ella left me to shovel poop and cut wood while she went to finish her new privy.

Ernie had left quite a few spruce logs for me to buck up, and I saw that there was a lot of dead standing willow around the house as well. Then I figured after there was enough snow on the ground, I would be able to take the dogs to help me haul more wood from elsewhere. I had my earplugs in, and was so intent on sawing up the whole pile of wood that I did not even notice the three-wheeler pull up until it was stopped right in front of me. I pulled my ear plugs out, and looked up at a little man wearing an orange wool cap pulled tight over his ears and a brown down jacket so patched with duct tape I figured it had seen better days. His cheeks and lips were rosy and opened up in a brilliant happy beam.

"It's nice to see a woman who knows how to run a chainsaw" he said.

Knowing that the latter part of his statement had been merely auxiliary, I ignored it and responded, "Yeah well, just wait, soon they'll be taking over the town."

"Er," he paused, "the females? Or the chain-saws?" I was pleased to have confused him.

"Both, rather" I responded.

"Well now," he said, "sounds like you've already been in Candle too long. I'm glad I didn't take even longer to introduce myself. I'm Bernie Scott — expert on Candle silver history."

"I appreciate your promptness" I answered. "I'm Heidi Ravison, and I've already heard famous stories about you."

"Hopefully not in books" he said.

"Oh no," I laughed, "only in the visitors guides."

"Well gee," he looked really serious, "seeing as how you're a newcomer to these parts, and seem intent to stay, you ought to have a little tour of the mine area."

I smiled, seeing right through this single bachelor's attempt to pretend that he was not trying to ask me out on a date. But I agreed anyway to have him pick me up in the morning and bring me back to his house for breakfast and a tour of the silver mine. Bernie was delighted with my pledge. His cheeks rounded out and gleamed under the orange hat. Even his three-wheeler seemed to hop with spunk as he sped away—most likely to the lodge to report his success to Herbert.

With the dust of Bernie's happy vehicle lingering in the air, I returned to my task of making my new home habitable. One can never underestimate the time consumption of basic survival. By the time I had chopped and split wood, rigged up a system for hauling water, which involved a skateboard and a cheap plastic sled, hauled enough water for me and the dogs, fed the dogs, and cleaned the dog yard, the sun was already gone and casting a pink alpenglow on the eastern mountains. A crescent moon rested in the sunset. I walked down to the beach of the tarn and listened to the waters gently lick the shore as I watched the sliver of moon.

My day with Bernie proved to be an entertaining initiation into Candle. He was very prompt picking me up with his fire red three-wheeler. Bernie's house which was by the silver mine, was actually quite far away. The steep road which led to the mine, was almost one-third of the way around the tarn from my house — about five miles. On the way, Bernie showed me the turn off to Kaluatna Lodge which was boarded up at the time, but according to Bernie kept the hills hopping with tourists in the summer. It was smaller than Candle Lodge, but "gives Herb and Louise a run for their money" as Bernie put it. He also pointed out Jack's Bunkhouse close to the Kaluatna Lodge which offered tourists a cheaper lodging option.

The road was very bumpy, and I did not want to give Bernie the satisfaction of having to clasp my arms around him to keep from falling off the three wheeler, so I contorted my back in odd positions, grasping onto the luggage rack behind the seat. When we finally arrived, he actually had a wonderful breakfast waiting of whole-wheat waffles with some of Sue Bean's jam on top.

During breakfast, and our tour, which I am pretty sure was not his average since he took me down some scary mine shafts, and our excursion back down the hill, I learned a lot about Bernie and his cohort Herbert, and just about everything else there was to know about Candle. There was more opportunity to talk than I had anticipated because on our way down, the 3-wheeler got a flat tire. Bernie assured me that the mishap was not a ploy to get me to stay the night, although he did offer to have me stay for dinner. I refused this offer having the excuse of the dogs to feed. But I did accompany him back up to his house and helped him scrounge around the house for the right tools, while he muttered about how Herbert had kept his 5/8 inch socket for six months. We then rolled the new tire down the hill, a very inefficient method, since the tire kept rolling out of control causing us to run madly down the trail and smash through thick alder to rescue it, and put on the new tire without proper tools. Between swearing, and apologizing to me for swearing, he assured me that this was not his normal everyday activity and that these tires were brand new and should have lasted longer and if he had the right tools bla, bla, bla.

While we walked up and down the hill, he told me his greatest desire: a wife; his greatest fear: developers in Candle; and his second-most great fear: environmentalists. It all beat me, but it was an enjoyable day, not to mention informative in a strange kind of way, and gave me a lot to laugh about with Ella that night over tea.

On Tuesday morning I went with Ella to mail. Going "to mail" meant going to the Candle airstrip in time to meet the bush plane arriving once a week from Cantwell with the town's mail—quite an event to anticipate. Within Alaska, postage for big packages is inexpensive. A 20-pound box costs only a couple of bucks, so I was able to mail most of my belongings and groceries.

I prayed that my groceries would arrive along with the dog food I had ordered, and pulled along my skateboard contraption for hauling them home. I enjoyed the walk to the airstrip with Ella, splashing though the leafy puddles on the road.

She told me about her own introduction to Candle in 1977. She was 23, and sick of her parents asking her when she was going to get her life together. So she pulled the bandannas and beads from her head, and left Missouri to find a couple of boyfriends who were working on the pipeline. On her way north however, she got side tracked by a guy she met on the ferry and he convinced her to go to Candle with him. She fell in love with Candle immediately, but not with the guy (much to his chagrin). He eventually left, but she stayed.

I was thankful to have someone I knew with me when we got to Zachary's house, because there were more people than I expected there. There is nothing more intimidating than walking into a big group of people where everyone knows each other very well.

I should digress a little and explain that Zachary Bishop was the postmaster of Candle. He only acquired the title I think because of the convenient location of this house. That is, his house, which was a period Candle home from circa 1927, resided practically on the airstrip. I am almost positive that Zach created the honorable position himself—having had the chutzpah to write the U.S. Post Office and suggest that Candle needed a postmaster. The Government not only bought the idea, they even agreed to pay him!

Actually, Zach's duties encompassed more than you would think. Zach would be the wonderful someone who would return the piles of mail that came for long gone summer seasonals: bills, letters, and jury duty summons that would have otherwise become buried and forgotten beneath piles of slippery catalogues. He also ordered stamps from the postmaster in Cantwell, and enjoyed the great responsibility of selling stamps and sometimes even envelopes! In his spare time, Zach built rows of mail boxes in his front room. Mail was an important event—a weekly social gathering. And Zach's house was very much appreciated as a warm and mosquito free respite in which to gather. People would bring thermoses of tea, or coffee and whisky, or some sort of treat, and hang out and chat and wait for the mail plane to arrive with mail to be sorted into the neat rows of boxes by Zach, and a few volunteers.

When we arrived upon this friendly scene, the first person I met was sitting on the front porch energetically wagging his tail. Rather, he seemed like a person the way he smiled and offered me his paw as I approached, but he really was a dog—a stocky husky type, mostly brown but for a black tail, a black splotch near his rump, and a black mask about the eyes. Around his neck was tied a plastic orange juice bottle filled with something that was clearly not orange juice.

"Aw, poor thing," I said noting his unconventional collar.

"He loves it" said Ella. "Come on, let's meet everybody. Zach can tell you more about Uncle Hickory."

Reluctant to leave the fine fellow without becoming more acquainted, I followed Ella into the house and was immediately surprised by the crowd inside. Some were sitting on chairs, others just standing around and waving their arms. The women formed their own circle segregated from the men, and I found myself automatically heading straight toward it.

Sue Bean grinned when she saw me. "You get acquainted with those dogs okay?"

"Yes, they put me right to work." Louise stepped close to me, put her hand on my arm and looked earnestly into my face.

"Did Ernie leave you with enough supplies over there?"

"Oh yes, I'm getting everything all together."

"You had firewood to get started?"

"Yeah, it was great. He left me a big pile of logs."

"Well good, and you know if you need anything just holler."

"Yeah it must be funny moving into a bachelor's home," added a woman with straight blonde hair who introduced herself as Lisa Kissell.

"Yeah, did he have any spoons?"

"What. Bachelors don't use spoons?"

"They never seem to have very much of any kind of kitchenware on hand."

"Or some have all spoons and no forks."

While Louise, Lisa, Sue Bean, and another woman named Beth O'Connor discussed spoons, I looked over at the other action in the room. Bernie was engrossed in conversation with Herbert about 5/8 inch sockets, and did not appear to see me. There were quite a few little people there too—running in and out the door, and always stopping to pat the dog on the porch. Three of the kids, James, JoJo, and Edward, belonged to the big smiling guy wearing red suspenders—Cal Jensen. The whole crowd appeared relaxed and happy, and had a lot to chat about as if they had not seen each other in months. Of course everybody was curious to know who I was, and was I genuinely prepared for a long dark and cold winter?

What I was most interested in, was the brown husky I had met on my way in. Ella told me he belonged to the postmaster and host, Zachary. So I introduced myself to the man with a big brown beard relaxing in a rocking chair, and holding a cup of coffee. He smiled and his eyes twinkled when I asked him about his buddy on the porch— apparently a favorite subject.

Uncle Hickory was a retired lead dog who had saved Zachary's life once by dragging him out of Raven's Creek after a bad ski accident had dislocated his hip. Unable to move, Zach would have probably let the waters of Raven's Creek freeze his leg off if Hickory had not dragged Zachary out, and then barked loud for so long that Lou O'Connor finally came down to see what was going on and found Zachary looking mighty pale. After that, Zach as a joke, fitted Hickory up with the orange juice bottle filled with Yukon Jack in the manner of a St. Bernard. Hickory appeared to really like it, so the bottle stayed there. Just at first meeting, I could tell that Uncle Hickory was a favorite of the whole town. He was the town sheriff, the paramedic, and a watch dog all in one.

My groceries did not arrive that mail day, but I did receive a few sacks of dog food which I supposed would come in handy if I became really hungry. I also found I was quite ready for the peaceful walk home. All the introductions had been exhausting even though everybody had been very friendly. Or at least very curious about a new female in town. Anyway, it was a good mail day, and I learned for the next time, that I should not refuse rides offered to me if I have a few hundred pounds of dog food to carry home.

Chapter 3

The days progressed very fast, and Candle started to grow on me. I realized that there is nothing that makes a place more beautiful than to be able to call it home. I began to learn Candle's secrets—the hidden trails, the funny stories. And I came to learn the beauty of Alaska hospitality. I never once went to visit somebody where they did not welcome me with completely open arms into their house. A pot of hot water sat on every person's stove ready to pour tea as soon as a visitor walked in the door. I always left a friend's home with a tummy full of cookies, or fish, or whatever goodies they ran to their secret stashes to pull out when a visitor showed up, and a happy warmth that would linger about my heart for hours. I had my share of visitors too, and I tried to learn from the good examples set by my friendly neighbors. I ordered a selection of tasty teas to offer people that walked in, and always tried to keep a few clean mugs on hand. Unfortunately, I had not lived in Candle long enough to develop a secret stash of goodies, and I always felt just a bit lacking in that respect. But to make up for it, I tried to always make twice as much dinner as I needed in case someone showed up—the Elijah phenomenon I called it.

I have always tried to hold onto that lesson I learned. When I went back to school and lived in a city, I continued to welcome visitors in the same manner. It lacked that "bushy" warmth though, because everybody including me was really too busy to sit around and chat over tea, and in a place where thousands of people entered a person's life each day, chatting with a neighbor did not have the same importance. But even so, visitors were surprised by my welcome ways, and it made me feel happy as well.

By mid-November, only a thin blanket of snow had covered the frozen ground and the tall *Dryas* plants were still able to stick their fuzzy seed heads through the snow covered rocks on the beach. The sun would catch their tufts of hair and these hearty plants would shimmer like silver feathers. That sun was disappearing fast, but on the beach, its rays would kiss my bare cheeks and caress me with a soft warmth. I loved to stand on the beach and watch the sun poke through the gaps in the mountains and shine on the freezing tarn. I loved the peace—broken only occasionally by a raven's cry.

Deciding not to wait for the tardy snow to cover the trails, I dragged a beat up old motor bike out of Ernie's little shop and rigged the dogs up to it in place of a sled. Like most vehicles in Candle, it had no paint, and very little metal too for that matter. It only had one and a half handlebars, and the rims looked pretty nasty. I did not even bother to check out the engine because I did not need it. When I think of it though, I am sure it would have run with a little encouragement—that was the nature of Candle's vehicles. But already I had seven good working motors jumping out of their skulls to run anyway.

I hated to see the dogs so out of shape and desperate to run. I made a silent promise that the following summer I would get them off the chain as much as possible. Popik was my leader. I hooked him up to my "sled" first, and while he waited for me to hook up the rest of the team, he barked and barked: "Let's go! Let's go!" Each dog leaped and barked with intense excitement. Some, wiggling with frenzy, were even too excited to let me put on their harness. I had to hold them between my legs as I threw the harness over their heads. Dog teams are hooked up two by two. With Popik leading in front, the two dogs behind him were "swing." It helps if the swing dogs have somewhat of a brain as well since they are directly behind the lead initiating turns and such.

The rear dogs are called "wheel dogs." I like to put my biggest dogs back there next to me. The rest of the dogs in between are "team" dogs. They just have to pull and pay attention to the leader. Finally, and not without great effort, I got the last dogs, Crocodile (I was certain I did not care to hear the origin of that name) and Tuska hooked up, and we were off like lightning from a cloud. Even out of shape as they were, the dogs were strong and this mushing season was destined to be a lot of fun. We rounded the turn around the yurt with few problems even though trying to steer the motor bike was very different from trying to steer a dog sled. I decided the day was a good opportunity to explore new territory and had Popik lead us across the frozen mud below Candle Tarn and to the other side.

The air was very calm, and the tarn was frozen on its edges, but the middle was still liquid. The waters swirled a marbly blue as they emitted subtle puffs of steam. We traveled out the Hemle Road and took a right—known as "GEE" to Popik—and on to the narrow road heading around the west side of the tarn. I watched the icy mountains as we glided by, and searched for straggler ducks on the water.

All of a sudden, the dogs caught wind of something—maybe a rabbit or a moose I thought—and took off at top speed. My stylish vehicle threatened to spontaneously combust. I hung on, and enjoyed the speed, knowing my dogs would eventually tire and slow down again. The sound of the barking of many dogs clued me in as to why I had gotten such a boost up the road, and unfortunately, all too soon, I saw that I was headed straight for a dog yard.

The only thing one can do in such a situation is to yell, "On by! On by!" with all gusto. That might have worked, except for then I heard a screech, "Don't hit the chickens! Don't hit the chickens!"

Oh my goodness, what were a dozen or so stupid feathered birds doing standing in the middle of the road? I squeezed the brakes with all my might. I was so nervous, I gave myself a blood blister in my left hand. What followed as the tires skidded dusty black, was a sensory overload: a hundred or so barking dogs—or so it seemed, me yelling and swearing words I did not know I knew, bad chicken smells, and an angry female yelling at either the dogs or the chickens, or maybe me, but I hoped not. Then somehow, after I had become frazzled enough, all was calm.

My dogs were tangled up in a ball, which appeared small even for seven dogs. They were looking innocently at me with their mouths open and panting. Also looking at me with great disdain, were 11 chained up dogs, a pig, quite a few chickens, and Joan Jensen holding two chickens in her arms. I was beginning to think that maybe I should have brushed my hair that morning.

"Er, heh, good morning" I managed to say giving her half a smile. She dropped the two chickens, who clucked away, not appearing to be disturbed in the least by the incident.

"I guess they need to get more used to you" she said flatly, looking at the tangled up mess of canines.

"I think you are probably right" I said trying to think of a plan for unscrambling the ball.

"Well, they're not going anywhere real quick like that" said Joan. "Come on in and get warmed up with some tea, and then I'll help you untangle them."

Gratefully I followed her into her house which overlooked the tarn. The construction looked as if it had been very time consuming, with both the walls and the hearth composed of careful rock work. Their "porch" was just a shallow bluff above the boat dock. At first the house seemed small for six people, but then, I realized most bush residents merely spend time indoors eating, sleeping, and getting warm. Their houses only need to be big enough to hold the essential amount of belongings, and no larger. Hence, a family of six may live in a house the same size, or even smaller, than most mountain retreats of the urban dweller.

Somehow, although I had never been there before, the Jensen's home seemed too quiet.

"Where is the rest of the clan?" I asked taking a seat.

"Well," said Joan, reaching for her selection of tea bags to offer, "Cal and the boys are helping Herb haul construction supplies, and Catie of course is in Fairbanks where she lives now."

By then I had become accustomed to and ready to participate in the Candle manner of inquiring into everyone else's business. "What's Herb building?" I asked selecting some cinnamon tea.

"He's expanding the size of his lodge."

"He can't do that!" I blurted without thinking.

"Why not?" Joan smiled. "He can do anything he wants to."

"Well, I-I," I stammered, "that will change a lot. I mean, lots of people will come here—they'll step on the *Dryas* and pollute the drinking water!"

Joan laughed. "You are green." She got up and fished through her book shelves, returning to the table with two photo albums. Opening one up she said, "Look at this. These are from less than nine years ago." The pictures, which were of Candle, took me by surprise. The main road through town looked almost as desolate as the road from Hemle. It was bare save Manny Kleinman's hangout.

"These are from midsummer" she said. "Don't see too many folks around do you? I don't think you could find a quiet moment like this last summer."

Awestruck, I flipped through the pages.

"Here, you should check these out too" Joan said, pushing me the other album, "but be careful, the photos are real precious." I opened the pages to yellowing black and white prints of the booming Candle teens. The streets were lined with buildings: there was a jail, two grocery stores, a hardware store, six bars, a school, a church, a telegraph office, and power lines! The Kaluatna River was dammed, and the water diverted into a power house, which among other sources of noisy power, housed a water wheel. There were hardly any trees on the hills — all cut for lumber I suppose. And in one of the fragile photographs, I could just make out horse stables up by my house.

"Pretty wild huh?" asked Joan, "I love contrasting these two periods. I would love to have been here for 60 years, and watch this place go through waves of change."

"Doesn't it bother you though?" I asked, "I mean, all this recent development?"

"Oh sure" she responded. "Change is hard to take. But I think I'm getting better at it." She smiled again.

I finished my tea and then suddenly remembered the dogs. I jumped up and ran out the door, but I need not have worried. They were all lying peacefully in their little ball. None seemed the least bit put out by having a paw or a leg buried beneath several others. It looked rather warm and cozy in fact.

Joan helped me untangle the mess. Perhaps it was sort of a bonding experience. "The first tangled and dog doo covered rope of the season" she called it. At last the dogs were all straightened up and ready to roll once more. I thanked Joan for the tea and pictures, invited her to stop by anytime for some of my own special blends, and tore off back home by the droopy trees and steaming tarn. I tried to envision the place a booming town, and hoped that I would never really have to see it that way.

In time for Thanksgiving, the snow finally arrived with fantastic abundance. It seemed to know it was long past due, and was trying to make up for it. Large flakes tumbled from the sky, and covered the frosty trees. The tracks of all creatures were covered faster than they could be made—including those ugly ones of humans—the rusty fuel drums and rotting trucks. The clouds surrounded the mountains and descended thick in the valley. The storm was glorious: silent, but secretly peaceful, and giving Candle clean new clothes to wear for months to come.

I love the snow. It can dump on me anytime. The dogs were happy too. As I watched the wondrous flakes pour out of the sky and blanket the earth, the dogs howled a long winter greeting. Popik led them in a chorus which traveled through the churning waters of Candle Tarn, and was answered by Zachary's team.

Louise and Herb at Candle Lodge invited me to join them for Thanksgiving dinner. Ella skied down to the Stevens' for the weekend, but Bernie, Sue Bean, and Fred Davison—another dog musher who lived far up on the mountain, all accompanied me at Louise and Herbert's table. Everyone, including me, had a few glasses of wine and eggnog before dinner, so conversation was pretty boisterous. Since Fred and Zach and I all ran dogs, we talked mushing a lot, and of course, you probably guessed it—dog poop as well. This time I, being slightly buzzed on three glasses of wine, was the one to bring up the subject. I was interested to know why everybody seemed to have nothing but dog doo on their minds whenever I would mention my occupation. The answer simply was quantity. We figured at peak operation, the kennel had anywhere from 17 to 26 dogs. An average we estimated, of 9 gallons a day of dog poop production. That would be (we had Louise fetch for her calculator), 3,285 gallons of poop a year! Unfortunately, none of us knew the density of dog doo, or else we could have determined actual poundage. Perhaps, my readers will consider this an odd conversation for a Thanksgiving dinner, but it was much lighter than the conversation that had potential to ruin our jovial evening when without thinking anything of it, I brought up Herb's expansion project.

"Well, we have to keep up with the competition you know" he responded to my inquisitions laughing, "but old Kaluatna Lodge will be digging in their nails when they see the luck I'm going to have when I open my place up for business next winter!"

Herb laughed again, but his mirth was not shared. Instead, Bernie put down his fork and looked at Herb intently. "You're opening up your lodge in the winter?" he asked straight faced.

"Yeah" said Herb, "as a ski lodge."

Bernie's forehead had drawn into a frown which did not go away with Herb's reply. The table became quiet. Bernie and Herb stared at each other with penetrating eyes—perhaps reading each other's thoughts. I began to feel like I belonged in that 3,285 gallon pile for starting this conversation.

"Well" said Zachary suddenly, snapping the tension loose, "if more skiers show up than these guys can handle, we'll just chase them away with some of that dog poop!" We all laughed, and Fred started a story about how he tried descending off his steep hill one spring without chaining up the sled, and what kind of dog dooey trouble that got him into. The conversation eased back into more pleasant (if you consider talking excrement pleasant) badinage, and we were all able to relax again.

Louise brought out a pumpkin pie, and we continued to stuff ourselves. Altogether, it was a very enjoyable evening, and I appreciated the opportunity to get to know everyone better. In such a small community, it does not matter whether your neighbors are sixty or six, born again Christians, or atheists. Everybody needed each other, and more than anything, I loved to sit around with a group of Candle residents, taking time to appreciate everyone for whom they were rather than how many books they had written, or what galaxy they had discovered.

Zach suggested we do some dog expeditions together and invited me over to his house to have lunch and look at maps. I accepted and the evening drew to a close with a ridiculous (and also probably quite dangerous) game of drunken darts. I put quite a few unexpected holes in Herb and Louise's wall, but Herb said it did not matter since he was going to blast that wall out soon anyway.

Finally, feeling woozy from the wine, I tugged on my boots, hoped I had put them on the correct feet, and trudged away in the snow feeling the same happy warmth I always felt after a good visit. The snow was piling up deep, but it was soft and harmless. I kicked the blessed stuff around a bit, and then scooped some up and shined my headlamp on it. Each snowflake had kept its form. They each had so many points. I picked up another handful of the flakes and sifted them through my mittens wondering at nature's artistry. I was awakened from my reverie by a shout.

"Hey you drunken fool! You're still here?!"

My slowed reflexes did not give me enough chance to respond to two figures descending upon me with large snowballs. It was Bernie and Fred.

"Hey no fair!" I yelled, "That's two against one!"

But soon Zachary and Sue Bean were out to my rescue. As I have said earlier, there are no wimps in Candle, and this axiom may be extended to snowball fights. Especially drunken ones. But fortunately, Alaska snow is too dry to compact until the warmth of spring, so none of the snowballs were too deadly (although I was dunked pretty good one or two times). Eventually my snow-logged boots were somehow able to carry me safely away up the road to my house. I whistled before I turned the corner, and was answered with a howl. I knew the dogs would be very excited about the scraps I had saved for their Thanksgiving. I let each dog kiss me good night, and then managed to crawl into my own cozy loft.

———————

On Saturday evening, the storm came to an end. The clouds parted, and revealed a gently glowing sphere. The almost full moon pushed the clouds further from its path and proceeded to stretch down to my world and dance on the fresh snow. Sleeping would be a waste of such a night. I slapped on my skis and headed out toward the tarn. By the time I had reached it, the clouds that had shed us so many gifts for the past few days had fully taken their leave. The whole world was a magic black and white except for the Ilkitas which shone silver in the moonlight. The moonbeams on the soft snow gave me energy. I headed up the shore—or at least what I thought was the shore—it was all one white world now.

Hearing no sounds save the swish, swish of my skis, I wandered in and out of the moon shadows trying to disturb the untouched blanket as little as possible. I had skied almost all the way to Zachary's house when I realized I was no longer confined to the shore. The untouched world of the tarn was open for exploration. The quiet of the open space felt sacred. The moon spread over each grain of snow and illuminated every ridge and bump on the glacier—a silver scape of wonder. I ski-skated around and around in circles, taking mental snap shots to hang in my mind, feeling vastly free and spirited in the empty amphitheater. I felt that in this snowy solitude, the earth had let me in on one of her most precious secrets.

The sky was crystal clear on Sunday when the sun finally made it over the western mountains around 11 AM. Zach called me on the CB and suggested I bring my skis so we could venture around a bit. I said, "will do," and packed them carefully on the sled.

There was definitely no sneaking up on Zachary with my dog team. His dogs greeted us with quite a din which did not subside until long after I had chained all the dogs to my picket line well away from Zack's dog yard. Most mushers travel with a picket line, which is often a metal cased cord to which clips are attached. Should a stop be a long one, a musher will ensure that the dogs are safely secured by stretching the picket line from two points—often trees, unhooking the dogs from the sled, and hooking them to the line. This is called, "picketing out the dogs."

Zach came out of the door holding a spatula. "Good morning! Just picket them out between those two trees over there."

Uncle Hickory ran up to me wagging his tail and ignoring my barking dogs as I took them out of harness.

"Hey Hick! How is it going?"

WAG WAG.

"Did you have a good Thanksgiving?

WAG WAG.

"Did you get any good turkey scraps?

WAG WAG WAG!

"Right on! Well let's go in the house." He turned around and led me into the house.

"I guess he's allowed in" I said kicking the snow off of my boots.

"Yeah" smiled Zach. "Sit down Hickory."

Seeing Zach still holding the spatula and standing over his stove I asked what he was making.

"Salmon burgers! You have to get creative out here you know."

They were delicious, and after lunch, Zach pulled out several maps, and we had a good time going through them and envisioning excellent trips we could take.

"Of course we can't do any trips for a while" he said, "it's way too dark, unless you really enjoy playing cribbage by flashlight. But it makes up for it to just look at maps."

I agreed, and quickly grew very attached to the idea of spending lots of time in the field. After a while of looking at maps and photos, Zach jumped up. "What are we doing? We're wasting a beautiful day! Let's get on our skis and look at the real stuff."

We bundled up and Uncle Hickory followed us outside. "Oh I love clear days like this!" Zachary said excitedly rubbing wax on his skis.

"Oh, it's not like this very often?" I asked.

"Sure it is!" He responded. "But that doesn't mean I should get jaded on it does it?"

Good answer I thought. Anybody who takes this beauty for granted should not live here. We skied down to the end of the airstrip and up Raven's Creek a little while Uncle Hickory happily broke trail for us. Zach pointed out to me the trip he wanted to do which was to go down the Kaluatna River and up the Talana River toward the Talana Glacier, then scoot around the mountains back there, and come down Raven's Creek. I was very intrigued by the idea of the excursion. Suddenly Zach interrupted our visual exploration of Raven's Creek.

"Look!"

I followed his gaze and saw large round tracks heading up the hill.

"Fresh lynx tracks!" he said excitedly. Then he pointed to splotches in the snow every eight of the lynx's steps. "See how he stopped regularly to sit down and check things out?"

I skied up closer to the tracks to get a better look at them.

"Hmm, haven't seen too many rabbits around lately" he mumbled. "Let's turn off the creek here. Lou has a trapline around here somewhere. If he has a trail in already we won't have to keep breaking through all this stuff."

We found Lou's trapline which provided very enjoyable skiing, but all the same, I was glad not to find our lynx in any of the traps. The fresh snow was already filled with many other tracks besides those of the lynx such as the sharp prints of the red squirrel which kept crossing our trail. Zach pointed out to me that the ptarmigan tracks were the three-toed ones with no beginning or end travelling from willow to willow.

"Mmm" he licked his lips, "have you ever tried ptarmigan? Great stuff, especially with a little rosemary and thyme."

"Can't say I have" I said. And thinking fondly of my usual diet of rice and beans which were grown somewhere far away, processed by machines, and then shipped to me in beautiful chlorine-bleached boxes, I declined to comment further.

"Of course, you need to get a lot of them to make a good meal," he added as he continued down the trail.

Uncle Hickory darted from tree to tree, smelling every scent and having a grand time, but for the most part he did not veer far from Zach's side—especially when we were in Raven's Creek. He found us several bear trees—poor old spruces stripped of their lower bark and covered with blonde bear hair. I managed to get a bit of the hair from some of the trees before Hickory peed on them. The hair makes great souvenirs to send home to the folks.

Zachary was just starting to tell me about the first aid properties of willow (they contain salicyllin which is the same as aspirin and that is why willow-eating moose do not get headaches) when we heard a plane.

"Shh listen" said Zachary, "It's skipping, it must be Jack. Hey, you wanna go say hi to Jack? He's right on the way home."

"Sure," I agreed, thinking it had been a while since I had experienced the opportunity to meet any more eccentric sourdoughs.

Jack Greely had already unloaded his plane by the time we made it down the hill. We found him by his plane swearing at his snowmachine.

"Hey old Jack" Zachary said as we skied up, his snow filled beard giving away our activities of the last few hours. "What are you doing in town?"

Like most Alaskans, (except the few who are female) Jack had a longish beard and a wrinkled face. He wore a beat up old down jacket, and despite the nippy temperatures, his only head covering was a dirty baseball cap that said, "The Best In The West."

"Hi" he grunted barely smiling, "I came in to check things out for a few days, and I brought in a few groceries for Bernie. I'd rather burn his wood than mine, so I thought I'd head up there right away, but I can't get this goddamned piece of junk to start."

I skied forward and unfortunately skied over the tips of Zachary's skis. "Hello, I'm Heidi" I said, as I tried to sidestep off of Zachary's skis.

"Pleased to meet you" he said as my efforts happened me to fling a big gob of snow at Zachary's waist. "You're the one taking over Ernie's place aren't you?" He asked leaning over and opening the hood of his machine. "I see you're hanging out with Zachary. You another one of those goddamned environmentalists?" He opened up the carburetor and started fiddling with it.

"Depends on how goddamned they are I guess" I said smiling.

Zachary wiped the snow off his pants and laughed. "She's not an environmentalist, she's a klutz."

I ignored the comment and asked, "You run the bunk house huh?"

Jack started unhooking hoses. "Goddamned piece of garbage. Nah. I don't run anything. I hire slaves to do it for me." Using his mouth, he siphoned gas out of the hose and quickly stuck it in the carburetor, spilling some on the fresh snow.

"We can loan you some dogs to get up the hill" teased Zach.

"Nah, not mechanical enough for me."

"Well, ya need some help?"

Jack started the machine which made promising efforts, but then quit. "Goddamned piece of crap. Nah, thanks. A little perseverance will get it." Then he looked up and smiled for the first time as he reached for the gas line again. "I'll do some coffee though."

"Sure thing" said Zach, "hop on over when you get this unit going."

I gave Jack my best wishes for a working machine, and we skied back toward Zachary's house.

While we waited for hot water to boil, Zach showed me more photos of his past winter exploits. Even in the dim light of his propane lights, I could see there was beautiful country around there to explore. But thinking of the new neighbor I met, asked, "Jack's a wild character eh?"

"Yeah" laughed Zach, "Sometimes I think it's scary he owns a plane."

"I think it's scary he owns a bunkhouse!" I said.

"Yes well, I guess you have to get to knows Jack. Living out here for 20 odd years can turn any ordinary guy into a wacko."

We were well on our way through our second cup of coffee, and Uncle Hickory lying on a black bear rug was engaged in some intense snoring, when we heard the unmistakable sound of a working snowmachine. Zachary opened the door for Jack who was still wearing his Best In The West cap even though when I had last glanced at the thermometer, the falling mercury was at -16° Fahrenheit.

"How do?" he said yanking off his large white rubber army boots, well known by Alaskans as bunny boots, "Certainly appreciate the warmth."

"Well," said Zachary getting out another mug, "You know you're welcome to spend the night if your house is too cold."

"Thanks." Jack put his hands over the stove. "I think I got that goddamned machine to work now. I should make it up to Bernie's okay." He happily accepted a cup of coffee. "Saw a bunch of moose coming up the valley."

"No kidding?" Zach's eyes lit up. "I'm surprised they are up this high right now."

"Wow, that would be neat to have them come up here" I added.

"You want some meat? Or you want to take some pictures?" Jack asked, and suddenly remembering cookies someone had given him, pulled a bag of crumbs out of his pocket.

"Neither, it just would be neat to have them around."

"Yeah, you'd probably get all mad and upset if we went and got us some for dinner then huh?" Jack's eyes twinkled under his cap. His quick judgements were beginning to get annoying.

"Where did you get the idea I'm some threatening radical 'environmentalist'?" I asked.

"Oh, you just seem like it" he said grabbing a handful of crumbs. "I can usually spot them."

Having lived in Alaska long enough to know his sentiment was common, I asked, "Well, what have you got against THEM anyway?"

"Watch it, she's feisty" Zachary said smiling.

"Oh, they always think they know what's best," Jack answered, "Always trying to change the goddamned world, save Alaska, and they're not realistic."

"Well, that's not me," I said, "I've lived in Alaska for a while, and I know what goes on here. I just think you feel threatened for some reason."

"Oh ho! She's on to you Jack."

"Well maybe she is" Jack responded, "I'm just sick of people coming in here: 'Oh you can't do that even though you've been doing it for 19 years, you might hurt this mosquito!' And goddamned tourists coming in: 'Oh we've got to protect this place — it's so pretty! Quick, let's tell all our friends to come here and help us protect it!'"

I could not help but giggle a little at the falsetto voice Jack used to imitate his enemies. And the way he put everything, it did sound absurd. But still, he was missing the point.

"What do you think 'environmentalist' means anyway before you go bashing them around?"

"Well, I don't know about a dictionary definition, but I just see them as a bunch of goddamned hypocrites who want to lock up Alaska so no one can use it, and so they can have some pretty place to talk about."

"Well maybe there's a lot of folks like that, but don't call them simply environmentalists. To me, an environmentalist refers to someone who has a concern for the impact of other's actions on the earth, and a willingness and hope to minimize the bad."

"Whatever." said Jack munching on another handful of crumbs. "You seem feisty enough to not let me get away with anything I say, so you'll probably do real good out here."

51

I smiled. I guessed it was not really fair to pick on a guy after he had just experienced a long and difficult journey and had even offered me cookie crumbs. The moon had risen once again, and it seemed it was a good time to start thinking about getting my dogs home.

I remained at Zach's long enough to make certain Jack's frozen fingers were able to start his machine, and then bid a fond thanks to Zachary and Hickory who both helped me harness up my dogs. They were anxious to get home for dinner and tore down the road. Popik knew the way well, and did not need to receive any commands, so the journey was silent — swishing through the aspen and poplar trees, the blue and silver mountains peering through them. The cold nipped my forehead, but the dogs loved it, and I let them tear around the moonlit corners, pulling me standing on one runner, and loving the stubborn wildness of the place.

Chapter 4

M ost Alaskans make a run for it sometime or another during the course of the winter. I know very few who will go a whole winter without some sort of excursion to Arizona, Florida, or Hawaii. Some are senseless and go to visit places like North Dakota or Minnesota, but most make a break for a few weeks of sun. I know none who will go two consecutive winters without a "vacation." Even so though, there were quite a few folks in town on December 21 for Candle Lodge's solstice party. Of course Bernie and Sue Bean both showed up, as well as Zachary, and Jack. Ella was gone on some wild excursion in the Himalayas, but Lisa and Ralph Kissell, who lived up in the hills behind Ella's house, arrived with their five year old son Zach, who was delighted to see that Jonathan and Hazel Cohen had brought their two young daughters, Esther and Sarah, who were aged seven and four-and-a-half respectively.

The Cohen's lived at the end of the road on the west side of the tarn three miles past the Jensens. There was no way the Jensens would have missed a party, and even the Stevens who lived on the Talana River 10 miles away, made the long mush up the Kaluatna River with their 13-year-old daughter Molly. Fred Davison had just left town but the dogs he had left with me had been pretty noisy the past few days, and more than made up for his absence.

It was 26 degrees below, and the skinny spruce trees were already silent in silhouette against the faint orange of dusk by the time I arrived with my dish of potato pancakes. Most of the folks were already there. I could tell by the large number of vehicles parked in front of the lodge. And I do not mean cars of course. By parked vehicles, I mean a couple of dog teams, a few snowmachines, one or two three-wheelers, and a pair of skis stuck in the snow. The latter belonged to Bernie whose vehicle had broken down — with no surprise to anyone except himself. Bernie, Herb, Cal, Sue Bean, Zachary, and Jack were on the porch sharing a smoke.

"It's the poop queen!" Herb said when I stomped onto the porch trying to get the snow that was in my boots to go elsewhere.

"Hey now, be nice" I said. I did not think I was quite ready for Herb.

"There's some home brew inside" said Bernie, "Here, I'm ready to go and warm up anyway." Inside, Bernie showed me the towering pile of coats, pants, hats, and boots on top of which I threw my own burden of wool and down.

The kids were already engaged in some major play which involved running with stocking feet at incredible speeds around the building, pausing only when the running course would take them under or over the legs of a parent who would suggest running elsewhere, and squeezing a rubber dinosaur which made a horrid squeak every time its poor gut was poked. Bernie introduced me first to a bottle of home brew, second to Sue Bean's blueberry brandy if I was so inclined, and third to Catie Jensen who was visiting her folks for the holidays. She and I hit it off right away — as I enjoyed her stubborn and dry humor. Despite her strange and isolated upbringing, she appeared to be a very normal and well adjusted person. She was working at some cross country ski lodge out of Fairbanks, and was training dogs there as well. Catie did not appear to be distracted in the least by the squeaking dinosaur, but I could tell she was not going to let her younger brothers or anybody for that matter, give her any trouble.

Joan brought a huge turkey and Louise and Herb contributed pumpkin and pecan pies, which were consumed almost as fast as Sue Bean's brandy. It was quite a party, and understandably, for when the shy sun shows its face only between 11:30 AM and 2:30 PM, the solstice — which means the darkness will cease to encroach — is quite a cause for joyful celebration. And despite the fact that its presence was strong and always there, no-one seemed to pay attention to the visqueen covered hole in the lodge's side wall revealing Herb's new building project.

When everybody at the party was sufficiently titillated on some form of tittlefier, Cal Jensen made sure his red suspenders were not twisted and inhaled deep through his smile in order to gather sufficient air in his chest to get everybody's attention over the squeaking dinosaur, stomping feet, titillation, and Jimmy Buffett music. The latter was quickly quieted when someone noticed Cal standing up and snapping his suspenders.

"Now here all!" As his voice boomed, the corners of his mouth forgot all rules of gravity, and brought themselves up as high on his face as they could go. "Seeing as how this day marks an important event for all Northern Alaskans, I brought my Hokey Pokey tape so we could do the day justice."

I thought Catie would be cringing with embarrassment at her silly father, but she just sat on her stool smiling at him along with everybody else.

Some, like Joan said, "Oh, no Cal," and sort of groaned. But Cal would not stand for any obstreperousness, and in a manner only a six-three and a half foot tall, 220 pound, 16-year resident of Candle, Alaska could do, Cal got the whole gang to move comfy couches and beer bottles out of the way to do a Candle Polka.

Edward Jensen put in Cal's tape, and with Cal as "caller," we did the weirdest sort of Hokey Pokey I have ever done. There was not much structure involved. The kids seemed to like it the best because we were in sort of a circle—maybe more of a rhombus, and they would run in and out of the circle and dance around giggling. (By that time, one of the grown-ups had somehow gotten a hold of the squeaky dinosaur and had hidden it under one of the cushions of the couch).

When we had poked Hokey enough times, Cal grabbed Catie and they danced through the circle—still to the stupid music of the Hokey Pokey. Joan yanked Bernie from the bar stool behind which he was trying to hide, and swung him through the collapsing rhombus. Through the din, Uncle Hickory could be heard howling outside, so nine-year-old Jojo Jensen let him in and holding Hick's front paws, did a dog paddle-jitter bug sort of a dance.

Louise was occupied with a proper box step with Zach, so Herbert tapped me on the shoulder and requested my hand. We swung around, and tried not to bump into Ralph Kissell and Sue Bean who were trying to teach Zach Kissell and Sarah Cohen the Tango. Little Zach and Sarah did not really understand the concept, but liked the cheek to cheek bit, and ran around showing everybody how their cheeks were "super-glued" together. Soon, what had been a mild rhombus of Hokey Pokey, had erupted into an arena of waltzing slam dancers. It was fantastic fun, and I think I had the music for the Hokey Pokey in my head for days and days after that. I will never be able to do a normal version of that dance ever again.

Eventually the kids displayed signs indicating the imminence of exhaustion-induced crankiness. The Cohens initiated the exodus, being the first to sift through the huge pile of coats and mittens. They were joined by their sleep-over hosts, Hickory and Zachary. Everyone else made certain that each party goer had a warm and nearby place to spend the night. I left with my usual dose of warm happy thoughts. I had felt so comfortable at the gathering—loving that everybody had seemed ready to help each other have fun. I learned then that I loved Candle for not only its unmatched beauty, but for its community closeness as well.

Shortly after solstice, the skies opened up. The atmosphere felt so thin that I thought I could reach out and grab a handful of stars at night. The low sun let the mountain ridges take turns casting shadows on one another, and in their play, I could distinctly view every single blue tipped ridge. The air was crystal clear, and too cold for even molecules to move about. The holes in the skies had let in 50-below temperatures. But there was not one whisper of wind, so if I stood perfectly, perfectly still, the biting cold could not get at me through all my layers. I fed the dogs lots of tallow, and figured it was a good time for repairing dog harnesses, sewing patches on my own gear, and playing the guitar.

I think I discovered my new game of sliding in my down booties to the outhouse the same day I discovered the feathers of ice that grew next to the spring. I ran out of water at what first seemed like a very inconvenient time, thinking no one should have to go mess with cold water at 50 below. Now, I am glad I was forced into my excursion to the spring, which was not only steaming like a geothermal plant, but was also frozen on the sides. On the frozen ice were tufts of white hairs. My first thought was that they were Dall sheep hairs. But it only took me a moment to laugh at my stupidity. Dall sheep reside on steep craggy cliffs, not on flat frozen lakes. Looking more closely, I realized that the hairs were ice. Crystals had formed into intricate feathers and had gathered together in one tuft. In fact, these tufts grew all over the ice shelf. The temperature was cold enough that I could pick up a feather, and study it in my mitten. It could have been a very pinnatifid leaf—frosted with snow, or a baby feather from the most delicate of birds. But it was a perfect wonder of nature, reminding me of her underestimated power and grace.

There was fresh snow on the ground the day Zach and I started our dog trip. The sky was clear, and the sun, back from its winter vacation, shone brightly on the fresh blanket. Thin slivers of white, so dry and fine are those Alaska snow flakes. The sun bounced off of their edges to sweeten the landscape with a sugary show. It was a balmy 10° and thin wisps of clouds surrounding the silent Ilkitas were no threat to our adventure. On beautiful, clear days like that, I understand what is meant by the expression, "painfully beautiful." I feel guilty not gazing at the mountains every second, thinking other thoughts, or even looking where I am going, rather than at the wondrous scene of depth, sharp points, soft shadows, and stripes of rock interrupting the gentle slopes of white.

The dogs knew we were headed for an adventure. They saw us load up our sleds with 10 days worth of dog food and tallow, stoves, sleeping bags, lots of warm clothes, and snowshoes — which would be instrumental in completing our trip. It was March 16, almost the Vernal Equinox, when 12 hours of night are matched by 12 hours of daylight. We no longer had to concern ourselves with the problems of not having enough traveling hours.

The Stevens' trail down the Kaluatna River was still well packed by snowmachines and other dog sleds, and thus our start was an easy one, a glide down familiar territory. I love the view of a traveling dog team. The profile of musher and dogs against a white landscape is a picture that could be placed in any time, from a century ago to the present. The 10 miles to Talana River were over quickly, and we were welcomed by the howl of the Stevens' dogs. The Stevens were happy to see us, especially Molly, who never minded a little company other than that of her parents. We brought them vegetables from Zach's root cellar, which they added to fish from theirs, and we shared a happy family dinner.

The dogs were very anxious to get going the next morning. They grew more and more impatient as they watched us carefully packing up our sleds, ensuring our loads were properly balanced. Their barking made me feel anxious. I snagged a thin willow switch from an exposed bush, and snapped it against the sled. The yard was silent, and we were able to pack in peace.

The Talana River is a large braided river with a wide river bar that is "unused" by the river most of the year. I both love and fear those large rivers. Their mighty summer floods of glacial silt provide vast open space and little vegetation. I sometimes feel very alone amid the sea of gravel, or in winter—field of white. Yet, also to stand so close to a great mighty being, one that is stronger, more dangerous, and more unpredictable than any animal, gives me a rush.

In the winter, these rivers overflow often, flooding their bars with a thin layer of water which freezes quickly on top of the original ice as it floods. With this constant interruption, in addition to strong winds which flow down river, snow has little chance to build up thick layers. Our travel thus, was easy, gliding smoothly on the thin layers of snow.

Occasionally, a chinook winter wind will warm the river enough to cause a surge of water to rip through the layers of ice it had created earlier. The river will tunnel through or push away these ice shelves and eventually refreeze in its new place. The result is, by the end of winter, a chaotic jumble of ice—chunky and smooth—a menace to anyone who dares navigate the water's path. But the river perseveres, finding a route through the complex collection of ice boulders and bubbles, often giving rise to gentle steam as it flows through the cold.

It was then, next to this quiet source of beauty and terror, that we travelled. My dogs were fresh, and excited to be in a new area of views and smells. They pulled the load well. Uncle Hickory ran behind the two sleds, certain to let us know if we had dropped anything. I felt wonderful standing on the sled and letting my dogs introduce me to this new scenery. Mushing was fairly easy, so I barely had to concentrate, but inhaled the serene boldness of the landscape.

We made good time traveling along the river that day—managing to cover a distance of about 11 miles. The valley had begun to narrow, indicating that we were only a couple miles from Marshall Creek—

the canyon that would allow us to climb up into the mountains. We would have preferred to continue on to the entrance of the canyon that evening, but our daylight as well as our energy was waning. We still needed plenty of it to make camp, get firewood, and melt snow for the dogs. As it was, the dogs had worked enough for the day. They displayed no qualms when we brought them into the forest a bit, unharnessed them, and clipped them to the picket line—strung between a few thin willow trees. Within the protection of the forest, we expected to be a lot warmer than if we spent the night on the exposed river bar. I broke a few spruce boughs off some generous trees, and offered them to my dogs for sleeping pads. They had already dug themselves little holes in the snow in which to curl up—their noses buried under their tails, and were happy with my gifts which they put in their beds.

That evening, we watched the sun nestle itself into a gentle dip in the mountainous horizon. Resting in its wake, a pillowy mass of cloud sufficed to scatter the departing light, giving the orange glow no choice but to suddenly burst into rusty hues, framed by the bluish peaks. In the foreground, the fiery display discovered the thin streams of overflow making their way through the white, and colored them swirly rose and orange. Popik was delighted with the show, and said so with a long throaty howl. The others soon joined in, a welcoming song for our journey.

Zach was almost positive that our present campsite was within barking distance of Marshall Creek, and he was certain that traveling up Marshall Canyon with the dogs would be too difficult without a packed trail. The snow was deep, and our dogs were not accustomed to plowing through it, so we decided not to break camp in the morning, but to do a trail-making day trip. Sure enough, our dogs had barely run 20 minutes when we hit the confluence of the two icy waterways.

Marshall Creek, although much smaller than the Talana, is no mere rivulet either. Do not be mistaken by the names Alaskans give to their waterways. If you have ever had chance to look at a body of water called a "bay" in Alaska, such as Bristol Bay, you will notice that it is in actuality, a small ocean or sea; in the same manner, what we are familiar with as to being a "bay" is called an "inlet." A mighty fjord is an "arm," and water does not exist as a "river" unless it is sent crashing and bubbling through voracious canyons, and over glacial carved valleys miles wide. "Creeks" are navigable waterways which rip out sturdy bridges year after year; and those many drainages which are unnamed, and sometimes even unmarked on maps, and which tumble down mountains so full and so quickly during midsummer that to attempt to cross them with four people locking arms is a tremendously harrowing experience — we call them "streams."

The area had undergone so many temperature fluctuations that winter, that Marshall Creek was a mess: convoluted shelf ice and surprise holes and cliffs throughout. We decided not to even bother trying to mush our dogs right up the creek. Instead, we unhooked our poor teams who were raring to run another 10 miles, and picketed them out once again. Even Uncle Hickory.

"Hick, you're too old to go breaking trail for us," Zach told him. Hick whined at first, but understood that the decision was in his best interest. It was time for me and Zach to begin the work. We strapped on our snowshoes, and leaving the two teams, began our stomp up Marshall Creek. We were going to make our own trail.

Alaska snow, at least that around Candle, is lighter and drier than most snow one will ever encounter anywhere in the Lower-48. It forms no base, but just piles up in lovely white dunes. Unfortunately, the thick powder then, is bottomless, and travel is restricted to trails for the most part, and huge rivers like the Talana. The wonderful secret that I am about to disclose however, is that the bushes are gone. The menacing gnarls of summer that cause one to beg for mercy should she stray from a path, are covered and forgotten. One may travel anywhere providing a trail is made first. Hence, the "stomping." Hiking in single file, we used our snowshoes to create a trail three snowshoes wide. Great care must be taken to make the trail as straight as possible, otherwise, a musher will find the dogs around a corner, but the sled sinking in powder in order to catch up. Where willow branches hung in our way, we sawed them off. If the creek was broken anywhere and a snow bridge needed to be included in the course, we had to retrace our steps and create a new, straighter on-ramp, ensuring that musher and sled could not miss a corner and tumble into the stream. Sometimes, stomping away to ensure a good, clean path, we had to retrace steps a quarter of a mile or so in order to find a better route that perhaps did not wind around so many trees.

We packed a trail for about six miles up the creek and then picked a campsite where we might find shelter from the wind. In hopes that disturbed snow would set up enough to walk on without snowshoes the next evening, when we would return with the dogs, we then stomped out a spot where we could picket out our dogs, and a spot for our kitchen. After hot soup of dried veggies, brought from Zach's cupboard, we then stomped our way back, smoothing out and fixing the trail wherever needed.

One may ask, why if all this stomping is needed, is dog mushing an efficient way to travel? True, by the end of our trip, we had traveled some or our trail three times if you add up the stomping up and back — certainly not an efficient way to travel. However, our whole purpose was not solely to cover as many miles as possible, but also to be out with the dogs, and enjoy the land.

Any dog lover will understand the joy of being able to camp out with 16 dogs, riding on a sled, and having dogs carry your gear and theirs. The non-dog lover may just assume leave them at home. Further up north, where the land is covered by ice, one does not need to stomp a trail. The world is open for travel. In fact, the dogs do not even need to run in single file, but can be hooked up all spread out in a large fan.

Our trail turned out to be more technical than anticipated. Mushing up it the next day was a chore — not as glamorous as the earlier mushing I have described. I was whacked in the face with branches quite a few times, which made me think that maybe we had ought to cut more brush. My dogs also cut quite a few corners, which led me to believe our trail was too crooked. I only crashed once when one willow refused to get out of the way. But Zach crashed twice, and the second time was troublesome. His dogs rounded a sharp bend in the trail okay, but his sled had not. Instead it tumbled sideways off the trail and smashed into a large bush. Zach was okay, just had snow up his nose (Hick was licking him anyway just to be sure). But the sled was broken.

"I'm going to have to give you a ticket for reckless driving" I said as I pulled out my repair kit. With string and a hundred-mile-an-hour tape (known by many as duct tape), the patch job met Uncle Hickory's approval, but tainted our trip, for Zach's sled speed would be limited by the repair tape to a 100 miles per hour.

The sky that night was cloudless — sure to be cold. Zach curled up in the basket of his sled under Uncle Hickory acting as a blanket. I dug a small pit deep enough in which to escape chilling breezes and lay my sleeping pad directly on the snow. Inside the comfort of a thick down bag, I lay on my back, and watched the thin light of stars penetrate the blackness. An occasional twinkling cascaded quickly across the dark arena. A faint utterance of green light steamed from the horizon. When I awoke later to a chorus of howls, the green light had flowed into thin streams which poured through the stillness. They moved in nano-breaths. Pulsating slowly, gently. The movements so slight, so sly, I never understood how they changed. A silent song—unearthly magical. I watched in sleepy reverence and the dogs sang. When I opened my eyes again, the lights were gone as well as the black. A hint of blue remained to welcome the early dawn.

Narrow Creek—our route from Marshall Creek to the top of the pass that separated us from Raven's Creek—was aptly named. Those old time prospectors sure had a way with words. As we climbed in our snowshoes up the drainage route, the sunny canyon became more and more narrow. The route was steep, carrying us above the scraggly brush as we turned snowy corners one after another. As elevation increased, so did the depth of the snow. Each step was an effort in the deep powder. Push, push. My legs were exhausted. I wondered about Zach. In spite of being 15 years my senior, and having a fair amount of winter insulation about his girdle, he was in excellent shape, working the trail like an ox.

The gulch, smooth, with sparkling crystals of snow, served as a solar collector. Bouncing from rim to rim, the sun reflected off the snow, charging my body with intense heat even though according to the thermometer dangling from my jacket, the temperature was only 16° Fahrenheit. The radiant warmth soaked in through my layers, and soothed my pale skin. We were in the heart of the mountains—the tips of peaks just out of reach, laden with quiet beauty. The canyon became so narrow that our trail occupied the whole bottom; all else were sides. The landscape was a dream-world, a playground really. With many options of gullies and tiny canyons to explore near the pass, it would have been a superb place to play hide-and-go-seek, or "house," with gently sloping white walls separating each room.

When our aching legs brought us finally to the summit of the pass, the sun was a giant orange ball nearly touching the rims of the gulch. With it at our backs, washing over the windswept snow, we looked at the birth place of Raven's Creek, and the shadowy world beyond it: the tip of the Kaluatna Glacier parading boldly in mounds of hidden snow, and surrounded by rocky summits and bowls filled with ice. I was in heaven. This was the Alaska I had chosen to live in.

Zach gave a thrilled hoot. As his gleeful sound spilled down into the Northern Canyons, I searched my backpack for treats with which to celebrate our accomplishment.

Suddenly Zach interrupted my noisy rummaging. "Shh. Listen!"

I held my breath and opened my ear to the wind. From a nearby canyon, I heard a long deep howl. The voice of a wolf. With excited astonishment, I turned my wide open eyes to Zach and started to exclaim to him, but he interrupted me by cupping his hands to his mouth and calling back, "Owwwwouoooo!" Then we looked at each other, smiling excitedly in silence as a low howl resounded again from below. Zach howled again and kept the wolf calling. The voice was quite close, but not eerie as it sometimes is to hear a coyote shrilling in the darkness. This was a beautiful sound, emanating from the far reaches of the canyons.

The fiery ball behind us disappeared, leaving in its wake an intense layer of rosy orange. In contrast, pointing softly to the loud sunset was our trail. Our narrow track, appearing blue now in the shadows, was the only interruption of the smooth snowy surface. I was proud of our trail. The product of much sweat looked neat. It was a minor disturbance, but had allowed us to achieve a great high.

If I thought I had used a lot of sweat in making the trail up Narrow Creek, it was nothing compared to the chore of pushing the sleds up the steep trail the following day. The night had been cold—too cold for our trail to set up solid, and so the dogs had little traction with which to grip the snow and pull. They barked with frustration as Zach and I pushed from behind. "Hup hup. Let's go. Let's go Popik. Hup hup hup!"

We had hoped to reach the summit before the sun of midday had a chance to heat up and loosen the steep sides of Raven's Creek Canyon. But we were still puffing and groaning on the Narrow Creek side of the divide when the sun's fiery head popped over the ridge tops. The light was blinding, and the temperature must have increased 30 degrees. We stopped to remove layers of clothing and apply sun protection. The dogs rolled on their backs and rubbed themselves into the velvet white powder—seeking to get as much of the cold substance between their hot oily hairs as possible.

We had not broken trail on the other side of Raven's Creek— relying on the elevation drop and the sweep of wind to permit us to descend into Raven's Creek Canyon. We were hot, and assumed the canyon's walls would soon be also—and therefore dangerous avalanche terrain. But the windy summit was no place to make camp, and we were sure as heck not going to climb back up to it again. No, down Raven's Creek was the way to proceed, and quickly.

The shallow bowl would have been excellent backcountry skiing. As it was, the mush down was very enjoyable. The dogs were happy also, as they plunged their paws down the hillside. Yeehew! After that mighty push up hill, I deserved the ride.

There was open water further down the creek, and somehow Zach had gotten ahead of me and out of sight, expertly maneuvering his sled through the willows and along the creek. Our route was flattening out. I figured we would have to stop soon. Probably Zach was anxious to find and make camp before light and energy faded. The day had been a very lengthy one.

Suddenly without warning, Zach's trail made a sharp turn and crossed a narrow bridge across the creek. It was a snow-covered log—just wide enough for a sled. There was no other way to go. The dogs followed the sharp turn that led to the on-ramp of the bridge.

"Popik whoa!" Anxious to catch up with Zach, my dogs paid no heed. "Whoa Popik! Whoa!" I yelled. Too late. I jumped from the brake just as the sled plunged into the water and wedged itself under the bridge. The dogs were already beyond the crossing, and barking with impatience.

I had already dumped my sled twice on the journey down from the pass. Righting the heavy load had taken almost all of my energy. I flopped myself down in a patch of sun.

"You wanted a break?" I yelled angrily to my barking dogs. "You're getting one! We're stuck!" I closed my eyes. I would deal with it after a rest.

My sled was completely and utterly stuck. I tried to get in the creek and push the sled out from under the bridge, and then above my head so the dogs could pull it to freedom. All I succeeded in doing was getting wet. At least the dogs could not go any where—even though they desperately wanted to. They were attached to a 250 pound anchor. I tugged and pulled. My sunny patch disappeared. My predicament became awful. The dogs were crazy with frustration and voices started becoming hoarse. "Shut up!" My frustration and exhaustion exceeded my enjoyment and patience. Eventually my dogs quieted and lay down. They had lost their hope in me. My feet were cold, but the rest of me was sweaty. I took another break.

As soon as I sat down, the dogs stood up and started barking again. Goodness, what now? It was a hello bark. They were greeting Uncle Hickory! Yay! Yay Hick! I was so happy to see him. He jumped up and down and wagged his tail. We gave each other a huge smelly hug. He was glad to see that I was not hurt. No, I did not need a drink from his orange juice bottle. Or did I?

"Go get Zach. Go on." Hick ran off, and I lay back down on the snow. When Zach showed up with Hickory 45 minutes later, he laughed. I could not believe it. His bushy brown beard shook as he sized up my situation with amusement.

"Oh shush. Come help me." My irritation fueled his mirth. He was slap happy from the rough day's exertion.

"I'm just so glad you're okay Heidi." He erupted into a new fit of giggles. I stepped back into the creek, not caring now that my immersion was wet and cold, and showed him how my escape involved a two-person chore. He did not stop laughing, but obligingly came to my aid.

"Don't worry Heidi. I've got camp all set up, and twigs ready for a fire. We're just a mile or so from the trail we broke last month. It'll be a real easy cruise back home."

Candle seemed like a city to me when Raven's Creek spit us out at the intersection of the road and the airstrip. There were our familiar trails, planes, and houses. Evidence of humans at every turn. I felt foreign, as if we had been away for years. Of course it had been only a week, but I felt as if we had traveled to another wild world.

Breakup came upon Candle quickly and early, and for me — without adequate warning. For those who are unfamiliar with Alaska's unmerciful change of seasons, "breakup" is a term referring to the transition between winter and spring that is neither winter-like nor spring-like. The April sun becomes more intense than you ever remembered, but the ground stubbornly remains frozen solid. Hence, the once beautiful blanket of snow turns into a nauseous quilt of muck and mud which freezes at night, oozes down the mountains in dirty avalanches come midday, and refuses to go anywhere productive.

Skiing becomes hopeless as skis ridden with gobs and gobs of klister (a kind of glue Nordic connoisseurs try to pass off as spring kick wax) surrender all too quickly to the odd mixture of mud and slush. Snow machining becomes a joke, and rubber boots never seem tall enough to prevent tablespoons of gooey glob from slithering down to your last pair of clean socks.

It becomes apparent to the breakup neophyte that transportation opportunities are strictly limited to traveling in early mornings, or by snowshoe. And anybody who has ever snowshoed very many miles will tell you that breakup is a good opportunity for catching up on letters you never answered, finally cleaning those tools that have looked dirty all winter, or building a new addition to your house. The latter is the most popular since the days are so sunny and long that staying inside is shameful. But going anywhere is impossible, so building outside is a pleasant way to spend the long days.

I'll tell you — in sharp contrast to the peace and quiet of winter, I never heard so much sawing and hammering going on. Everybody had something to build. You wondered why there are so many abandoned buildings in Alaska?

The dogs were not quiet either. They were in their prime of shape. Having just completed a grand finale to their winter, they were ready to pull 25 miles a day, and here they were sitting on their rumps. And you bet they felt they should complain about that! I tried to get up early and take them out in the mornings, but that is asking a lot when they howl all night long. BUT, the snow did start to go away, and days did get longer and longer. And on April 18, I heard my first varied thrush.

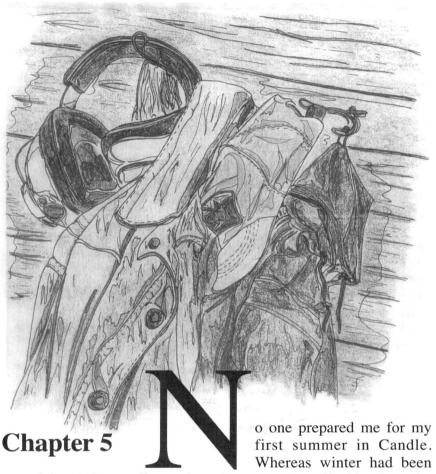

Chapter 5

No one prepared me for my first summer in Candle. Whereas winter had been peaceful and slow—all sounds and movement muffled by the quiet blanket of snow, the summer sun brought the warmth to melt the glaciers and cause the rivers to roar. Birds and buzzing mosquitoes filled every sound space of the day, and people arrived. Lots and lots of people. I was astounded by the number of tourists that seeped in through corners everywhere. Suddenly, vans continually stirred the dust on the road between Candle Lodge and Kaluatna Lodge; people walked about exploring the remnants of buildings at all hours of the day; the tarn's waters were rippled by canoes; and the beach was always occupied by at least two couples searching for shiny rocks, or just marvelling at the awe-inspiring beauty of blue ice and black rock cascading from towering mountains.

Ella, who was in Candle for a few days off from guiding, must have noticed me shying away from this sudden hustle and bustle and retreating to my dog yard, for she tromped on over to my place in her large plastic mountaineering boots one Tuesday morning in early June, and demanded that I follow her on to the glacier for a bit of exploring.

"I see you moping about those dog houses" she said, "One would think you'd forgotten that summer could be magical as well."

"Oh Ella," I protested, "I haven't been moping. I just wanted to fix up these ratty old houses. You know the Stevens' are bringing over their dogs for the summer this week."

"You can fix them on a cloudy day" she said, and handed me plastic mountaineering boots to try on. Then she added with a sly smile, "You know, most people have to pay me to take them out on a glacier." I cheerfully acknowledged my great fortune in having such a talented and generous neighbor as she, and jammed my feet into the glowing green cement blocks that attempted to pass for shoes.

When Ella finally succeeded in pulling me away from my house, I became excited, and realized I had never traveled on a glacier before. In introductory college geology, we were taught about U-shaped valleys, tarns, and cirques, but never about what it was like to be on a glacier—to experience the body and mind of a moving mass of ice.

We bumbled down the road in Ella's 1954 Willy's Jeep. In between bumps, she told me about the trip she had just guided up and down Mt. Enser—laughing about the rich engineer who had dragged his unwilling wife along on the trip, and how Ella had managed to tame them both.

It had been a while since I had hung out with Ella, and as usual, I enjoyed her inspiring tales. She showed me a secret trail she had cut around Candle Tarn through Alder Hell, and we pushed through the bushes to the moraine where she finally admitted to me that her real reason for wanting to come on the glacier was to look for a snow picket she had left behind last fall, and that she now needed.

"I knew you couldn't just be taking a day off just for me, I teased.

"Yeah, but admit it" she grinned, "I got you out of that dog doo."

The glacial moraine itself was a wondrous new world to me. Although I have never been on the moon before, I instantly understood what people mean by "moonscapes." What foreign desolation. On the brown gravelly surface, even the big boulders seemed lonely. The ground up rocks slid beneath my feet as I tried to walk, and I was not sure if I liked it.

"Just wait" Ella reassured me happily and plopped herself down on a boulder. I could tell she was in her element. "And I suppose you're taking it for granted that there's no mosquitoes around here?"

"Hey, you're right!" I spun around in a circle suddenly noticing the freedom in the air. The silence had returned. Ella started putting on her crampons and I quickly followed her example. She stopped for a moment looking at my feet, and then at me — softly smiling:

"The points go down." I caught her eye, and then laughed fixing my error. There was no use in feeling embarrassed around Ella.

We stepped on the ice and I felt a wild shiver in my body. I was standing on a mighty being — unknown to most of the world's population. Ella showed me how not to trip in my crampons which proved to be very pleasant to walk with, and we ventured out into new realms. Having envisioned a glacier to be a sheer block of ice — like a frozen river, I was unprepared for all the new surprises Ella showed me: valleys, ridges, crevasses, and deep, deep holes she called moulins (pronounced Moo-lawns). If I had a good foot hold, I could look down toward the dark depths of these things. It always felt sort of sneaky, as if I was peering down into the secret hollows of the earth — where I was not really supposed to see. The ice in these holes was crystal blue. Cold and hard with mystical beauty.

Down many of these moulins flowed the water that created them. Gushing, tinkling, "gallooping," and gargling, each waterway had its own sound. It was an orchestra conducted by the sun. Ella did not laugh at me — wide eyed and gasping at every corner — instead she shared my delight.

"It's different each time I come out here. Last time this was a tunnel you could crawl through a ways. Now its a mere valley. Oh and look here — this wasn't here before at all — it's a huge moulin!"

I opened my mouth right under one little waterfall and took a gulp of the blue fluid. It was cold and shocked my teeth, but tasted like I had drunk from the fountain of youth. Pure H_2O, lacking any minerals, or human additives too for that matter. We did not tire of looking down every bottomless hole, climbing up and down every valley to see new surprises, and finally Ella shouted, "Aha!" and pointed to a hint of metal capturing the sun. We had found her picket. The day had been a success.

It was Louise who had the bright idea that I should give dog demonstrations and sled rides for extra income to young visitors. I decided I would go along with the philosophy of, "if you can't beat 'em join 'em" and accepted the eager tourists she sent over to me. At first I enjoyed it. I was happy for the extra cash. I got out the sled and showed them how the dogs were harnessed and attached. I taught them to say "gee" and "haw" and showed them the brakes on the sled and the bungee cords that prevent supplies from falling out. I even put a couple of kids in the sled-skateboard contraption and let Tuska and Popik pull them around a little. And I answered questions: what kind of shoes did the dogs wear on their feet? How did the dogs stay warm? How many times had I been attacked by a dog? Didn't I feel lazy just standing on the sled with the dogs working? How could I tell the dogs apart? And wasn't it mean to keep them on a chain?

Then the tourists started coming everyday, and I found myself telling them the dogs had to wear basketball shoes. Then they started coming twice a day, and I told them that I put an electric heater in each dog house on cold nights, and I had super-glued name tags on the dogs' backs to tell them apart. Then the tourists came over whenever they wanted and it was too much. They would knock on my door and expect me to talk to them while I was eating dinner or brushing my teeth. They would go into the dog yard uninvited and set the dogs to barking a 50-dog-din at 11 PM. One guy even unchained one of the Stevens' dogs to take back to show his wife. It got loose, and I could not find it for days. Finally, I put a sign up that read, "DANGER: WOLF/POLAR BEAR MIXES RAISED HERE, STAY AWAY" and they left me alone.

On the Fourth of July there was a town parade. The event brought out some great creative efforts. The Jensen's tied one of the leaky canoes on top of their big truck. They had painted all sorts of fish and Octopi and sea horses on the truck and the kids sat in the canoe with their life vests on. Joan, who was driving, threw candy out the window, and when people came to pick up the candy, the kids, "bailed" water out of the boat and splashed it all over the eager sweet-seekers. Zach and I put one of our sleds on a red wagon. Zach wore a dog costume made out of a few cardboard boxes and Zach and Popik pulled me in the sled — wearing my winter coats and pants. Popik must have been nervous with all the people watching him because he stopped right in the middle of our cruise through town and dropped his own version of "candy" on the street.

Herb and Bernie, who were likely drunk when they thought of it, in addition to drunk at the time, showed up as a two-headed miner. They marched through town in a sheet stapled together and sprinkled with silver glitter to look like silver dust. They wore miners' hats and head-lamps and carried pick axes. As they stumbled down the road, they kept arguing about how the other person was walking too slow or too fast. James Jensen perfected their costume by discreetly sticking a large KICK ME sign on their back.

The Candle Lodge employees put an old carpet on top of the lodge van and tied balloons on the edges as tassels. Then they sat up on top of it, their legs in Indian style, with towels tied up on their heads like turbans. One of them played on a recorder and made a coiled up green garden hose that was painted with pink and yellow stripes dance about. I guess they were supposed to be on a flying carpet. Manny just walked behind the floats playing his accordion, and people threw their candy back to him. We drove around town a couple of times, throwing and receiving candy, and getting the spectators wet, and then everybody played some organized games: an egg toss, a tug of war where the losing team got tugged into the pig slop, a beer drinking contest, an Uncle Sam piñata for the kids, and a canoe race on the lake.

It was not long after July Fourth when the first big bus rolled into the parking lot on the other side of Kaluatna River. Twenty-three Germans spilled out of the bus with their cameras, and wanted to know where to go to the bathroom. They all stumbled over to Cal's ferry landing on their wobbly bus legs, and lined up behind the door of his outhouse and quickly proceeded to use up all the toilet paper. Then the leader of their clan approached Cal who happened to be there assisting his hired help.

"Allo, ve go to ze Kaluatna Lodge for lunch, and ve need ze ride across zis river." Cal smiled and told them it was $1 per person, but since they were a big group and since he was such a nice guy, he would let them across for $.60 each.

"No, no," argued the guide, "Ve eff reserwations at ze lodge. Ve ef payed. Okay?"

"Okay. Okay." Cal continued to smile, "You still have to pay me. It's for insurance reasons." But still the guide did not understand and demanded ze ride across. Now Cal, was not really one to enjoy arguing with tourists. So after snapping his red suspenders against his chest a few times, he finally decided to let them on board and then bill the lodge later. Julianne, Cal's employee, tried to hand out life jackets to the customers. They were those funky old orange vests that wrap around your neck and are generally only used by families on canoe outing in small local ponds. There were only five, which was the maximum capacity of the ferry. Poor Julianne could not get anyone to receive her colorful wares. They all rushed past her as she cried, "Um, er, uh excuse-um-you really must, ah hello, um-yes you need ah er" and they clambered aboard. Cal ran to her rescue, seeking out the leader and explained to him that only five people could go at a time.

"No, no!" yelled the guide, "Ve eff only one hower. Ve eff to hurry to get there." That was it. Cal's smile faded and he snapped his suspenders rapidly.

"I can only take five at a time. You need to all get off." The Germans gradually mumbled their way off the ferry, and poor Julianne smiled weakly and put the life vests on the customers. She made five round trips across the river. At four minutes each, one-third of their precious hour had lapsed by the time Julianne returned, weary and bug-eyed from her final round.

The Germans were reported to be seen being escorted up the road to Kaluatna Lodge at a record setting rate — flying over the potholes and washboards in a manner that surely reduced the life span of the van six or so years. Twenty three bowls of mountain chowder and 23 Kaluatna salads were consumed in a speed competitive with that of sled dogs. From the Kaluatna Lodge porch, 384 pictures of the tarn and the mountains were captured for posterity in 9.6 minutes, and then 23 Germans were reported to be once again packed into 15-passenger vans setting new figures for the life-span of a Dodge suspension.

Julianne and Cal who had been keeping themselves busy scrounging around the boathouse for a German-English dictionary were surprised to see their foreign friends so soon, and hence spent 2.75 minutes longer than scheduled bringing the tourists back across the river — much to the guide's great annoyance.

"Dees delay has been very, very bad. I am not heppy. Next time I hope — no waiting." Julianne and Cal looked at each other. Next time?

Norton Hoover was the owner and proprietor of the Kaluatna

Lodge. He was in his early 40s and being an ex-big wig of fisheries management, was a very proper and clever businessman. He spent little time with the locals, and set himself apart from the rest of the Candle occupants by always dressing in clean and classy clothing. Because of this, he was known by his staff and by many of the locals as, "Sportin' Norton."

The day following the German parade, Norton himself came sportin' down to the boathouse where Cal was whistling away, applying glue to a new hole in one of the canoes. I happened to be there visiting with Catie who was in town for the weekend, so I got to see the exchange myself. Norton stepped into the boathouse with, as Catie called it, a, "no-teeth smile" on his face. Cal was his usual boisterous self.

"Oh hello Norton. You lookin' for some beer?"

"No thanks Calvin, actually I came to discuss matters with you concerning the Germans yesterday."

"Ah yeah, weren't those guys a bunch of clowns? Watch out for this stuff now—it can give you quite a high." Cal squirted a big gob of the stinky glue on the hole.

"Actually Cal, they were very important people. They were a tryout run for the weekly Sunshine Tours that are going to come on in here." Catie and I stopped clanging around with the paddles we were to use on the tarn, and began to listen discreetly. Norton went on, "They were very unhappy with your treatment of them, but they still enjoyed Candle."

"The heck with them. We treated them wonderfully. For God's sakes, they got my poor employee over there studying the German-English dictionary—scared to death of their return." With his gluey hand he motioned toward Julianne who sat huddled on the dock, her nose buried in Larousse.

"That's not really a proper attitude regarding a large group of people who could bring a lot of income into Candle." I was surprised such a busy man as Sportin' Norton was spending this much effort on a conversation with Cal. I kept my ears perked up. Cal put his glue down and snapped a suspender with his less sticky hand.

"Norton, you know as well as I do, that with a group staying here only 20 minutes, the only pockets in Candle they're filling is yours." Norton pursed his lips tightly.

"Well, I can see you are not going to be very cooperative in this matter" he said, and started to walk toward the ferry landing where

Julianne was practicing saying in German, "Can't cross without this!" "Need this to cross!"

"I guess not if it means being a tight ass!" Cal yelled after him. "Tell them to mellow out. They're in Candle!" As Norton got back into his van, Cal yelled after him, "And thanks for the friggin' tip!"

Catie and I timidly finished selecting our oars and boat for the day's outing, and Cal returned to his work. He did not say anything to us, and his whistling had ceased.

"See ya in a little, Pop" Catie said as we passed him with the boat.

"Hah? Oh—be careful with that thing." Cal's tone was stern and cranky. "Don't get a hole in it. And don't stay out too long. I got to rent those to customers you know."

Catie and I both felt tense from the altercation. Gliding out into the smooth waters of the tarn was a cleansing relief. The day was pleasantly warm, and the mountains mirrored themselves perfectly in the soft glassy blueness. But swirly grey clouds were forming over the northwest peaks creating bold patterns on the tarn.

"A storm is coming I think" Catie said softly.

Chapter 6

In the third week of July, a couple of Kaluatna Lodge employees pulled into the parking lot across the river with a heavily loaded truck which they proceeded to unload—not at the ferry platform as usual, but further down river just a bit. Out of the vehicle came a large cable, bundles of shiny new lumber, bags of cement, a small inflatable raft and paddles, and 13 spanking new PFDs (personal flotation devices) priced at $86 each. While the town waited in awe, the lodge employees worked long hours hammering and sawing. They paddled the raft furiously across the river holding the cable and securely anchored it to a new cement anchor. Their efforts drew attention from tourists who cheered when the employees in the raft made it safely to the other side with the heavy cable.

Meanwhile, when tourists would step aboard Cal's ferry, they would ask Julianne what was going on. She would shrug her shoulders. But Cal Jensen knew very well what the Kaluatna Lodge employees were doing and he ignored it. "Glad they've found something to entertain themselves with" he would respond if you mentioned the new activity.

Four days after the work began, the Kaluatna Lodge employees were heard yipping and whistling upon the unveiling of a handsome seven foot by ten foot wooden raft. Hand railings bordered all the sides, AstroTurf to prevent slipping covered the surface, metal hooks were placed along the railings to store the 13 life vests, and there was even a wooden bench for those who needed to sit during the short crossing. I must admit it was a fancy looking barge. At the new landing there stood a big green and white sign, "KALUATNA RIVER FERRY. FREE FOR ALL KALUATNA LODGE GUESTS. ALL OTHERS 70¢ ROUND TRIP."

On the same day as the unveiling, a large bus pulled into the parking lot. Julianne recognized the smiley-faced green sun on the side of the bus and prepared herself to meet her fine German friend once again. When all the passengers had managed to wobble down the stairwell of the bus, Julianne ran to greet them with an armful of life preservers and a nervous smile — ready to practice her newly learned German phrases. But when they greeted her with "Où est la toilette?" her smile fell and she did not need to get a French dictionary to find the one word she needed.

"Merde."

As the french tourists lined up behind Cal's outhouse, the driver of the bus walked straight over to the new Kaluatna Lodge ferry and smiled at the employee awaiting them. When all of the toilet paper was gone from Cal's outtie, 12 tourists at once stepped onto the new Kaluatna Lodge cruise-ship and were whisked across to the van waiting on the other side of the river.

Secretly, some of the Candle residents were pleased with the new development at the river. Now there would be less competition for space when hauling supplies across. Some were disgusted and talked about how neon signs were next to come. The Jensens did not say much about it and appeared to be indifferent. I did not anticipate it would be Herbert and Louise who would freak out about Sportin Norton's aggressive move. I was hanging out at the Candle Flame Bar shooting pool with some Italian women who kept telling me jokes in Italian even though I told them I no-speaked-Italian, when I overheard Herb saying to Cal, "You can't just sit back and watch this yuppie steal your business away from you like that!"

"Why not?" Cal said crushing his empty beer can with one hand, "He saved me from having to buy new boots to kick him off my ferry with."

I scratched on the 8-ball, and as the Italian women started to rack up the balls again, I thought it seemed unusual there was not more competition for the table. Come to think of it, the Candle Flame Bar was unusually empty for a midsummer evening. Then I realized, Cal was not the only one whose business had been threatened. Herbert was losing his walk-in clientele to people who would take a free ride across the river to stay at the Kaluatna Lodge. It would only make sense for Herbert to form some sort of partnership with Cal regarding the ferry.

The next morning after shoveling the dog yard, I realized I had not done any visiting with anyone since just after spring breakup. Everyone had been too busy for visiting. I decided to ride my one-speed Schwinn over to Lou and Beth O'Connor's gift store. Sue Bean happened to be there with new carvings to sell and so we oohed and ahed over those for a bit. I enjoyed the opportunity to chat—mail had been so hectic lately with all the seasonal employees about, and all their mail confusing the sorters, that I had not even been going. So it was nice to chat with a few locals. Inevitably though, the conversation swung over to the new ferry at the crossing.

"Well it was a smart business move on Norton's part" Lou contributed.

"I don't know. I hate to see squabbling going on" Beth added. "As far as business, it's one thing, but as far as the community goes, it was a lousy thing to do."

"Yeah, well now Herb's dragged into it" Sue Bean sighed. "It's bound to get more messy."

"Can't say I mind more crossings though" said Lou, "with the ferry getting all bottled up there on busy days, it was a real potential hazard in emergencies."

"Well it shouldn't be at the cost of friendships!" Beth interjected quickly, "Why the Jensens always used to help the Kaluatna Lodge with their parties and such."

I did not quite know where I stood on the issue. But I certainly felt that having only lived in Candle less than a year, I had better keep my mouth shut. Two cents was worth a lot.

"Well, they never were such terrific friends anyway" Lou muttered. I realized I was tiring of this conversation quickly, and tried to bring it back to Sue Bean's carvings. She had done some really wonderful things with that wood. It was not just a bunch of conversation piece type paper weights, but earrings and pendants as well. But eventually, the conversation always slid back into the town politics. I guess I had not been in Candle long enough to understand how much a little squabble would effect people. Either that, or they were just really bored and it was the most exciting topic.

Cal ended up dropping the price of crossing on his ferry to 65¢ and making a deal with Herbert for the Candle Lodge guests to ride for free. Their partnership seemed to pick most of the Candle Lodge business back up, but a lot of tourists who had no reservations at either lodge would be confused upon arrival of which ferry to take. Most of the older folks and people with high standards would go straight to Norton's ferry, and most of the long time visitors would head straight to the institution they knew well— Cal's ferry. But many others would get quite perturbed at the crossing. Julianne and I started to call it, "the crossing of anxiety" because we would sit at the other side and watch tourists frown in confusion as they read the signs of each ferry over and over. Often if it was a couple, they would disagree on which one to take. Sometimes they would split and take both—just to spite the other person. When they would arrive at the other side—each would say their ride was better. One time I saw a couple who had just driven the 78 miles down the road from Hemle, arrive at the crossing of anxiety, and get into a worse-than-usual altercation over it. I could not hear them over the river noise, but watched them point and holler, and then turn around and get back into their car and drive back out.

Meanwhile, Cal and Joan—whose income had taken a bit of a dive—were thinking of buying new boats to add to their rental fleet. Cal said he could make them, but Joan said the money they would save by making their own, they would spend on glue to repair them. I do not think Cal debated that one.

The tour busses continued to show up on the other side of the river every week despite the hardships they had to endure on the drive in. The road became so bad that the state actually came in and tried to grade out the washboards. It was the first time they had been out in six years. Meanwhile, Candle Lodge's expansion project was completed, increasing their house capacity from 22 to 48 persons. Herbert and Louise had a big grand opening party with a band from Anchorage that stayed the weekend. Domestic beers were 10% off, and the Candle Flame Bar was packed. The seasonal employees whooped it up under the midnight sun until the dusky streamers of last light began to be replaced by the glow of morning rays. I stayed away from the fiesta — somehow not feeling overly joyous about the occasion. But from my house, my dogs howled and barked at the dancers in the road, perhaps hoping their music would make up for my hermitage.

I saw little of the other locals. The Jensen's had their hands full with the boats and the garden, Bernie was keeping very busy entertaining many of Herb's guests, and everybody else including me was either too occupied with their gardens or not brave enough to battle the bus-loads of tourists that continued to visit the town. I had 32 dogs that summer, and they were keeping me fairly busy, for I was trying to get each one off of its chain at least once a week.

One late evening as I was walking down the fireweed-laden road with two of Fred Davison's dogs, I spied a friendly spot of gold wagging hello from the top of the tree. This first golden aspen leaf was a very pleasant sight. Fall was ready to bless us with sweet berries of all kinds, colorful canopies to guide the lowering sun, and the return of the peace.

No-one, not even Sportin' Norman seemed to complain when the needles on our thermometers took an abrupt dive counterclock-wise in early September. A dense fog rolled in and an unscheduled arrival of lovely white flakes descended to cover the ugliness of summer. Tourists disappeared as abruptly as our autumn, and a sigh swept over the town. Kaluatna Lodge boarded up their windows and sent their employees packing. Zach and Sue Bean made a noble attempt to get all the berries off the bushes before they became covered, but the snow ignored the fact that it was only September and continued to blanket our earth. It buried both ferry landings and the boat docks, and everybody appeared to have a smile on their face as they gleefully drove themselves in vehicles over the crossing of anxiety.

Best of all, Ella came back. She came stomping in her big boots over to my warm house late one evening as I was stirring a big bucket of dog food. I was happy and excited to see her and quickly set out a cup of coffee.

"Whew!" she exclaimed through purple lips. "Glad for the fire! That was one heck of a drive in! The roads were completely dry coming out of Fairbanks. I had no idea about this mess!"

"Want some dog food?" I grinned at her holding up a spoonful of the stuff I was stirring.

"Gee I'll take anything at this point! I'm so glad to be here. It took me eight hours out of Hemle—stopping all the time to saw away downed alders and what have you. I got stuck three times. Good Lord what is going on with this weather?" She gulped down her coffee and began to pull off her heavy and wet clothing. "So, anything exciting happen this summer after I left?"

"Oh Gosh, Ella," I sat down with her at the table. It felt good for some reason to tell all about the summer's hectic events. As if I was getting rid of them as they spilled out—the squabbling, and the tourists everywhere—cigarette butts on the trail, no T.P. in the outhouse—I had not realized the whole summer had been so noisy. Ella listened as she warmed up but did not say much. Just wrinkled her brow and shook her head.

Finally after what seemed like endless days, the snow stopped falling. But the low fog stuck around in a heavy wet ick that made me want to just sit inside. But leave it to Ella to get me going. She interrupted my trance one morning staring at the tea leaves in my empty mug wondering what fortune there was to tell in them with a WHACK at my thinnest window. WHACK another snowball.

"All right, all right!" I stepped outside to see her awaiting me on her skis.

"Come on. Get your skis on let's go play on the tarn!" There was never any refusing Ella. I threw on my duds and joined her outside.

"What's your hurry?"

"What do you mean?" She feigned surprise. "This is a record setting day! Skiing on the tarn Sept. 17! We have to say we did it!"

Despite the soupy atmosphere, the giant flat world of the tarn made my soul breathe easy—no boundaries, no hills. No other tracks save ours. How rare I thought, to enjoy an untracked world. We danced about on our skis, skating, and drawing snow patterns and feeling very free, when suddenly Ella stopped still and held her head up high, her eyes stern in concentration. I stood still as well—wondering what made her pause. And then I too heard an unmistakable sound—getting louder and louder every second. A sickening drone of high pitched buzzing—coming closer and closer—an unhealthy din of angry bees. Multiple snowmachines were speeding down the snowy road from Hemle making their way with no time to waste. Days and days quicker than a skier or even a dog sled could manage—heading straight for Candle Lodge. Ella turned her head and looked at me with her intense blue eyes for a piercing second. Then, as abruptly as she had stopped, she began her dance around the lake once again.

Shortly after our big September storm subsided, the sky was blown free of clouds by an unusual wind that swept through Candle. It hollowed out the basin—whirling through empty dying buildings, slamming shut long forgotten doors, and ripping off pieces of the wooden roofs. The last leaves desperately clinging to aspen branches to survive the snow storm, were sheared from trees with a vengeance, and carried away forever. Fine new grains of snow slithered across the tarn in hasty emigration leaving behind lonely foliated white dunes. Plumes of white danced from the tops of all the peaks signaling the dangerously strong winds blowing up there.

Bernie and Herbert bundled themselves up tightly in wind resistant clothing, and like two young giggly boys, ran down to the frozen tarn where they unleashed Misty—their large pink and orange kite. Misty struggled to become free from the hands of her masters, and instantly flew into the blue sky. She dove and wiggled—riding the battling winds while her masters nipped away at a bottle of Yukon Jack and giggled in glee.

The next morning while enjoying my last sips of morning coffee, I overheard Herbert anxiously trying to get Jack on the CB.

"Yo Jack, you there? Yo Jack Greely, you gotta copy? Jack Greely, come in please!" And then calling Ralph Kissell over and over. His voice sounded unusually urgent. Still no answer from either.

Then I heard Bernie's voice, "Yo Herbie, what's going on down there?" As I know most Candle residents do when little action comes in on the CB radio, I turned my squelch down and the volume up in order to overhear the discourse better.

"Hey Bernie," Herb's voice continued to sound uneasy, "Manny was supposed to show up this morning to help me with my new generator. He's crazy, but he always shows up on time. His house is cold and his plane's gone."

"Did he take off for a little flightsee yesterday?" Bernie asked.

"Break, I saw his plane fly over my house yesterday around 3:30" broke in Ella.

81

"Tell ya what," Bernie came back on, "I'll buzz down to Jack's place and wake him up and we can go look for him in his 180."

"Break Bernie," broke in Zack, "Don't bother foolin' with your broken vehicles. I'm much closer, I'll run over there."

"Great," Herb came back on, "and then get back to me." Two clicks of transmit from Zach meant okay, and then Ella's voice came back on again.

"Herb you still there?"

"Yeah Ella, go ahead."

"Yeah Herb, you need me to come with?"

"That would be great Ella."

"Okay, I'll be over with some rescue gear."

Click. Click.

I continued to sip on my coffee—wondering what to make of all the CB banter when I heard Ella stomping on my porch. I got up to let her in.

"Got some warm clothes?" she asked, "I want your help too."

"But don't you have enough people in the plane already?" I asked.

"Herb hates flying and we need your eyes," she answered flatly.

I put on my boots and jackets, and walked with her over to the airstrip where we met Zach, Uncle Hickory, Herb, and Jack who was warming up his plane and checking the fluids. Over the noise of the propeller Ella shouted to Herb, "If you want to stay here, Heidi can come instead."

"That's a good idea," he yelled back, "That way I can stick around and monitor the radio."

The fact that we all had to shout over the noise of the plane made the scene feel more tense than it was already, and I noticed Uncle Hickory looking concerned. I went over to him and with his front paws he gave me a big hug which I happily returned.

"Hick's worried," I shouted.

"I'm sure Manny's alright," Jack responded, "This isn't the first time he's spent a night out there. I just hope he has a goddamn sleeping bag this time."

"Where do you think he went?" Zach asked while scratching Uncle Hickory's head.

"I'm gonna look for him up the Talana River Canyon," Jack shouted back, "Ella said he flew over her house, and also I think he was looking for a couple of moose that headed up there. He's a goddamned bastard for going out in that wind."

We got in Jack's plane with Ella's backpack containing a

sleeping bag, a thermos of hot water, and food, and took off leaving Herb, Zach, and Hickory to shield themselves from the cold snow blown from the plane. I had flown in a small plane several times before. It is perhaps the only way to see much of Alaska. Flying high over long blue icefalls, one can learn of the desolate and frozen world up there without a lot of suffering and hard work, swooping over treacherous crevasses and untouched snow, or maneuvering through narrow canyons past long waterfalls. But this time I could not permit myself to look at the fantastic scenery. I was there to look for a small orange plane—possibly smashed, and I had to prepare myself for that sight.

From the corner of my eye I saw a large flock of sheep on a steep mountain side, but as much as I wanted to, I did not dwell on that sighting. I systematically scoped the landscape as we flew over— feeling a burden of obligation as my drawn together eyes strained to look for Manny's plane through the thick glass. Ella and Jack talked to each other up front. I could not hear what they said, but remembered that Ella said my eyes were important.

We were fairly far up the Talana Canyon when Jack—responding to a blinking light among all his dials, swooped up and over another ridge—the light was an ELT (Emergency Locator Transmitter). We flew along the ridge and I felt myself becoming nervous until we saw it—a tiny orange plane stuck in the wind drift on a flat ridge top. From our height, the orange plane looked alone and helpless. A very small existence in a vast land of emptiness and cold. The little plane was turned up on its end. Was it smashed? Was its passenger okay? I was ashamed to admit it, but I was a little afraid. We circled the plane while descending, and then we saw him. He was sitting next to his plane tinkering away, and sure enough, there was Ol' Griz sitting next to him too.

He stood up and waved to us with both arms, and then went back to tinkering with his plane. He looked just fine, in fact, I began to wonder where his accordion was. We circled him and circled him. Was Jack trying to land? Obviously there was no room on that little ridge top for us to land. We would end up like Manny. We circled and circled while Jack talked to Manny over the aircraft radio. I thought I would get awfully dizzy. Finally Ella opened her door and dropped her pack which went flying with the wind down onto the ridge top for Manny, and we flew away. Once again, we were back down the Talana river. I could relax now and enjoy the beautiful scenery—the narrow gorge and the steep snowy peaks beside it.

Uncle Hickory greeted us when we stepped out of the plane. He still had that concerned look on his face. I petted him, and even gruff Jack gave him a pat on the head. Herbert and Zach were right behind Hickory.

"He's fine," Ella smiled when she stepped out of the plane.

"One heck of a place to land," Jack said.

"Do we need to get ahold of Ralph so he can pick him up with his super cub?" Herb asked.

"No," answered Jack, "he wants to get his plane out himself now before it snows more. He thinks he's almost got it fixed. Though I suppose the goddamned bastard will want a little of his orange juice when he returns."

Chapter 7

Candle Lodge had seven guests on Halloween. A couple of them skied in, and the rest rode snowmachines in or had even brought their skis with them on the mail plane. Most of them were friendly folks, but I could not suppress a selfishness in me that caused me to think of the visitors as intruders. While the summer had been trodden with tourists, I came to expect Candle to be empty in the winter. Strangers in town did not seem right.

Bernie drove his three-wheeler through deep snow down to Candle Lodge to have a chat with Herbert. This time he did not bring his kite nor his Yukon Jack, and he did not seem gleeful when he left either. He came up to my house afterward. After he had shed his snow suit and had a cup of hot coffee in his hands, he exclaimed, "Well, its nice to be able to sit down with a friend once in a while without strangers bobbing around!"

"How are Herb and Louise?" I asked.

"Oh, just swell. Well actually, how should I know. They don't have the time of day to talk with ya now. They got all those folks running around." Bernie was upset. He was drinking his coffee fast and talking rather loud. I think he was disappointed. He wanted a Halloween party so he could be a two-headed miner with Herb again, but did not want to party with tourists. Negative talk of tourists made me uncomfortable, so I moved the conversation along to his Halloween batch of home-brew, which made Bernie smile again and relax. We played a quick game of cribbage in which he almost skunked me, and then it was time for him to take his leave. I walked outside with him so I could water the dogs, and watched him try to start his three-wheeler.

"Ohhhhhh!" I heard him wail as he discovered his dead battery. While I gathered up dog bowls, I heard him pulling and pulling at the pull cord, and then a barrage of unusual words as the pull-cord disintegrated in his tight fingers. I tried not to laugh at poor Bernie's misfortune. He was having a bad day.

"Look, Bernie," I said, "the dogs need running, I'll take you up the hill and you can come back another time with a fresh battery or something." He brightened at the idea.

"Yes, if I could only get my tools back from that lousy Herbert..." I did not wait to hear the end of his usual rantings, but went inside to fetch the dog harnesses.

Bernie must have been enjoying the dog sled ride. He was quite talkative as we swooshed up the road. He told me stories of past winter exploits with Herb getting stuck together up the Talana River for days setting trap line, skating on the tarn, and crashing into Herb by accident giving him a black eye. I did not say too much being partly out of breath. I was running along side the dogs to stay warm. The early cold that had arrived in September had never taken its leave. Being that it was only Halloween, I was still in the denial stage and just was not dressing warm enough yet. When we passed the boarded up Kaluatna Lodge, Bernie interrupted his story:

"Now see, there's a lodge that closes in the winter. Does its thing and leaves. None of this hanging around stuff."

It was a tough push up the steep trail to Bernie's but I was looking forward to the ride down. Bernie invited me into his house to warm up. I knew full well that Bernie would have been pleased if tribulations with my source of transportation had prolonged my visit. But having no intentions to be prolonged or to even remain more than a few moments, I trusted my dogs with just a snow hook to hold them in team instead of picketing them out during the quick visit.

I enjoyed a quick cup of hot cocoa with Bernie, after which I said my goodbye, and got back on the sled. All eight of us were anxious and excited about the steep run back down to Candle. I made sure my breaking mechanisms were in place, put one foot on the break, one on the runners, and called out, "All right. Let's go!" We yanked full speed ahead toward the silver mine road. But I had barely set the snow hook back in the basket, where I kept it when it was not it use, when I heard a frightful commotion of buzzing and had to stand on the brake with all my might to get the dogs to stop. Four snowmachines shredded past me down the trail at near lightning speeds leaving a smelly trail of exhaust behind them. "ZZZOOOMMMM!!!" and they were gone. Bernie came running out his house and down his trail to me. He was livid.

"Christ! What is going on? Those guys could have killed you! What the heck are they doing up here? Are you okay? My god, this isn't a war zone! Miserable, stinking, filthy, scum of the earth...."

My team was antsy and barking so I did not stay around to learn any more new words from Bernie. We tore down the trail. My dogs were excited to run fast and I enjoyed the speed myself. But I was looking forward to getting back home and having a little peace.

The next day Bernie skied down the road and shut the gate that separated state and private property from silver mine property. This gate that blocked the road was just a facade: it was always open and was only put there by the silver mine to remind folks who owned what. But Bernie closed it. He even put a lock on it.

I remember that day well because that was the day I was teaching Lou and Beth's visiting niece, Skyla, how to dog mush. The plan was to go back up toward Bernie's and ask if he wanted to bring down a fresh battery for his three-wheeler. I had split up my team and had given Skyla her own four dogs to mush. Following behind me, she was doing well—getting the hang of how to lean and balance, turning corners without smashing into trees or dumping upside down, until we hit this unexpected obstacle.

I yelled to Skyla behind me to hit her brakes hard, and threw in my snow hook. I hopped off the sled—trusting the snow hook to hold my dogs in place, and ran to the gate to investigate the situation. Just as

I reached the gate, and had an opportunity to note that it was locked, I heard a zip-zip-zzing and along came Sue Bean from the other direction in her four-wheeler heading to Herb and Louise's kitchen with a big load of cranberries. She greeted me with one of her flashy smiles, and then a frown as she discovered the locked gate.

"Now who on earth...?"

I shrugged my hands with an expression of disgust, "One can only speculate." I had by then realized that only a hacksaw would allow us to get through.

"Well shoot Heidi," said Sue Bean, "this gate would be a stupid reason not to get to town. Clear out!"

Next thing I knew, Sue Bean was ramming her way around the gate trying to maneuver through and over the thick bush that outlined the road. One minute she was driving that machine like a crazy woman—a look of sheer determination on her face as she punched through the deep snow and brush, and the next minute she was down—cranberries all over, staining the snow a blood red and giving the scene a very dramatic flair. I ran to her help, and unfortunately, so did Skyla, who upon jumping from her break to run toward the accident, left no one to hold her dog team. Sue Bean was delightfully covered with snow and cranberries (a beautiful holiday-like combination if I may add) but fine. Or I should say she was fine until she saw four dogs and a sled heading her way.

"Skyla!" I yelled. Skyla ran to catch the excited dogs who must have been hoping for a cranberry dinner. By some acrobatic feat she was able in a bounding leap to reach for the handlebars. She nearly had control, but was distracted by a "Whoah!" from James Jensen who just happened to be skijoring up the road that day. Rather, he was trying for dear life to stay standing up, and his two dogs were tearing up the road to join our excitement.

Skyla could not get her feet on the sled, but held on, and the dogs dragged her through the snow covered bushes—her stomach nearly touching the ground, and the toes of her boots making cute gouges in the snow.

"Whoooahhh!" James' dogs were way too excited to listen. They bounded in the direction of Skyla's tangle of dogs and driver.

"Come Gee! Come Gee!" he yelled trying to get the dogs to turn around. They did eventually listen for some reason, and took a quick about-face only to wrap up Jamie's feet tight in his bungee cords—a marvelous trick. He took a dive into the snow, and the dogs, unable to rescue him from his soft and snowy plight, took a rest.

Skyla had meanwhile managed to tip the sled sideways, and the dogs — wrapped around an aspen tree — lay down as well. I looked at the situation. Sue Bean, covered with cranberries and trampled by paws, lay in her self created ditch, her head resting on her crashed four-wheeler. Jamie was wrapped in bungee cords, his legs attached to skis that were nowhere to be seen in the powdery snow. Skyla lay flat on her stomach, her arms outstretched and panting like a dog. The dogs also wrapped up in some form or another, were barking with impatience.

Never have I been good at separating humor from other's misfortunes. When I was young, I always used to laugh whenever my little sister would fall down the stairs or spill her milk. I was no different now, and a loud giggle erupted from my mouth. It was followed by others I could not suppress, and soon joined by a few from Jamie, then Sue Bean, and finally Skyla, sputtering snow as she gulped for air. The dogs barked, and all four of us just rested there, laughing until tears dripped from our eyes. Bernie was not going to live this one down.

Unfortunately, Herbert did not laugh when Sue Bean told him about the entertaining series of events that occurred at the closed gate. He was even less joyful when Louise told him five influential guests wanted a refund because they came out to see the mines and they could not get there because the road was closed. Sue Bean, and whatever sauce and liqueur she was able to make of the survivor cranberries was sent back up the hill with a message for Bernie: "Open that gate!"

Bernie, of course, ignored the message. He was probably appreciating an interlude of snowmachine-free peace. He even turned his CB off. I know because I tried to get in touch with him. I still had his three-wheeler and did not want to be responsible for keeping his dead battery from freezing. Knowing Bernie, he would not remember about his vehicle until he needed to go somewhere.

Despite his many worn years in Candle, and his somewhat wacky disposition, I do not think anybody in Candle expected Herbert to do what he did in response. I remember I had been outside watching the birds at my feeder flit about — their bright and bold colors decorating the plain wooden box. Jojo Jensen had made me a wooden bird house, and Joan had loaned me some seed. I had been enjoying watching the downy woodpeckers, the chickadees, and the grosbeaks all taking turns at the feeder. Rarely would all three kinds eat at the feeder at once, but I watched them all equally. Without any politicians or rules, they managed to maintain some silent cooperation at this commons of theirs. As I marvelled at their harmonious cohabitation, I heard the unmistakable sound of a loader. Good lord, were they plowing the road at this time of the year? Well, maybe it would lessen the snowmachine traffic. But no, that loader was not state operated, it was Herb in a D6! Herb drove that thing up the road to the gate, and did not go through it, but right around it. Made a new trail. He and his hired maintenance man got out and whacked away the bushes and felled a few trees, and cleared a new road—right around the gate.

The tourists on snowmachines were once free again to roam the world. They zipped happily up the road to explore the mine buildings and terrorize Bernie. They were happy, Herb was happy. Surprisingly, no one in town said much at first. I think everyone was sort of in awe of the whole situation. Bernie was fuming. I know because he would not come off of his hill, and I could not raise him on the CB.

I finally decided to head up to Bernie's house. I did not want to have to worry about his battery any longer. I met him at his trail hauling water. He greeted me with a smile.

"So nice to see a real friend for a change," was his greeting. He was very grateful for the battery, but it was not enough to relieve his bitterness:

"Well, you could have used it yourself you know—if you had needed one. Come in for tea. I mean, you would have been welcome to use it. I know you would have returned it unlike other people in this town who never return any tools I loan them. I mean, for crying out loud, Herb probably used my tools to cut that road! Peppermint okay? It's amazing he even knew how to do it!" I accepted tea from Bernie but refused lunch thinking I did not want to listen to him for that long. He apparently had been in need of a vent of some sort.

"You just wait until the DNR and Wells and Company hears about the new highway Herb created. Milk? And you can bet they'll hear about it!"

I decided not to wait for my tea to steep and added more milk to it to cool it down faster.

"Wouldn't mind if they closed his place down. If you ask me, that place doesn't know a thing about regulations anyway."

I took some big fast gulps from my mug and burned my mouth.

"And you know, I can do jolly well without any of his business.

People come up here anyway, and Lord knows I don't need that many folks tromping my soil."

I added more milk to my tea and downed it in one big huge swig.

"I sure as hell don't need his friggin beer. Now that place—well you sure finished that tea fast. Like some more?"

"Oh no, thanks so much, I really have to go. Lots to do at home." I realized I really did not feel like listening to anymore. Bernie got up and walked me to the dogs. He looked a little dejected—like an abandoned puppy.

"Well, I sure enjoyed the visit. Not sure if I'll be down there real soon. I'm not quite sure where I threw the key to that gate, and I'm not about to take Herb's trail."

I felt a little sorry leaving Bernie. He obviously was in need of a hug or two, but I had no time for soapboxes that day, and so I hailed my dogs and held on for the fast ride down the mountain, steering clear of speeding snowmachines.

Herb and Louise invited me again for Thanksgiving dinner, but instead I decided to go to the Stevens' with Ella. We mushed together down the Kaluatna River on Thursday morning, which was a good day for mushing—beautiful crisp weather. The land was covered with snow but the high bush cranberries had managed to still hang on to their mother branches. Frozen, their bright redness against the pure white of the snow provided a holiday decor to our journey down the river. The rock walls enclosing our canyon dripped with thin ice, the peaks in the far distance were blue and white mystics. I breathed deep, inhaling the clean fall air, and absorbing more precious Candle moments.

I appreciated spending Thanksgiving with a family. The Stevens' house was much more homey than my bachelorette pad. They had a small split level log house built by both Mary and Bruce. The ceiling was high, creating a roomy free atmosphere even though Molly's loft covered half of it. Molly was very excited to see us arrive. She ran out upon hearing their dogs bark at ours, and helped me unharness my dogs. She obviously had little contact with folks other than her parents—a common phenomenon which I think is a little sad in Candle. Kids need other kids I think, in order to grow up as healthy functioning human beings.

After my dogs were settled, Molly grabbed my hand and skipped around their dog yard quizzing me on whether or not I could remember them all, and asking me how I thought they all behaved in the summer. She showed me her tree fort, and her snow fort, and once inside, she showed me her loft, and her bookshelves, and paintings, and would have enticed me into building a marble machine with her, but Mary rescued me from repeating my childhood by calling us down for eggnog. I resumed normal adult behavior as we sipped homemade eggnog and relaxed in the quiet of their house, savoring the smell of turkey.

The next morning was clear again, and cold. The kind of cold that freezes the insides of your nostrils, and gives you long thick lashes of white icicles unless you blink hard enough to melt them. Ella and I covered up in scarfs, fur hats, and down jackets, and loaded with turkey sandwiches hit the trail when the first hues of soft sunlight hinted at peering over the mountains.

Ella tucked her small body under the skins in my sled basket and I let us go, whishing through the mountain shadows among the stillness I savor. In contrast to our trip down the river, when we filled the still air with our babble, both eager to share our newest ideas and philosophies that had been cooking all fall and summer, we both kept silent on our ride home. I was enjoying the clear view of the Ilkitas against the bright blue sky, breathing in the scene through frozen nostrils. My mind was clear as if the river's peace had reached an equilibrium in and out. I was in my own world. Ella must have been in her own Zen world too, for when we both heard a sudden "ZZINGG!!" she sat up abruptly and shook her head like a wet dog shaking off after a dip.

A herd of snowmachiners was headed for us at close to 40 miles per hour. I sank in the brake and called Popik to go haw. Ella jumped from her cozy bundle into the snow to grab Popik and lead him off the trail. No sooner did she have him by the collar, than the snowmachines were upon us. As Ella stumbled into the deep snow with the team of dogs, the driver of the first snowmachine smiled and waved and plowed his big machine right around us and continued on. Six drivers behind him then proceeded to do the very same—each waving as they passed us at 30 miles per hour.

Ella, after regaining her stance, put her hand out in effort to stop some of them, but they all smiled and waved, and were gone. I knew Ella had wanted to tell them off. She was fuming. I had never seen her angry before, even though I had witnessed several opportunities for her to become so.

"Those bloody scumbags! They have no right to knock us off the trail like that! Short of causing a mess of tangled gang-line, they could have run us over!"

I threw in the snow hook and ran to help her free Popik of his entanglement.

"Those bastards!" she went on, "I can't continue to live like this! Anybody has a right to be here, but I shouldn't have to exist in fear that I'm going to be overtaken by several tons of metal every time I go out!"

I was not really sure what to say. I was not particularly pleased with the incident myself. But I was also more accustomed to dodging traffic in dangerous city streets and had more recent insight into the mentality of our visitors.

We finished untangling the dogs in silence. I could almost see smoke coming from Ella's ears.

Then she said, "Okay, enough of that. Let's eat our sandwiches and talk of nice things. Let's talk about Molly, and what she's going to be like when she grows up."

The dogs lay down and rolled in the snow, and we sat on the sled with the sandwiches, our tongues remembering the pleasant dinner of the night before. We made up boyfriends for Molly and laughed, and the rest of the way home was filled with light chatter. But our journey had been tainted. Our peace had been broken once again.

Christmas came and went without much flair. The Jensens went down to Idaho for the season to visit relatives. The lodge had two shy guests from Switzerland who did not speak English. For Christmas dinner, they politely sat in silence while Herb and Louise downed shots of rum, toasting a night of loneliness. Sue Bean, Fred Davison, Zach, and I had a quiet evening together. Zach cooked a goose he had bagged early in the fall. We decorated a spruce tree with popcorn chains and beer bottle caps painted red, and played Hearts into the wee hours of the night (that is 10 o-clock). Zach invited Bernie, but he did not show up. Sue Bean went to check on him on her way home the next day. Found him passed out next to an empty bottle of Wild Turkey. She stoked his fire, put spruce bows in the empty bottle, and went home to carve more alders.

The new year brought the warm winds of a chinook. Suddenly in January it was 30 degrees out. Tee-shirt weather. I could not stand to chop wood because I would get too hot. Everyone was appreciating the warm weather and all showed up for mail. It was the first time I had seen the Cohens for some time, and even the Stevens decided to mush up the river and get their mail. I enjoyed seeing everybody and their dogs. Uncle Hickory was delighted, and ran from dog to dog, from person to person getting a pat from each.

Many of us were too warm to stand inside, and were chatting in front of Zach's house, opening our mail when Herb held up a letter and exclaimed, "Listen to this everyone! Some woman—Adele Hugston—is coming out next month to look at this place. She wants to make a ski resort here!"

Mouths dropped. People, accustomed to Herb's odd sense of humor were not sure whether he was serious or not.

"Give me that." Sue Bean snatched the finely woven satin paper from Herb's hands and Bernie rushed to her side to read over her shoulder.

"Sure enough" she said after looking it over. "She's going to stay at the lodge."

"Is this your idea Kramer?" Bernie shouted at Herb. I think it was the first word I heard Bernie say to Herb in some time. "Did you invite her here to stay in your whorehouse of a lodge?!"

"I don't think I have to answer that question Mr. Tourists-are-only-allowed-here-when-I-want-them-to!" Herb snapped back. Sue Bean and Louise exchanged quick glances.

"I have a right to my privacy!" Bernie was red in the face." I have a right to—"

Herb interrupted, "Everybody had a right to come here. If you can't handle it then LEAVE!"

"I can't believe you guys," Lisa Kissell interjected calmly, to my surprise. "Take your problems somewhere other than where we are. Nobody needs it."

"And I agree" said Bernie in a voice twice as loud as that of Lisa. "Nobody needs it." And stepping up to Herb: "Nobody needs you ruining our town!"

All of a sudden, Herb lost control—it took me by surprise, and I think Louise screamed when Herb reached up and punched Bernie. Bernie was no fighter. He was a skinny little guy really. And Herb was on him fast. In shock, I rushed to grab Herb. I do not know what I thought I might accomplish. Those two could have probably spent some vicious moments rolling in the snow. But fortunately, my attempts to pull Herb away were instantly aborted when Uncle Hickory appearing from nowhere pushed me aside and jumped onto

Herb and knocked him down. Then Hickory stood over Herb's chest wagging his tail but looking sternly into Herb's eyes.

Bernie brushed himself off, and got on his three-wheeler which had a flat tire and rode away without saying anything. Herb gave Hickory a pat on the back and scratched his head "Good boy," and Hick let him go. Then with no further ado, Herb and Louise hopped on their snowmachines and were off as well. I gave Uncle Hick a big hug and we went inside to tell the others what had happened.

Scratching Hickory underneath his collar, Zach shook his head when he heard the story.

"Ms. Hugston wrote me as Candle postmaster a month ago telling me of her plans and asking where she could stay while checking things out. I was the one who told her to write the lodge."

"I punched my best friend once," said Bruce, "felt like hell afterward."

"I punched my brother once," someone else added.

"Everybody punches their brother."

"No one punches their mother."

"Or their dog."

"Why punch your dog when you could kick your dog?"

"Say you broke your foot?"

The conversation got sillier and sillier until everyone had forgotten everything—sort of, but not really, and we all gathered our mail and went home one by one thinking about the days' events.

Adele Hugston arrived as she said she would in early February—a beautiful time to visit Candle. The days were becoming longer so there was plenty of light with which to gaze at the snow covered mountains, bare of vegetation save a few spruce trees here and there. Perfect terrain for a ski resort. Ella and I had in fact climbed up past the mine a few days earlier with our skis and had enjoyed making turns through the bottomless powder the whole way down. The soft sun provided us with plenty of warmth. The skiing was perfect and Adele Hugston knew it.

Bernie suggested spray painting the whole mountain below the mine with a big poison sign to drive her off. Fred Davison suggested haunting the mine when she went to visit and convincing her the place was cursed. Ella thought of shoveling away all the snow so it would look like Candle never gets any. Hazel and Jonathan Cohen thought the town should work with her and suggest creating a minimum impact educative ski resort. A sort of resort slash university.

Nobody did anything though. We all just politely ignored her when she stepped off the mail plane in her furs and painted fingernails and let Herb lift her heavy suitcase onto the sled behind his snowmachine. She smiled tightly and blinked her eyes at us all in our dirty work clothes as she climbed behind Herb on the vehicle and was whisked away.

She spent a week at the lodge. Herb escorted her around Candle and up to the mine where the resort would have its lobby if she decided to buy it. They snowmachined over the hills looking for prospective runs. And she and Louise played with the calculator every night coming up with deals they could make with each other.

To be quite frank, many residents were scared. Almost too scared to even talk about it. Developments were happening far too fast. Jonathan Cohen even went all the way down to the lodge to meet with Ms. Hugston—bringing with him his proposal for an educative resort.

Jonathan's report of the meeting was that she blinked her eyes at him as she poured lots of sweet and low in her coffee and said, "That's so cute of you locals to want to chip in ideas. However, they don't seem to fit with those of our corporation. We would love to employ you though—perhaps as a mountain host or something?"

Ella skied up to the Jensens to study their 1920s pictures and look for good photos that might somehow indicate that Candle has a long history of snowless winters. Meanwhile, Fred started digging around in his shed for any odd and scary contraptions he could set up in the mine buildings. And Bernie, he just moaned and grumbled.

Louise called me on the CB one day and said that Ms. Hugston would like to go dog mushing and wouldn't it be nice if maybe I could take her? I sure did not want to take Ms. Hugston on a special dog mushing excursion, but I said I would let her mush with me to mail if she cared to.

Sure enough, she arrived Tuesday morning over at my place just as I was scrounging around for a stamp to put on my letter. A week of being in Candle and spending the days outside seemed to have taken its effect on Adele. Her hair was a bit mussed, her fingernails less shiny, with perhaps even a chip or two; and somehow she had an air of being a little more rough. But still, she kept herself wrapped in a cloak of dead animals and was all talk, talk, talk.

"What a darling little place! I can see how you just love it out here. Oh these dogs are so sweet. What's this one's name again? Oh isn't it a dear? Hullo you Tuskie Tuska. You are excited aren't you..."

96

The Stevens were out for a week, and had left me their dogs, so I figured I could put two teams together. I thought Ms. Hugston would enjoy running her own sled. The mush to mail was fairly easy, and with me in front, there was not much she would have to do except hang on and lean. And anyway, then I would not have to listen to her talk. I showed her how to harness up the dogs, (she kept putting the harnesses on backward anyway) and gave her a few hints of how to lean at the turns, and made sure she knew the number one rule of mushing: Never ever let go of the sled.

For a beginner, Adele did fairly well coming out of the dog yard. That is always the hardest part. A dog team does not accelerate easy and slow like an old Volkswagen. It does not even glide into speed like a turbo charged sports car. But one second all is motionless and barking, and the next instant YANK and you are speeding quietly at the fast rate of 28 paws. No problems around corner number two either. She seemed to have a pretty good command of the sled.

After a few minutes, Popik had to relieve himself in a solid sort of manner. Funny about dogs, a short run always makes them have to go. But I always figure better on the road than in the dog yard where I have to take care of it.

While we were stopped, Adele yelled up to me, "Um Heidi! What do you do when you need to pee while you're mushing?"

Well, other people might tell you this story differently, but I did not mean to mislead her at all. In all honesty, I had no plans for what happened. I did think her question rather peculiar, but that was the extent of my thoughts. I simply answered her.

"I just pull down my pants and stand on the mat or the runners, hold the handlebars, and pee right there on the trail." That is what I do. I thought she was just curious—that maybe the dogs' actions had triggered her curiosity in the subject. And as I said, I was not really thinking, so I neglected to tell her that I also usually throw in the snow hook to anchor the dogs while I take my time.

Well, the dogs were ready, so with an "All right. Let's go!" I resumed travel up the road. The roar of a plane overhead reminded me that we had little time to spare if I wanted to send my mail off that day. I urged the dogs on. I hated being the last one to arrive at mail. With all the people and dogs there, the potential was always high for things to become very hectic with my team. When we passed Lou and Beth's house, my dogs caught wind of the other dogs at mail and they took off in a hurry. I love those bursts: the dogs are excited and happy whizzing through the snow with the wind in our faces and whipping past my ears. I was also thankful for the boost, because when I reached the end of the road, I saw that the mail plane had already landed. I hoped that I had time still to anchor the sled and get my mail in the outgoing bag. We pulled into the airstrip where everyone was standing around unloading the mail plane, and as I reached for my snow hook, I heard a high screeching from I behind me.

"Aaahh! Whoah! Whoah! Stop it! Stoppit! Aaah! Stop! Stop!"

No one was unloading the plane, they all had huge grins on their faces and were looking in my direction—or rather behind me where Adele Hugston, hanging on to the handlebars for dear life was squatting on the runners with pants and panties wrapped around her ankles, and her pink bottom and more—exposed for the whole world to see. The dogs were dragging her in this helpless fashion at record speed toward the whole congregation of delighted mail-goers! I threw in the snow hook and rushed to her rescue. But it was too late. Everybody was whooping and hollering.

"Yee haw!"

"Nice one Heidi!"

"Way to go Heidi!"

I had never seen so many shit-eating grins in one place before. Everyone was wearing one. All except for Adele Hugston of course. She was mortified. Absolutely red, she stood and pulled up her pants as the dogs finally calmed down. She would not let me help her. She was furious at me. Just down right outraged. She wrapped her furs around her and without saying a word jumped into the plane and would not look at a soul. Did not even talk to the pilot. We never saw or heard of her ever again. Everybody said I was a genius. To this day, I bet they would insist I planned it all. Honest to God though, I'm innocent.

Chapter 8

Not even two weeks after Adele Hugston had hitched her britches back up around her waist in a huff and taken her angry leave from Candle, a dense fog rolled in and socked us in. Wet snow, from who knows where, mounded up outside my door faster than I could shovel it. The whole world was lost in a cloud. The view from my window nil. I brought in a big load of wood and enjoyed the coziness of my wood stove. No sounds dared penetrate the fog. The dogs were still and peaceful in their houses, there was no wind, and the squirrels had tunnelled themselves deep under the blanket of white. The only sound interrupting this severe silence was the mild cracking and bellowing from my wood stove. I enjoyed those peaceful times curled up under a cheesy green and yellow afghan. I found the weather opportune for repairing dog harnesses and drinking lots of coffee.

My crackling stove and hissing of the water pot on top of it however was not loud enough to keep me from my discontented thought that Herb and Louise were somehow mad at me for "chasing away" their client. I felt too restless to carefully poke the awl back and forth through the smelly chewed up material. Instead, I put on my wool pants and parka, and surprised my comatose dog team by rigging up the sled. It was a lousy time for traveling. The fog was so thick I could scarcely see Popik in the lead, and the damp air chilled through all my layers.

When the fog suddenly gave away to the cheery lights of Candle Lodge, I was surprised to see a large number of colorful snowmachines lined up by the door. In so much fog and silence, I had forgotten all about them. These folks must have been fog bound. I secured my team and knocked the snow off my boots before opening the door. Herb was sitting with his guests looking relaxed, but occupied with telling a story. Guests in stocking feet, who were drinking coffee and engrossed in Herb's narrative, filled all the seats. Their shiny colored plastic helmets were lined up on the walls. Beyond, I could see Louise bustling about in the kitchen.

I instantly felt uncomfortable when I walked in, as if I had intruded upon something. Herb interrupted his monologue for a moment as I opened the door. He looked at me long enough to see me smile at him, but not long enough to respond. He returned his attention to his group and resumed his story.

A wave of loneliness swept down my back. I suddenly felt akin to the many Candle residents who had been shunned by a friend. The heated room felt cold. I backed from the entry way and slipped quietly back out the door. I had come to apologize but had probably now made things worse by leaving. My dogs were happy to see me, and I them. They took me back home where I let Popik into my cozy cabin to help me savor the peace and escape the loneliness brought on by a crowded room.

My days of hermitdom curled under the green and yellow afghan did not last long though, for the silvery days of March soon beamed over the bluish mountains to Candle. March is my favorite month. The days are long and sweet. The sun is warm again, but not enough to melt away the lovely quilt of snow. Ella and I were both excited for the season of extended outdoor expeditions. We were not the only ones however. Our earlier cause for complaining about the disruption of peace by snowmobiles now seemed like a joke. Folks looking like space explorers hidden under great big helmets, and sporting large shiny machinery arrived in throngs. They zipped all over the country spewing exhaust and making new trails. The once still white dunes of snow were now tracked up like an Indy 500 course. Candle had become a playground for snowmachines—their haven.

Toward the end of the month, with Ella's encouragement, I decided to do something I had sworn I would never do. I took a trip without my dogs. Though Zach promised me he would use them, I felt guilty. What kind of musher was I? Maybe I was only a poop shoveler. But I could not resist the call to get way the heck out of snowmachine country, and that, I could not do with my dogs.

Another woman, Denise, joined us for our adventure. She sometimes guided with Ella, and the two of them wanted an opportunity to practice and discuss new teaching and glacier travel techniques. Thin and tall with short black hair, she had no shortness of confidence. I must admit, being completely inexperienced myself, I felt a little intimidated to be venturing out with these two very competent women, who were surely capable of accomplishing more without me. Even so, I hugged my forlorn canine friends goodbye, and eagerly climbed aboard the Cessna 180 that would land us out in virtually unexplored territory. Our lives were in the hands of our mail pilot Dale, who was at the time the most experienced bush/glacier pilot in the area. I was bundled up practically from head to toe in borrowed gear: the lime green plastic boots again, and more petrol chemical clothing than I thought I would ever own—certain to protect me from any element we might encounter. With everybody's warnings to "be careful!" (Why did everybody have to say that?) we were in the air, and very quickly away from familiar territory as well as snowmachine country.

In that little plane, we flew for nearly 45 minutes. Flying through narrow valleys, by hundreds of snowy peaks, ice and whiteness dripping from each, I felt almost suspended in mid air—a white, white world below us. As we neared our landing destination, a large glacier surrounded by cold foreboding mountains, I literally began to shake with anticipation. He was going to leave us here in this vast world? A place for no humans.

I was relieved when the skis of the plane hit the glacier and we glided to a smooth stop. With our feet on the snow, and the sun beaming down from all corners, our home for the next eight days lost a little of its foreboding feeling. The little plane took off to get Denise. It became miniature quickly and the hum of its roar lingered long after its departure like hanging curls of smoke from a wafting cigarette. I stared for a while at the emptiness the plane left behind, feeling only ice and snow around me, until I was awakened from my reverie by Ella who already had her shovel and snow saw out of her pack and was beginning to dig in our campsite: a deep square pit for our tent, a kitchen equipped with benches and counters, and of course, an out hole.

Once Denise arrived, and our base camp was all set up, we roped up for a little exploratory excursion up the glacier. With Ella and Denise on both ends of the rope to do the thinking, I had only to worry about keeping the 40 feet of rope in front of me taut enough. Though weighted down with heavy clothes, rope, and pack, I felt incredibly free skiing slowly up the glacier. It was exciting to be part of that bold landscape. Just us, sun, wind, and snow. The ice was endless, and yet at the same time, the edge of the world was right there. I was hooked.

That evening, the wind picked up and slammed hard snow against our tent. It shook and rocked us all night long. Cozy in my sleeping bag, I once again felt insignificant. Here we lay in our orange tent — the only thing orange around for hundreds of miles, and nature would do her best to cover up this unnatural existence.

At 7 AM Denise's alarm went off. She leaned forward and unzipped the door and groaned. We were socked in good. The world was gone. She could not even see our kitchen. Another morning groan and she zipped the tent back up and buried herself back inside her sleeping bag.

The wind continued to hurl snow at our tent all day. We read, played cribbage, slept, talked, and took turns crawling out of our orange cave to ensure the rest of our camp was still existing through all the bleakness. It was not until after Ella had beat both me and Denise at several games of cribbage that I stepped outside the tent and noticed the massive peaks in the south glowing orange pink in the alpenglow, and the remaining swills of fog rolling away down the valley. I pressed my lips to the darkening blue and inhaled the enchantment, feeling ultimately lucky to be there at that moment. I called to Denise and Ella to come out and bring my mittens while they were at it. Together we stood in our down booties watching the sky clear and fill with stars, and rejoiced that we would get to play outside our tent after all.

Early the next morning as the yawning sun was beginning to stretch its first rays over the mountains into our day, we got up — eager to get out of the tent. We would not be able to climb a peak yet — for the preceding day's wind and snow was certain to cause dangerous avalanche conditions. Instead, we decided to goof around on the glacier another day, allowing Denise and Ella to discuss and practice route finding skills.

Making sure to empty our bladders beforehand, we once again locked up access to our clothes with harnesses, coils of rope, pulleys, carabineers, snow pickets, and ice axes. Feeling like a mail-covered soldier, I took my place between Ella and Denise, and we ventured slowly down the valley.

The sun apparently had been eager to come out of its hiding, for now it streamed intensely through the snow. Having been just dim bluish images a few hours earlier, the peaks enclosing our valley were now bold and provocative in their new light. I did not dare remove the protective glacier glasses from my squinting eyes.

Ella steered us gently toward a side canyon—an intersection. Even my untrained eye could tell that we were coming up on a large depression. Ella planned a careful course on one side of the thing— yet for some reason this unfriendly hole evoked a strange intensity in me—an unfamiliar feeling of nervousness.

Ella turned to me and Denise and said, "Now, watch me" as she prepared to pass the hole. She plunged her ice axe shaft methodically into the snow before each step. When she was safely past, she called out, "It's fine Heidi, come on."

As I approached this monster in the ice, I became aware of its beauty. It was an elongated oval, pointy on the ends, and about 12 feet wide in the very center. Hardened windswept snow curled over the edges and pointed at the abyss below: a beautiful secret blue that darkened mysteriously with depth. Ella and Denise let me pause to stare down its throat for a few moments, and then I moved on. I was free of it.

We climbed up the valley further and I began to bake. Maybe the ambient temperature was only 29° or so, but with the sun penetrating all that snow so deeply, and bouncing from every corner back onto my vulnerable body, I was sure that I was experiencing heat of 90°. We paused to loosen clothing and open zippers everywhere, but Denise would not let me stash away any of my clothing.

"You must always be prepared to drop unexpectedly into an icy cold freezer at any minute," she warned. "If you're sweating, drink water and move more slowly." I told myself I should take her on a dog trip sometime and let her be the novice, but obeyed her expert advice.

After passing more crevasses further up the valley (they were nothing to me now), we probed a wide circle of safety and stopped for lunch. We were nearing the head of the canyon, and did not want to find ourselves in a cozy avalanche bowl at the heat of the day.

I found it to be a relief to sit down on my pack and cool off. The sun was gorging upon us. We munched on pilot bread and dried fruit and as we did, happened to see quite a show. The sun's intensity reached the sides of the mountains and stirred up fantastic avalanches. It was like watching lightning and thunder in a way. For if our brains were quick enough to identify the source of a terrific roaring magnified by echoes bouncing across each valley, we would be lucky enough to watch the snow spill down opportune gullies with marvelous speed. They were white waterfalls with on-off controls. Sometimes a larger one would spew forth great clouds of snow and cover our view. Of course, we were safe on our probed island—not too close to any avalanche run-out zones. Yet it was a thrill to watch nature do her stuff, and affirm the wisdom of confining ourselves to the valley floors.

The collapse of the snow on the mountains before our eyes that afternoon, followed by colder temperatures, assured us that our avalanche risk was significantly lower. So, if we started early enough in the mornings, we would be able to safely venture up a few peaks in the days that ensued.

I cannot believe how much I learned from Ella and Denise. I quickly became accustomed to the use of snow pickets, my ice axe, traveling belays, and my crampons beneath the lime-green plastic boots. The crampons were the most frustrating because they would constantly collect huge clumps of snow. I felt like I was walking on top of tennis balls. I would bang my ice axe on my feet to shake off the snow, but two steps later they would ball up again. Ella was very patient, and never let me feel that I was an annoying beginner, or that I was holding her back. I loved learning from her.

The scenery made me want to keep moving. Never did I lose my excitement for the views of crusty white peaks stretching for ever and ever. From the top of one of these fortresses, our camp would be only a very small orange dot in the midst of a great huge arena of glaciers and mountains. How amazing that we had been able to make ourselves comfortable in the middle of all this. As we would descend from a peak, I would watch our camp grow in size, but as we approached the friendly orange tent at the end of a day's journey, it always seemed forever far away.

When I look back on it, I think my most memorable day was our sixth. We actually did not summit—probably because of my nervous snail like pace. But that did not matter because we had fun regardless, and we all stayed warm. We tried climbing a very steep route (for me anyway) of solid ice and snow that required the use of our ice axes, and anchors placed along the way, which Ella removed as she brought up the rear.

I was nervous with this challenge, but both Denise and Ella were very encouraging—coaching me with each scary step. I suppose that at the time, I did not find that ascent so enjoyable, but definitely afterward, I was thrilled that I had partaken in the challenge. As I edged my way upward, I saw only the solid face of white and occasional swirly blue before me, and the unfriendly beckon of slippery slope below me. I thought only of my feet and hands making the correct moves with the appropriate force. The snow squeaked and groaned with my kicks and the metal hardware on my harness clanged away in prime distraction. I urged myself sternly: "Go Heidi, Go!" and plodded along.

At last we reached a false summit, and a sigh brought from every nerve in my body eased my tumult of tension. At this point, it became clear to Denise and Ella that we were too tired, and I too slow and inexperienced to summit that mountain. So we took advantage of a sunny rest stop and made the decision to bail. But the terror of our exit far surpassed that of the climb. Ooh, I definitely did not enjoy that bit of the journey, for our escape route required that we do a scary traverse—travelling horizontally across the steep face of the mountain. This time, I was certain that one misstep on my part would lead all three of us down the rocky mountain side, for we were still all three roped together. It seemed when we reached the end of that nightmarish crossing that I experienced the happiest moment in my life. What a lovely cozy gully we found! It was the most wonderful place on earth.

We detached ourselves from each other, carefully tucked in all loose clothing, and jumped off for the best part of the day— the descent. Using our ice axes to arrest ourselves and control speed, we glissaded down about two-thousand feet on our bottoms. How relaxing that method of travel was in comparison to our frightening traverse! Careful not to tumble on top of one another, we laughed as we each became a colorful snowball. Perhaps I was the most amused by our carefree descent; here were two competent alpine guides whose movements were always efficient—never stumbling nor falling—now hurling themselves carelessly down a hill like young children. With this activity, no one had to drop me hints either. I was as expert as one could already be.

The night before Dale was supposed to pick us up, we were all a bit melancholy about our departure. We sat bundled up on top of our sleeping pads in our kitchen and watched the evening shadows creep across the valley, slowly down the peak we had climbed on Tuesday, gently encroaching upon the orangy glow on the wind-paved glacier, and finally up the dark mountains with the choppy black bands on the other side.

Ella placed a lit candle on our kitchen counter. We focused on its warm radiance and recapped the highlights of our successful outing. We had been blessed, for the most part, with extraordinary weather. Our faces had a tight sheen from five and half days of streaming sun, and our bodies felt relaxed from good old-fashioned strenuous use. In addition, with only having basic survival to worry about, our minds had experienced a chance to file and sweep away a lot of clutter. Funny that the best way to relax is to put yourself through high energy life-threatening situations. But then it was hard to prevent my mind from fast forwarding to the weeks that would follow. I had experienced on that glacier, the ultimate peace. Was this euphony now to be interrupted with crashing percussion as I returned to snowmachine terrorized Candle? And having grown accustomed to Ella's charms and support, now to have her leave again until climbing season was over at the very earliest. Ah, but there was my dogs to return to.

The moon had long ago slipped down the gullies on the opposite side of the mountains, but Ella's candle nestled safely within the walls of our wind-block sent its bouncing flame to all sides of our pit and back again, providing us with ample light in which to watch each other's glowing faces and flashing teeth as we laughed. With the last of the peppermint tea, we raised our insulated mugs to a toast of our successful journey, strengthened friendship, and a farewell.

In the morning we awoke early as usual, but instead of gathering up our harnesses and rope to wear, we prepared to break camp. As with the days before, the morning was glorious: there was no wind, and the awakening sky was an intense blue—distributing high energy to the glaciers and surrounding mountains — still just barely touched by the morning light.

"What a fantastic day for flying," Ella said when we had all had a chance to peek at the day's greeting. "There should be no reason why Dale can't make it up this valley this morning." With those words of comfort, for there was always the concern that bad weather could leave waiting passengers marooned for days, we all began to get ready for Dale's arrival. That meant having all our gear ready to go, for you never want to make your pilot wait. We placed our skis sticking up in the snow in front and behind our campsite so that Dale would be able to see us clearly from the airplane, and in the case of flat light, could get an idea of the topography of the landing area. We expected him at 8 AM, but wanted to be plenty ready before hand. How strange to think that we would soon be whisked away from our blissful spot and brought back to our bustling lives. And how much stranger yet that I considered returning to Candle a return to hustle and bustle! Eight AM came and went, and Dale did not arrive.

"Well, he's sometimes late" Ella was able to remark from experience. So we sat on our heavily loaded packs and waited. The sun enveloped the valley and spread its penetrating rays over our bodies, and we continued to wait. Ella looked toward the ridges of broken ice curling over the mountain tops and ending abruptly with shear smoothness.

"One time I was stuck for five days by myself up near the Hansen Glacier. Our pilot was able to pick up all my clients, but when it came time for him to return to pick up me and the rest of the gear, the clouds had closed in good. These mountains make their own weather fast."

We said nothing, but focused on the penetrating warmth of the spring sun. "Yup, I could've gone nuts up there by myself. The wind was relentless and the noise of my tent shaking and zippers hammering away for five days was enough to make anybody turn religious or something."

I laughed. "So, what religion did you turn?"

Ella wiggled her feet up and down to keep them warm. "Actually, I decided it would be a great idea to learn how to meditate. But I didn't. I sewed every single rip and tear in my gear, reinforced all the seams. Finished both my books, read every single critic's review in each book at least three times, and slept a lot. Oh, and ate a lot of oatmeal."

"At least you <u>had</u> oatmeal," Denise said. "Once I was flying out with this pilot in the Southern Alps in New Zealand, and his engine failed. We were up there for almost four days with no food before another pilot picked up his ELT and came to rescue us. All we had was a box of cough drops."

The sun crawled over the sky, and the snow got mushier. I said, "Well, once I had to wait an eternity in a Health Maintenance Organization hospital for my yearly checkup, and all they had were those orange plastic chairs to sit on that are harder than sitting on concrete."

We continued to wait sitting on our packs and listening to every sound lest it was a plane. The sun spilled into the western sky, and shadows sneaked down the valley.

"Okay fine," Ella finally said abruptly, "Let's set the tent back up." Reluctantly we unpacked our bags, and unsheathed the cold tent poles. The sun at last yielded to a fuzzy show of pink and yellow on the horizon briefly illuminating the peaks behind us in a rosy spotlight. It was obvious Dale was not coming that day.

Fortunately, years of waiting for planes in bad weather had taught Ella to always pack a couple extra day's worth of food. So at least, for the time being, hunger was not one of our worries. That is, if we did not mind that our surplus happened to be in the form of mostly oatmeal. But our morale was not anywhere near the height it had been in the preceding evening. As I watched the surrounding peaks send moon shadows parading across the glacier signifying another crystal clear night, I thought surely the weather in Candle and Cantwell (Dale's home town) was this clear as well. What was the reason for our delay? Ella, buried in her bag and already reading, had not said too much and seemed to want to keep it that way. I wondered what sort of speculation of our plight was going on within her experienced mind.

Dale did not show up the next day either. I started reading Ella's book, she read Denise's, and Denise played a lot of solitaire. Our waiting was more agonizing than cabin fever. There were a few lenticular clouds in the sky, but the weather was still terrific, and now we could not take advantage of it for fear that if we left our camp, Dale would arrive and find us gone. No, we had to stay put. And put we stayed until I thought that the piercing sun was going to drill holes in my brain.

Our third day of oatmeal was considerably more cloudy. It appeared that if Dale did not show up soon, he, or we rather, would miss his chance. Denise had started to mutter a few words here and there about unreliable mail pilots, and Ella's thoughts had obviously progressed from our relaxing trip to her next employment responsibilities.

Finally, at 2:15 that Thursday, I was just about to come in for the kill in a hand of Gin Rummy with Denise when Ella raised her head from her book sharply. "Shh, listen."

The past few days we had participated in quite a few "Shh listens" as jets passed over head, but this time the sound was unmistakable. It was our plane! Hallelujah! Our card game instantly was aborted, and we scrambled to pack everything up. We were stuffing the icy tent in the stuff sack once again when the plane approached and passed us overhead—apparently somehow not ready yet to land.

"That's not Dale! That's Jack!" Ella exclaimed in astonishment as the plane buzzed our camp.

I thought of the day I met Jack and his broken snowmachine, and shuddered. He circled overhead quite a few times before making the approach. Clearly, he was hesitant to land.

"Oh great, and he's got wheel skis instead of regular skis," Ella rubbed her face with her gloved hands. Jack's landing was a little shaky, but okay in the firmly packed snow. He opened his door quickly and Ella ran up to him with her pack.

"Jack! I didn't know you were a glacier pilot!"

"I'm not. Hop in, There's goddamned clouds closing in over us as we dilly dally." Ella grabbed the skis,

"I'll stay. You two go in the first run."

"No, all three of you. Let's go."

"All three?"

"Yeah, get in. Is that all the packs?" We piled in timidly. Ella sat on top of our packs in place of a seat in the back. Looking at Denise and Ella, I could tell that they shared my hesitation, but were also glad as heck to get off that glacier at least.

Once in the bumpy air, the noise of the plane was too loud to hear Jack's response when Denise, sitting next to him, asked what happened to Dale. All I caught was "plane crash," and "hospital."

You know, life seems to unfold in the darndest ways. I gave up long ago trying to guess how things are supposed to work out. All I can tell you is that I was glad as all get out to shake Uncle Hickory's paw once we had landed safely on the Candle airstrip.

Chapter 9

Soon after we returned from our trip in the mountains, Ella and Denise left Candle for their season of guiding. I had a happy reunion with my dogs, and proceeded to mush them as much as possible in the few remaining weeks of snow. Already, many roofs were bare and trees had little snow left in them. Candle as well, was already preparing for a busy summer. The first day I passed through town, I was surprised to see a new building in progress between Candle Lodge and Manny Kleinman's place. Next to the tumble down ghosty looking building, the new lumber looked very squeaky. A bearded man, quite tall, and maybe in his early forties, was operating a Skil Saw while a youngish boy hammered away at the frame. Figuring I should be neighborly in the Candle tradition, I walked over there to introduce myself. The man saw me and put his work down.

Smiling, he lifted his chin and shouted over the obnoxious drone of his generator. "Howdie. Sam Hoina. You new over here?"

I shook his hand. "Actually, I was thinking it was you who was new."

Sam chuckled. "Well, I guess it's how you look at it. Compared to that building, I'm new, but I've been coming here for some 17 years. I'm sorry, What did you say your name was?"

"Oh, sorry. Heidi. Anyway, your construction looks awfully new."

"Yessir ma'am. Well, you wouldn't be the first person to ask what I'm building. That over there is my nephew Josh," Josh waved, "and his father and I are starting a flight business out here. This will be our office. Maybe finally I can start living out here full time again if we make it."

"Oh. Wow."

"Yeah, I'd like to do some comp-flightseeing trips for locals and their employees so they can help sell us. Maybe we can get you in the air. What do you do?"

"I run Ernie's dog kennel."

"Oh! I heard about you. Yeah, well good to meetcha."

"Yeah, I'll let you get back to your work. I'll be seeing you around."

I was awed. Candle was growing. But at least so far there had been very little competition. Little did I know what other changes were in store for Candle until mail on Tuesday.

Dale, our mail pilot, had survived his plane crash and was convalescing at home in Cantwell. In the mean time, Ralph Kissell was filling in for him. Everybody at mail wanted to hear how our climbing trip had gone. I enjoyed seeing all the neighbors and telling about the huge crevasses and flowing avalanches. Unfortunately our pleasant conversations ceased when Jonathan Cohen voiced the rumor that someone was going to hire out motor boats on the tarn the coming summer.

"Where dja hear that?"

"Oh, I've got my ears open."

Cal Jensen frowned and snapped a suspender.

"I know that doesn't sound too good for you Cal," Jonathan continued. Cal shrugged and snapped both suspenders a couple of times. "But maybe Cal isn't the only one bothered by this. I frankly, don't want to see any more impact on the tarn, and I think we can put a stop to it by getting special wildlife refuge status."

"There ain't no goddamned wildlife on that lake besides Cal and his goddamned customers!" Jack blurted out.

"Well yes there is. It's a fragile ecosystem and motor boats would have a large impact."

"Wait a wait a minute" Herb interrupted putting his hand out, "Are you suggesting that we get the Feds involved to give this place park protection or something?"

"Well, along those lines."

"I don't think you know what you're saying!" Herb became excited. "They'd be all over this place: no this, no that, no motorized use at all. Scrap your snowmachines and your generators. Let's go back to the 1800s."

"Bernie would like the part about snowmachines" Fred chuckled, jabbing his elbow into Cal's side. Bernie was not around to defend himself for he was still boycotting going to mail.

"Bernie needs to relax" Herb said. "You and I all know that if he had the money, or the knowhow for that matter, he'd be all over this place on one of those things."

"Well frankly Herb," Jonathan's voice was calm and mellow, "I'm not really so hot about all this snowmachine traffic in my backyard either, and I'd like to see some limitations."

"LIMITATIONS?" Herb was really getting worked up, "You ask for limitations, you'll get them! The environmentalists in government would be more than happy to give us all limitations out here. And me, I'd personally like to shoot myself in the foot!"

"Well maybe there's something we can do." Joan Jensen joined the debate, "You got to realize Herb, our livelihood is being attacked from all sides now."

"Joan," Herb's face became wrinkled like a used paper bag, "You know I've always supported you guys 110%. But you had to see this coming. Don't you people realize? People are coming! There's business for everyone. Another boat company isn't going to put your family in the bread lines! Don't you people realize? They've found out about this place! You're not going to fight it! If you don't join in, you're going to lose!"

"Well, I'd like to see a little regulation," Jonathan stated. "I don't think we have to give in to the destruction of this area."

"Business isn't going to destroy Candle," Jack snorted in his usual cynical tone.

Herb interrupted him, shaking his head, "You guys are blind. This is a new time for Candle. The days of us jumping in the lake naked are over. But we can live prosperous lives!"

"Whelp, I'm just not sure we're seeing eye to eye on this one Herb," Cal finally said slowly.

Herb sighed heavily. I was listening, but keeping my mouth very shut. This was no time for my wit.

"Look," Joan said in an almost pleading tone, "We're a small growing community. We need each other. We've gone through so much together. We have plenty of time. We can work together. You guys have got to quit bashing heads."

That was it. The voice of reason. But reason does not come easily, and nothing was resolved that day. I went home feeling rather depressed despite my fine stack of mail, and I am sure I was not the only one. Candle had split herself yet once again.

I could often hear snowmachine traffic from outside my house, and I hated to hear it. I wanted to hear the grosbeaks and chickadees singing at my feeder. I wanted to hear the Kaluatna River growing larger as ice chunks jockeyed for position at the tarn's exit. With the horrors of breakup imminent, I was not quite sure whether to rejoice that soon I would not hear another snowmachine for seven months, or feel disheartened that the faucet of tourists was close to being turned on. I decided on the former. More pleasant to rejoice than to pout. None the less, I knew my dogs were beginning to mourn the approaching loss of snow. I decided to take them on one last good super mush. I figured there would not be too many snowmachines up Raven's Creek, and headed there with my whole team hoping that Zach had packed a trail up there.

The dogs recognized the canyon from which they had so happily descended a year ago. I was dismayed to see that already there were fresh snowmachine tracks up Zach's trail. It was a beautiful clear day, and the sun beamed down and surrounded us from all directions. The narrow canyon was like an envelope of sun and I basked in it, appreciating that this was one of the warmest times of the year. The crusty snow curled over the rocks and trees, smooth and shiny. Conditions were fast—even travelling up hill. Coming back down was going to be a thrill of a ride around those corners!

Suddenly my dogs picked up a brilliant speed. Popik had caught wind of something.

"Ayeeeeee!" I called to them, loving the boost up the hill. Rarely do they burst up a slope like that as mild a hill as it was. Happily I pretended I was a sled dog racer, and expertly picked the sled up on one runner as we tore around a sharp curve. When I rounded the bend (being the very last to do so), I was surprised and horrified to see a large cow moose standing boldly and angrily in the middle of the trail ready to defend herself, and maybe—as my worse fears would have it in those few seconds—her young calf as well. Knowing moose to be more than fierce and able fighters in face of attack, I was stricken

114

with fear, which of course hampered my reaction time. I jumped on the brake but the dogs were excited and had already brought me to the moose's lap. Snorting angrily, she thrust her powerful legs aggressively into my team. Her head rolled about her shoulders, her eyes were intent and fierce.

My hesitated jump on the brake had not been enough to halt the dogs either. Barking and frothing at the mouth, they lurched for the moose and attempted to pile up on her. With the gang lines tangled about her body, she became a monster—violently kicking and thrashing. In shock, and having no idea of what to do, I reached for the snow hook and as I bent down to place it, the moose gave a powerful THWACK against the sled.

Had the moose kicked my head, I am sure it would have killed me. As it turned out, my head was shielded by the handle bar of the sled which bashed forcefully into my face. I am sure I must have screamed as loud as the blow was strong, but above the uncontrollable noise of the dogs, neither the moose, nor the dogs, nor even I for that matter, heard it. Hot blood dribbled down my face and spattered the snow. Holding my head with pain and fear, I abandoned the sled and made for the closest refuge—a friendly spruce tree with lots of branches which I attempted to climb and escape danger. A moose can and will stomp a human to death.

From my greenish vantage point, I watched helplessly this most ugly display of nature. It seemed evident that there would be no winners in this fight. Most of my dogs appeared to clue in eventually that moose attack is not as great as it is made out to be, especially when everybody is all attached —all except for Crocodile. Oh that useless dog! He continued to aggravate the moose who proceeded to kick the sled violently, smashing bits of it to splinters. My head throbbed, my heart pounded with adrenaline. I was barely aware of the tears streaming down my face. Never have I felt so vastly powerless. I feared for the dogs, but in my terror and anguish, I could do nothing, not even yell.

After what seemed like hours sitting cramped and frightened on that friendly branch, I was brought out of my hysteria by a gunshot. Once. The moose turned and lifted her head. Twice. It was down at the sled. Three times, and the beast lay motionless. It was dead. Still I could not find the power or courage to budge from my perch. I ached too much—both inside and out.

Descending the trail on snowmachine, appeared Herb Kramer. I watched as he dragged the tangled dogs and shredded sled away from the moose so that it would be away from their reach, (Easier to move seven dogs and a sled than an adult moose), and then paused briefly to study my bright red addition to the snow. Agitated, he then called me.

"Heidi!"

For some reason, only one word managed to escape my bloody mouth. "Hi."

He saw me and walked over to the tree. "DOGS SHATTUP!! Heidi, you're okay, right?"

I slid out of the tree. By now I was able to add embarrassment to my long list of emotions.

"Can you ride on the snowmachine?" I nodded.

"The dogs—"

"They'll be okay." He paused and looked at them. Their dark eyes watched him carefully. "All right, whaddya got to tie em up with?"

Still shaking, I briefly looked over all of the dogs. They were still alive, but no one looked too cheery, or very interested in moving much. Herb helped me chain Popik to a tree in front, and the two wheel dogs in back to another tree. Without picketing them out, they were in risk of getting out of harness and starting a fight, but at this point I did not think any dogs were in the mood. In any case, that was all we could do. Herb wanted to get me home, and I appreciated it.

We drove down the windy trail with Herb handling the vehicle probably more gingerly than he had ever handled it before, and looking back all the time to check if I was okay. Once I was able to eke out a smile, and his wrinkled forehead smoothed over as he smiled back gently. When we reached the road, we were greeted by Zach skijoring with Uncle Hickory.

"What's up?" He asked, "Hick was acting all weird, so I followed him over here." Hickory sidled over to me, put his paw on my knee, and looked at me with his foggy old eyes as he wagged his tail. It was soothing to pass my mittened hand over his fur as Herb gave Zach a brief account of the event as he understood it. I did not pay attention. I did not want to think or talk about what had just occurred, and I do not think they expected me to.

Zach and Hick then followed us over to my house. I was reminded of my terror when I saw the empty dog lot, but never so thankful to see my house. I think it was the first time Herb had ever been to my place.

"Now you get yourself cleaned up, and lie down, and I'll send Louise over to see how you're doing," he ordered.

"Nah. Nah, I'm fine. I'm okay." By then, I just really wanted to be alone.

"Heidi, you could have a bad concussion. You shouldn't be left alone." Herb seemed so gentle and caring, so different from the goofy bastard I had met on the road a year and a half before.

"No, I don't need—I'm okay." I really wanted to lie down though.

"Heidi," Zach's tone was gentle but matter of fact, "Me and Herb are going to go take care of your dogs and that moose. I'm going to leave Uncle Hickory with you."

Herb turned and gave Zach a look as if to question "What the hell are you thinking?" which made a tiny laugh sneak past my lips.

"See? He's making her feel better already. He can push open the door and get someone if he don't think she's all right, and this way she can sleep."

"Whatever. Let's leave her alone."

They left, closing the door softly, and I lay down on my makeshift couch with a wet washcloth to mop up my face. Uncle Hickory snuggled next to the couch on the floor and rested his chin just above my shoulder, squishing the orange juice bottle against the side of the couch. I lay my hand on his neck, closed my eyes, and thought about what a sweet dog dear Hick was.

I was out for a few days. I did not look in the mirror, but I am sure it would have been an ugly sight. Zach let Hickory stay with me. Or rather, Hickory did not decide to leave until he figured I was back to normal. It was wonderful to have my doggy nurse by my side, but I wished Hick could have hauled water or chopped wood. This was my first serious ailment, and it had not hit me before what it means to live alone in such an environment. It is not just having plenty of your own space and cooking whatever you want, and being a little lonely every now and then, but it means you have to take care of yourself when you get sick. There is no such thing as staying in bed for three days watching TV. Someone has to get the wood and start the fire or the house will freeze. I do not know how Sue Bean and everybody has managed all those years. You have got to give them all a little credit. No wonder they get grumpy now and then.

Fortunately, Zach came over and fed my dogs. That was a long distance for him to travel just to tend dogs, and I certainly appreciated the gesture. He even hauled the water for them. I think he also missed Uncle Hickory a lot, and wanted to check up on him as well. My dogs were okay by the way. Bruised I am certain, because no one seemed to be complaining that we were not running anywhere, but they all seemed to fare okay. Even stupid Crocodile. Beth came over once too to make sure I had enough aspirin on hand. She did not stay very long though after noting that I was neither dying, nor ready for too much visiting.

In a few days I was ready to stay out of bed and get chores done. I had no sooner linked myself back with the rest of the world by turning on my radio and CB, when I heard a voice booming my name over the airwaves.

"Heidi. Heidi Ravison, are you alive?"

"Hey Herb."

"Well hey! You are alive. You haven't been for a few days. I was going to go over and check on you, but a voice said, 'No, no! Thou must not cross the barriers of the deep!'"

"Good thing you listened to that voice."

"Yes, you know I'm brave, but not stupid."

"No, not you."

"Hey, I got Polly the moose over here. She sure looks good between two slices of bread and some cheese. Want some?" What a horrible memory. I winced at the thought.

"No!" I voiced adamantly, "No. I don't want to have anything to do with that moose. I don't want to see it or hear anything about it." Herb laughed into the CB.

"I bet your dogs do."

"Sure, you can give them some, but I don't want to think about it. Another moose, another day."

"Okay" Herb laughed again, "You won't recognize it when you shovel it later." I rolled my eyes well enough for him to feel the vibrations through the radio waves.

"You're so thoughtful Herb."

"Yeah, okay, anytime. Well, have fun over there."

"Thanks. We'll see ya."

Click. Click.

———

By the end of April, our slushy, sludgy, gooey, rubber boot, breakup season was more than half way over: a stuck vehicle caught in the grips of an emerging ditch, or a thawing road glacier was a common sight; nobody had any clean clothes left, and the shrill song of the varied thrush rang throughout Candle welcoming back warmth and humidity, wildflowers, and....mosquitoes. Snowmachines were put away. Sam Hoina and his nephew Josh were over half finished with the new office for Candle Air Taxi. It was looking to be a beautiful office. But if I thought their project was the end of new construction in Candle, I had more thinks coming.

A young couple who had just purchased a lot in Candle was fixing up one of the old buildings to turn into a bakery. I am not sure if Louise was worried or not about a little breakfast and lunch competition, but if Herb's prophecy about Candle having plenty of room for businesses was true, then she had nothing to curdle her milk about. I had not heard much more about the plan to request zoning restrictions based on wildlife protection, but I did see a truck drop off a big load of materials on the other side of the river near the lake. And it sure made sense that it was materials for a new boat launch. I apparently was not the only one to notice this development, for then Cal and Joan panicked and started ripping out a wall with plans to expand their office into a grocery store.

May 6, and almost all the globby goo was gone from Candle streets. Candle Tarn had finally freed herself of her cover, and reclaimed her swirly turquoise blue character. I became excited when I noticed my first calypso orchid on the hill behind my house. It seemed safe enough to break out my poor old purple Schwinn. I pumped up the tires and rode to Zach's house, knowing that he would share my delight in the find. He was outside.

"Yeah I know! I saw a couple on the other side of the road yesterday I bet there's some anemones on the beach."

So I parked my bike, and we walked slowly along the beach searching for flower secrets hidden in the rocky shore. We were startled by the giant noise of a large plane approaching. We watched attentively, expecting it to land on the airstrip, and for the passengers to possibly need to use Zach's CB.

To our surprise, it passed directly over head, and made to aim for the beach we were on. "Wow. It's a twin otter!" Zach exclaimed. "I've never seen one of those over here before." The floatplane landed smoothly on the water, driving ripples across the lake as a duck does when it lands. We ran up the beach to greet the plane which pulled up along the edge of the lake like a docked boat.

We knew who the passenger was right away when the pilot pulled a shiny brief case out of the plane. Out stepped a well dressed man, clean shaven, and full of confidence. It was Sportin' Norton.

"Well Hello there Zach. And Heidi. Nice way to arrive eh?"

The pilot continued to hand him things, and we figured we might as well help unload. There was a whole plane load of supplies for the Lodge. Many boxes of food, a few chairs, a rug even. Enough stuff to make me wish we had not been quite so eager to greet the plane.

"Well, it looks like it beats driving the road in." Zach answered as he reached for the heavy rug.

"Sure does. Thanks for the help. By the way this is my pilot Tucker."

"Pleased to meet you guys." Tucker managed a brief smile between ducks in and out of the plane.

"Tucker's going to be bringing in Kaluatna Lodge guests," Norton explained.

"Oh," I pondered out loud without thinking, "Are you Sam Hoina's brother?"

"Not that I know of."

"What does Sam Hoina have do with anything? Careful with this box Zach, its got wine glasses."

"Oh, he's starting an air taxi out here this summer," I answered.

"He is, is he?" Norton chuckled, "Tucker, hear that? We've got competition already. (Can you handle this one Heidi?) Well, tell him to get one of these." Norton lifted his head indicating the large floatplane as he handed a big box to me. "You can bring in a lot more people." And he laughed again, knowing full well that a small starting business like Sam Hoina's could never afford a large floatplane, let alone a twin otter.

Chapter 10

Mosquitoes were particularly bad in June. When I gardened I resorted to wearing one of those mosquito netting hats that are practical, but for some reason look extremely dweeby. Determined to have a good crop of peas and broccoli that summer, I resisted all artillery the insect kingdom set upon me. Clad in army-green netting and surrounded by burning Buhach, I enjoyed the summer warmth and light. I thought about what made me dread the summer so much when the dirty patches of snow were shrinking in front of my house. I finally decided that if I had originally arrived in Candle in midsummer, as a tourist, and had just happened to linger on until winter, I would have seen a different view. It was all Ernie's fault that I had just come to think that the peacefulness of winter was the way things were supposed to be. Knowing only solace in Candle, naturally I should feel invaded when the brightly clothed seekers of summer thrills strolled into my town. I decided then that I would pretend I had never known a quiet Candle winter, and that I was a newcomer to the valley. Then, I thought, I would enjoy dear Candle.

What I saw when I imagined myself a tourist was a surprise. After a nightmarish drive down a lonely pothole-ridden road for five hours, I certainly would not expect to be joined by crowds at a river crossing. And instead of marvelling at Candle's gate way, the lucid blue waters mirroring the towering Ilkitas, I would be confused by the juxtaposition of the two ferry crossings. One spiffy and new, the other so clearly identifying herself as an old Candle institution. Once I paid my fare however, I would embark upon a foreign experience. As a tourist, I walked through Candle and saw weather-beaten Alaskan eccentrics running around trying to act like Los Angeles businessmen, beers for four dollars, and odd accordion music for nothing. It was hilarious actually. But there was much to offer. The scenery was free, there was much to do, and I could see that Herb was right. Welcome to the Malibu of the north. Make your bucks and enjoy it, or hide and pine away. I heard more and more inquiries about where to buy land, talk about future restaurants, campgrounds, bed and breakfasts, galleries, cottage rental, even a plan for a gas station on the other side of the river.

Meanwhile, the Cohens and the Jensens continued to collaborate on a plan to submit to Congress requesting wildlife protection status for the tarn. Lisa and Ralph Kissell left for the fishing season, but had given their full and avid support to the plan. The Fallons agreed to it also, but the Kapps said they did not care. The Stevens indicated they were not sure yet. Lou and Beth said they would support protection for the tarn, but not for anything else. Jack of course, was utterly against it, and told us so very often. Bernie did not mention anything about it oddly enough. Either he was scared, or he was plotting something of his own.

Interestingly, the issue had the two lodges in agreement for once. Sportin' Norton said he had more political influence than anybody in the area, and there was no way the issue would get past him. He was going to land his twin otter as he pleased, and continue to offer his guests as many recreational opportunities as he could.

Despite Sportin' Norton's obstinacy, a petition was designed which circulated at the ferry crossing, Cal's Boathouse, the gift store, the air taxi, the bakery, and Manny Kleinman's rocking chair. The petition read as follows:

"We as visitors to and enjoyers of the Candle area hereby state that the fragile Candle Tarn ecosystem, namely the Kaifrie blue-tipped spider, is being exceptionally threatened by overuse of motorized traffic on and around the tarn. We

request that protection be instated to protect this fragile region from further destruction, and maintain it as a beautiful spot for all to love and enjoy."

I should, by the way, mention that a small motor boat business had indeed begun operation on the parking lot side of the ferry. Glacier Sounds Boat Rental was owned by Axel Bend who owned the small house across the road from the yurt which made him my closest neighbor. He was a pleasant guy, really. I admired his pluck and business sense. A couple of kids worked for him cleaning the boats regularly and maintaining the motors. The fact was though, that Axel had only five boats to rent out—not enough to encompass the blue world of the tarn with the din of outboard motors. The tough truth for both Cal and Axel was that the glacial wind was a familiar force often driving scathing whitecaps across the wild waters. To be in a small boat when those waves were rolling, was akin to crossing a stormy Atlantic Ocean in a skiff. Certainly in those instances, boat rental was not a popular option. So it was not as if Axel was suddenly making a killing with his new business.

I felt sorry for Axel despite my obvious distaste for extensive motor traffic in Candle (mainly speeding snowmachines). He had been in operation only a few weeks, and already folks were plotting against him to destroy his business. He did not understand it, and initially even offered to circulate the petitions in his office. Of course, when he read what they said, he decided their use was more effective as notepaper. Even stranger to Axel, was that folks as gruff as Jack Greeley, and as opposite to each other as Sportin Norton and Herb would be overly friendly to him, while others, such as Bernie and Beth O'Connor would give him a cold shoulder. Sue Bean was the only one who gave Axel any normal attention (or so he thought). Very often she would bring him down some cranberry jam or cranberry liqueur to share. But we all knew this was only because earlier in the summer, Sam Hoina—the other new bachelor—had indicated that he was not interested in the jam, or any of the tools used to make it.

While my peas blossomed, and the dog poop pile behind my yard grew, groggy tourists continued to spill out of the dusty tour busses decorated with cans of fix o' flat on the tires, and Sportin Norton's Otter took any chance of calm wind to disrupt the glassy tone of the tarn's surface with the large floats. Sam Hoina and his brother were having great success with their business. In fact, they had already hired on two college students to work in the office since both brothers were constantly in the air, and Josh was overwhelmed with maintenance duties. It appeared evident as the incredible scenery of Candle was becoming better known in Alaska, that there was room in the air for more planes. Already, others had flown in looking at possibilities of building a new flight company. Tucker, who kept the Kaluatna Lodge filled with high dollar customers, was presenting no competition to Sam whatsoever since the otter was incapable of covering the exciting terrain that Sam and his brother could in their small planes. Likewise, with their days already beginning at dawn, and not ending until light was encased in shadow, Sam and his brother had no interest in flying charters from Cantwell or Fairbanks as Tucker was doing.

An interesting situation did arise as more and more Candle Lodge guests expressed an interest in touring the silver mine property. Still feuding with Bernie, Herb was hesitant to give Bernie any business, and yet, his customers wanted a tour.

At first Herb would tell the interested guests, "Eh, well you can go up there and look around, and maybe you'll run into somebody who can answer your questions." This was a shame, because Bernie really could give an informative and very entertaining tour. Then, Herb and Louise decided they would provide their own tours to their guests who requested them. The funny thing was that first they asked me if I wanted to do it. I gather they figured I had acquired enough of Bernie's knowledge along the way somehow. It was nice of them I guess to ask me, but it also seemed like a rude slap in Bernie's face. I did not know a sixteenth as much as he did, not to mention, I did not live up there.

Well then, and get this, they got James Jensen to do it. He was getting on 13 by then and I suppose Joan and Cal did not need him helping in the grocery store, or to feed the chickens or the dogs or the pigs, or to work in the garden, or to make dinner, or to do the dishes. So Louise loaded him up with books and pamphlets on the mine's history, and gave him the keys to their '78 Dodge with a very firm warning to keep his right foot light as a chicken feather while driving the clients around the tarn and up the hill.

Still pretending to be a summer newcomer, I found new delights in Candle. I went bush whacking up Gem Creek with Zach one day, and climbed up on the ridge. There were tons of alpine flowers I had never seen before, and we crawled on our hands and knees investigating the tiny hidden world among the lichens and mosses.

The two women working for Sam turned out to be avid explorers as well. I took them hiking on the glacier a couple of days, and they were both astounded by the tremendous foreign beauty. We also spent a long day climbing the mountain west of the Cohen's house. Even Willow and Tuska were tired when we returned home at 1:30 AM. Despite my muscles and eyes becoming droopy with fatigue, I was enchanted to be able to explore the world in the dusky shadows of midnight. And a few times, I had the opportunity to fill a vacant seat during Sam Hoina's flightsee tours. We sailed over the swirly tarn and up the glacier, loving a taste of the intensity of the banded icy creature. I even saw sheep run up steep creviced cliffs as we flew by. After each flight, I would return to the ground with even more love and appreciation of my home.

It rained on the fourth of July. But there was a parade anyhow. There should have been mud wrestling. The streets were sloppy and gooey as the old beat up trucks splashed through them. There was no two-headed miner that year, and we all missed its goofy presence. Bernie did not even come down for the parade. Rumor had it that his three-wheeler would not start. Sam and Josh had a good float going though. They designed a big plane out of cardboard boxes, painted the wings red white and blue, and marched down the street together with Josh at the throttle, and Sam buckled up and fearing for his life. Appropriate for the weather, the Jensens decorated their Chevy as a large whitefish with a mouth that opened and closed. The kids wrapped themselves in layers of mosquito netting so as to look like the fish's fins which flapped as it swam down the street.

I cannot recall what the lodge did that year for a float. It must not have been very exciting. I think Herb and Louise were too worked up about the Kaifrie blue-tipped spider petition to think up a good one. Since the petition was posted at the ferry, and at the air taxi, it was receiving a plentiful amount of signatures. Eventually Herb asked Cal to remove the one on the ferry. When Cal refused, Herb cancelled the deal they had made the previous summer regarding the ferry. I suppose there was no longer a reason for Herb to offer free rides for his guests across the ferry anyway since the Kaluatna Lodge was usually filled with floatplane arrivals, and had no space for walk-in guests. But Herb's action sure did not help Cal's situation. Still envisioning myself a tourist, I admitted that with a shinier ferry next door, a five cents savings was not much incentive to board Cal's "classic" barge. At least it had one thing going for it, the construction did look period.

Forced to drop their ferry ride price again to 59¢, almost one half of what was charged the years preceding, the Jensens set out in their battle against motorized boats with an even more spirited gusto. They plastered propaganda all over the grocery store, and encouraged every customer to sign the petition at least once. They drew up posters of the Kaifrie blue tipped spider with a balloon coming from the spider's mouth crying "Save me! Save Me!" and nailed them to trees. They even convinced Manny Kleinman to tape the posters onto his rocking chair and accordion case. Manny got into it, and as he showed off souvenirs to the passing tourists, he also urged them to sign the petition.

"Don't forget the poor blue kefir!" he would call out.

The whole thing put Herb into a continual state of crankiness. "These people are idiots! Idiots!" I heard him say to Jack at the bar one night. It was too rainy for flying, and so Sam had enticed me in for a drink and a game of pool. I spied Sue Bean there with Axel Bend. She seemed to have been dappling pretty heavy in the cranberry liqueur that evening for she did not appear to be very inhibited about playing with Axel's shirt collar.

"They're gonna get this thing passed," Herb went on, "And then when no one allows them to drive to their front door, they'll all be begging the state for motorized access. I can see it all coming."

Jack swirled the ice in his drink around and around. "Why don't we write our own goddamned petition?" Herb swallowed his gulp and looked at Jack who continued with his idea, "Yeah, I mean if they can gather so many goddamned signatures, why can't we? We're where the people stay huh?"

My turn at the pool table was up. It was a tricky bank shot, so I did not pay any attention to the rest of the conversation between Herb and Jack. But I did not need to hear what was coming. I knew.

Louise ended up firing James Jensen. At first her reasoning was that he drove too fast up the road. But when James, who had agonized his passengers in the Dodge by crawling carefully up the muddy road like a blue-tipped spider asked her, "Are you sure this ain't 'cause of you being all worked up over my Dad's signs and stuff?"

She replied honestly, "No."

Norton and Herb drew up a new petition together. Designed with fancy computer graphics, and printed on a state of the art printer, it read:

126

"We as people who fondly recreate, work, and live in the Candle area, seek to preserve Candle's qualities as an enjoyable resort town and home. We request that the tarn and surrounding areas be maintained as a region that will continue to provide boundless recreational opportunities of any sort to all who wish to enjoy them."

The new petitions were posted at Axel Bend's boathouse, both lodges and Jack's bunkhouse, Sportin Norton's ferry crossing, and Manny's rocking chair. Of all businesses, it was Manny who collected the most signatures. I gather that this success was due to Manny's prime downtown location, and the fact that he himself was a free tourist attraction. Joyfully, and with satisfaction, both Jonathan Cohen and Herb would each collect from Manny the papers filled with the scrawlings of innocent tourists, and praise him for his help as they replaced his supply with a fresh new stack of empty petitions to be filled. Unbeknownst to them, the tourists were signing both papers at the same time. If you read them, (which most people did not do any way), both petitions seemed to help the community. They both sounded like good causes, and the tourists were all eager to help the town they had come to love.

A renewed anger sprouted inside Bernie when he read Herbert and Sportin Norton's petition. It even got him to come off of his hill. With a four-wheeler borrowed from Sue Bean, he stormed down to Kaluatna Lodge with a scrappy piece of paper he had jammed into his manual typewriter. Smiling sweetly I suppose at a house maid, he convinced her somehow to let him use Sportin' Norton's copier to make 100 copies of a new petition. A giant crease ran through the center of the page, but it was still fairly readable:

"We're not worried about spiders. We just want to get rid of all the snowmachines driving around our backyards all winter. They are a public menace spreading pollution and noise everywhere. We can't hear ourselves think, We're scared to ski on a trail because they'll knock us over at 50 mph. We have no privacy or quiet. The snowmachines run everywhere and there is no escape. They're destroying our town. We want legislation that will outlaw snowmachine use in the area."

He posted a couple on the bulletin board next to our mailboxes, and kept a large stack for his tour business customers to sign. Moved by the exclaimer, Jason and Polly Fitch (the new bakery owners) also agreed to take a few, as well as Axel Bend, and of course, Manny Kleinman at his rocking chair. Now it became not uncommon to hear Manny, surrounded in papers, some petitions appearing smarter than others, singing along with his accordion. If you were not close enough, the words sounded muffled, since Manny was short, and the large instrument partially covered his face. But if you paid careful attention to his old wiggly voice, you would understand his catchy song:

> *"Sign away these papers!*
> *Prevent any or all of these capers!*
> *Be it a blue spider, or a super snow glider,*
> *They're all sure to be some sort of raper!"*

This new found song writing talent was quite exciting for Manny. Awed by the strange mixture of Alaska eccentricity and original musicianship, many more visitors stopped by to hear Manny and his sales of "precious pieces of history" increased fourfold. He became one of the attractions people told their friends they "simply had to see." As he became more famous, travel writers stopped by to interview him and learn more about him and the petitions. After pulling up a dynamite box and chatting with him a bit, maybe even tasting a lick of his "orange juice" the writers returned to Fairbanks and Anchorage with shocking stories of how a small town in the mountains had been caught in a fierce battle between developers and environmentalists.

> *"A lodge fiercely wants to defend its right to provide tourists with access to beauty and recreation,"* they wrote. *"But environmentalists prove that snowmobile use and excessive summer traffic will cause the poor Kaifrie Blue-tipped spider to become extinct."*

The stories rolled throughout Alaska papers and public radio stations, and inevitably slipped into the Seattle Times. Once word was out, nationwide concern spread over the Kaifrie blue-tipped spider. The hot issue hit the press throughout the country and suddenly folks without enough good causes to pursue, had found their calling.

Special interest groups such as Sierra Club and National Rifle Association began lobbying the capital in Juneau heavily. They wrote their members urgently begging for money to fight the battle. Universities entertained guests who lectured impressionable students about the near extinction of the helpless Kaifrie blue-tipped spider. Northern rural areas across the Lower-48 became dotted with homemade signs that said "THIS HOME SUPPORTED BY SNOWMOBILE USE."

With the incredible increase in publicity, tourists began to flock to Alaska to see for themselves what was so wonderful about Candle. Hal at the Hemle gas station was overwhelmed with tire repair jobs and oil pan replacements, and the Candle bus expanded its service from four days a week to six. There was a constant wait of at least 38 minutes at each ferry so some entrepreneur set up a soda stand at the parking lot. Because all three lodges were booked solid until Labor Day, a campground was created on the west side of the river. Axel Bend started sleeping in his office and renting out his house; and the people who owned land in the vicinity sold almost all of it within a month and a half.

Meanwhile, relations in the community were getting pretty wacky. Herb and Louise were mad at Axel Bend for circulating Bernie's petitions, so they stopped sending him business. Lou and Beth, agitated that they were being associated with the snowmachine movement, took away the spider petition in their store and exchanged it for Herb and Sportin Norton's. Their sudden change of support upset Cal and Joan, so they stopped sending customers to the O'Connor's gift store and started selling knickknacks and cards at their own grocery store instead. Bernie was all out of sorts because the world was calling him an environmentalist, and Jack—he could only swear in response.

After a while, when I went to mail I would discover Zach sorting mail alone. Only a few seasonal employees would be loitering outside his house waiting for him to finish. It was weird. Our weekly social gathering I thought I could always count on, was becoming like many friendships, a thing of the past.

"No one comes to mail anymore Heidi," Zach confessed. "People don't have time, and they don't want to see each other. No one cares for each other anymore."

"Well, Sue Bean cares for Axel. You care for Uncle Hickory."

Zach laughed. "That's good Heidi. Humor is what we all need. I just wish the others could stay lighthearted like you."

It was easy for me to keep a light heart though: I only ran a dog kennel. I had lived in Candle a mere two years. That was barely enough time for me to grow very attached to the view from my outhouse. I had little to lose by accepting change.

I stopped pretending I was a tourist. It was getting too darned confusing, not to mention too competitive. Instead, I focused on my garden (my peas were doing marvelously, but the broccoli was looking droopy) and getting the dogs out on long hikes. With at least two dogs on every excursion, I explored more of Candle than probably anyone else had ever explored. I summitted at least six rocky peaks with eye boggling vistas, became an expert at alder whacking, and came to know the Kaluatna Glacier intimately. Hiking a few miles up the bumpy blue ice, I found ridges became more compressed, and small crevasses more frequent. Traveling closer to the ice falls, I found myself repeatedly jumping across rushing blue water slides and deep narrow slits. I became very fond of Ella's lime green boots and rusty crampons. Their ability to bring me up and down nearly vertical terrain gave me the power to discover wonderful untold secrets of the glacier: a brilliant 40 foot waterfall on the west side, and a giant blue river snaking its way down the very center of the ice mass. The gurgling, swirling, grinding, and smacking of the water and ice was calming. Free from the chaos of the community, it was a world that did not care.

Chapter 11

When a member of the governor's staff came out to Candle in August to investigate the Kaifrie blue-tipped spider situation, no one seemed to be able to tell him who had done the original study on the tarn's ecosystem. A few weeks earlier, Jonathan Cohen had abruptly decided his family needed a vacation in the Lower-48, and had left no address at where he could be reached.

"Uh huh" was the administrator's only response to the absence. He remained in the area but a few hours before his government plane whisked him back on his way to Juneau. But just a week or so passed before the official returned with a team of biologists who carried large boxes of equipment to their reserved rooms in the Candle Lodge where they stayed for 11 days. Despite the whole town's deep curiosity, the group did not talk to any of the locals. Early every morning they were up at Axel's boat dock where they loaded their expensive equipment into one motor boat. Usually they would work out on the water until mid-afternoon when they would return to the lodge and remain in their rooms compiling data until late evening.

I met one of the scientists — if you want to call it a meeting — during a walk along the beach with Popik and Nali. The water was smooth and glassy, lapping softly at my feet as I looked for flat stones to skip across the perfect surface. An elderly couple shared my peaceful shore. They did not speak much, but walked along slowly, watching the gentle ripples tinkle and chase each other along the tarn's edge. The woman bent over and dipped her wrinkled fingers into the milky water. She dug them into the fine silt, carelessly loving the clammy texture of the ancient dirt.

"You're going to frostbite your fingers that way Eunice," her husband scolded. She ignored him and continued to swirl her fingers in the glacial remnants like a child. Further up the beach where my dogs were chasing each other, one of the biologists was walking toward us carrying a trowel and a backpack. Every few yards, he stopped and shoveled a bit of silt into a zip lock bag, labeled it with a fat magic marker, and walked on. We watched him with bewilderment. Even the woman turned from her play to look at him. The thin scientist ignored our curious gazes and worked quickly and methodically as he approached the old couple and me.

When he reached us, the old man nodded to him politely and said, "Good Evening."

"Evening." The biologist paused, not to chat, but to stare intently at the woman's fingers which were splayed out and moving slowly through the thick cold silt.

"You know," the elderly man told him, "You're not going to find any bait in this mud. This here's a glacial lake. There's nothing in it but silt and rocks."

The biologist's brief effort to smile was transformed into a glare as his intense annoyance sabotaged all thoughts of being friendly. The old man, obviously shrouded in oblivion smiled with satisfaction. "Thought you'd appreciate the advice."

Suddenly the biologist was angry. "Look, I'm not quite sure what you and your wife are trying to do. But if you're trying to sabotage this soil, or this government study, it's a five-thousand dollar fine." With that, he walked off, leaving the couple stunned and hurt.

After the 11 days were over, the biologists paid their bill at the lodge, and took off with their equipment in the government twin Apache. They did not say goodbye to anyone. But that did not matter since they had never said hello in the first place. Not much more than a week later however, an article printed in the front page of the Anchorage Times reported "**Kaifrie Spider a Fake.**" The article went on to report that no evidence of any organisms or food sources had been discovered in the waters of the tarn or surrounding soil. Plainly stated, the article explained that there was no way any arachnoid life could possibly exist within the icy waters of the glacial tarn.

By the time the article made its way around to my hands, there had already been an environmentalist backlash. Radio stations and newspapers throughout the country voiced the angry outcries:

"Conservative Alaska Government Hides Behind Faulty Claims Denying Spider's Existence."

"Overuse of Snowmachines May Have Already Caused the Extinction of Kaifrie Spider."

I could not believe it when I heard that environmentalist groups and ecotourism travel companies were calling for a boycott against Alaska tourism until the issue was resolved. As far as Juneau was concerned, they had resolved it, and refused to do anything further. They had learned throughout the history of Alaska not to take small bush communities too seriously.

Initially Herb was incensed by the boycott. I was in the new grocery store splurging on a fresh bag of coffee beans the afternoon that Herb barreled into the canoe rental office with the news.

"Is this what you wanted Cal?" Herb raged, "Was this your plan? Can't run your own business right so you have to go and ruin everyone else's?"

Caught off guard, Cal's large body stood rigid. Fibrillating his suspenders with his thumb, he muttered softly, "I guess you'd better leave my office."

"No problem Cal." Herb's voice was stormy and quivered as his eyes narrowed beneath his wrinkled heavy brow. "You're just darn lucky there's someone here to leave it. Next year at this time 'cause of you, maybe there won't be." He slammed the screen door behind him, and James, who was running the cash register, and I looked at each other exchanged "Uh oh this ain't good" glances.

The only one who did not mind the boycott news was Bernie. For the first time in ages, he was even sort of happy. He managed miraculously to fix his three-wheeler and came down to visit me, apologizing for the past few months of aloofness. He was freshly shaven and even wearing clean clothes. His mirth stemmed from the fact that he expected the boycott to put a halt to the winter snowmachine invasion. I gave my visitor a tour of my burgeoning garden. I was very proud of it. The pea yield was plentiful and tasty. With a handful of blissfully sweet pea pods in his pocket, Bernie left my sunny pea patch to go visit Manny.

Remembering the incident at the boathouse, I carefully took the liberty of warning Bernie to stay clear of Herb. I need not have been concerned with Herb's bad mood however. For when Herb came back from Cal's in a virulent rage that unfortunate afternoon, Louise was able to calm her spouse by showing him the reservation book for the winter. As it turned out, the kinds of people who boycott tourism over spiders are not the same sorts of tourists who like to ride snowmachines and eat good food over the holidays. Thus already in late August, the lodge was nearly booked solid for all of the December holidays, for much of March, and parts of February. Herb and Louise never expected so much success. Mere months earlier, such attention to Candle had been unfathomable, and yet, much of it was due to the National debate created by the three petitions.

In early September, not long after the boycott was announced, a budding new environmentalist organization decided to make a group outing to Candle in order to see the damage for themselves. The air was brisk and sharp when the group of 16 arrived in town. There were still plenty of vehicles in the parking lot, but activity had begun to wind down; one could plan to cross the river without needing to bring a coloring book or a novel for waiting entertainment, and the extensive colorful display of nylon tents at the parking lot had decreased.

Accompanying the crisp aroma of freshly decaying vegetation, were long lasting rosy sunsets which dipped silently into the curling Kaluatna River which was shrinking day to day as the glacier closed down her faucet of fresh melt water. The growing hours of darkness allowed Sam Hoina and the other exhausted business operators to shut their doors at decent hours of the evening instead of staying open dreary eyed until 11 PM.

The group of 16 remained in Candle only one day before Sam loaded the conservationist adventurers three at a time in his 180 and flew them to a remote location deep within the heart of the Ilkitas.

Safely armed with Nikons and Minoltas, the group trampled gently on the fragile land for six days of blissfully clear weather before Sam brought them back. When they returned safely to Candle, their muddy backpacks were brimming with containers of exposed film heading for major outdoor magazines published across the nation. From their pictures of blue hued mountains marching boldly before amphitheaters of ancient ice, rolling alpine meadows interrupted by nothing but clear sweet streams and footsteps of mountain sheep, spilled the secrets Candle's residents had cherished selfishly for years. The published prize winning photographs were usually accompanied with the caption: "A land worthy of our protection."

Two young members of the environmentalist group became so enchanted with our charming town and surroundings that they decided to take sabbaticals from their jobs back home in Minnesota and winter in Candle. The owners of a little house located not far from Lou and Beth agreed to let the young Minnesotans live there the winter in exchange for fixing up the place. That way, the two adventurers figured, they would be able to really help the town fight its vicious battle.

Gold and russet leaves clung to branches. A few mornings of blue toned frost sweetened the leaves on my broccoli plants. It was time for me to give up hope of them somehow turning into strong rich vegetables, and harvest the lonely greens. The river sounds quieted, and various birds were spotted resting in colored trees on their way South. But still, tourists lingered in town.

I was surprised at myself one morning when I became angered by my discovery of two tourists sleeping on the beach behind the air taxi. I practically stumbled over their frost covered backpacks which had been carelessly left beside their fire ring. I kicked the ugly charred circle of rocks apart and picked up the shiny foil which had been left inside it. I had not expected the offenders to be at their camp still, so I was startled when a groggy head popped out of the yellow tent.

"Eh, Hello?"

"Oh. I didn't know you were asleep. Sorry."

"Okay. No problem." The dark headed man started to zip the tent closed again.

For a brief moment, embarrassment shielded my fury. My congenial manner dominated my desire to affect change, and I almost backed away quietly and let the campers sleep peacefully in their illegal camp

135

spot. But then I realized that I was angry. This was not a campground, and Candle was not an amusement park. Why did all these people have to come and cause deep friendships to fall apart, sweet respites to be ravaged by poisonous noise? Why did I have to feel that I was on show all the time? Why did I have to feel always afraid? Afraid that the grandmother trees would soon know the fatal sword of chain saws, that the tarn would become oily, our drinking water impure. Why did dear Aldo Leopold have to be so right on the money when he explained that we destroy what we cherish by cherishing it too much? Why should I back away? Scared to offend. Lose respect. Here was my chance to stand up to the horror I was witnessing.

"Hey!" I called back to the man in the tent. The head popped out again. But this time less groggy. It yielded a dark face which wore a smile.

"Yes, hello."

"You know, this is private property. You can't camp here."

"Oh. We didn't know that."

"Yeah, you know you can't just go around making fire rings whenever you want either. They are a huge negative impact on this fragile land."

"Oh. Sorry. We didn't know that either. We'll be moving today anyway, and we'll clean up. Sorry."

"Okay" I said. He zipped the tent back up and I could hear the two people shuffling around inside.

My outburst turned out not to be so satisfying after all. I had been mean. The tourists were not to blame. They were not responsible for an atmosphere of greed and disrespect. I felt even worse actually, because I had lost my scapegoat. I was not sure there even was a scapegoat. Perhaps that was our problem. We all needed a scapegoat and could not agree upon who or what it was. Better I supposed, to pretend again to be a tourist. That was the easiest way to look at the world.

I went berry picking with Zach a week or so after Labor day. Our blueberry crop had been terrible that summer, but there were plenty of cranberries to be picked up Raven's Creek, and so we headed there with our buckets. How I love the satisfaction of picking berries. The search for bright red gifts from the bushes is a wonderful excuse to mindlessly linger on the path, listening to the groans and creaks of trees as the wind gently caresses their golden leaves. Or to sniff the pure sweet odor of autumn—a cold freshness brought forth from the decaying fruits of summer simmering in the warm streams of thin light.

"Plod Plud." A handful of the shiny little balls rolled around in my bucket. I recalled my mother sitting on the foot of my bed when I was young, reading *Blueberry Sal* in her tender voice. On Blueberry hill, Sal's berries went "kerplink, kerplank, kerplunk" when the fresh bulbous fruits hit the bottom of her pail. Only hers was tin, mine— plastic. Did they even have plastic pails in those days?

I sat down on the spongy floor of the forest. My quest for berries was the only thing that mattered. How wonderful it feels to satisfy your only goal. Buckets brimming with goodness. But Blueberry Sal never met that one goal: she kept eating the berries from her pail, as well as her mother's.

Quietly content in my thoughts, soaking in the year's last warmth from the sun, I had quite forgotten about Zach until he said, "Hey you know Heidi, I've been thinking. Wouldn't it be great to have an end of season party for everyone left in Candle?"

"That's a great idea Zach! We all need something like that!"

"I know!" Zach continued excitedly, "I was thinking we could have a bonfire behind my house on the beach, and it would be a great way to relax and end the summer."

"Yeah! And we could have Manny sing some of his new songs with his accordion, and I could try to pick along with him and maybe we'd inspire some dancing!" Zach laughed.

"Yeah. Except, maybe Manny shouldn't sing because his songs are about the petitions, and we don't want to think about that." I wrinkled my nose.

"Yeah, you're right. Maybe we could just bring a radio out."

We buried ourselves in our happy thoughts, and continued "Plud Plod"-ing away. My hands were becoming stained even though I was taking great pains not to squish the berries.

After a while, Zach broke our contented silence again. "You know though, we probably shouldn't have both Herb and Bernie at the same party. That would be uncomfortable for everyone."

"Yeah. You're right," I said. "That's good thinking. But actually. Bernie probably wouldn't come anyway if he had the slightest inclination that Herb would be there so we probably don't have to worry too much about that."

"Yeah that is true." More silence. Then I had another thought. "I suppose it would be kind of mean to have both Cal and Herb there at the same time. They're pretty touchy with each other these days also."

"Oh really?" Zach said, "I had not thought of that."

Plod. Plud.

"Well, Herb and Louise are so busy, they never make any events these days anyhow."

"That's true."

The air felt moist. Glancing at the sky, I noticed clouds gathering. Swirling, whishing. The dark shapes were moving quickly.

"On that account," Zach added, "it probably would be sort of uncomfortable to have the Jensens and Lou and Beth at the same party. Whooh boy you should have heard Beth go on the other day about that new grocery store at the boathouse. Have you been in it lately?"

"Uh, not since I ran out of coffee."

"Gad, they have all these trinkets and cards and stuff. Tee-shirts that say Candle Tarn. You know."

Plud. Plod, plod.

"Well geez Zach, let's just forget those people. Let's have a small shindig. We'll sip wine by the tarn with just Sam and Josh and Sue Bean."

"Can't really invite Sue Bean and not Axel Bend. She won't go if Axel's not invited."

"Okay. So Axel too."

"Well that would be pretty rotten to invite Axel and not the Jensens. I mean, that is rotten." I felt a couple of drips on the back of my neck. The trees swayed and rocked.

"So forget Sue Bean then. Some party, and Sam can't drink any wine because he has to be on call to fly."

The clouds unleashed themselves and rain spilled out. Drips rolled carelessly down my nose. They gathered on mushroom tops and slid down the waxy rims, hung onto the gills, teasing the ground, then dove to the spongy beckoning floor. Our buckets were not quite half full. We headed for home, and did not speak anymore of a party.

The soft rain fell for days. Showy leaves were washed to the ground where they became a soggy carpet of color. Giant puddles formed in the street—slippery mud. The tarn, bubbling with raindrops, became swirly grey, pushing waves in slow rhythmic whooshes onto the beach. People left. Tents disappeared. Town was quiet. Nights were dark but for the silent glow emanating from the Candle Flame Bar. With most of the tourists gone, the small smoky room lured me in once again. That was where I got to meet my new neighbors. I had forgotten about the two Minnesotans who were renting the house near Axel Bends's for the winter. Occupied with canning berries and fish, I had not thought to go over there and introduce myself. And mail had stopped being the sort of event where one got to know newcomers.

They were Cassie and Jake Thompson and they were quite good at pool. But one would never guess it from first glance. Cassie had silvery blonde hair which tumbled in curls just past her shoulders. Her handshake was loose and relaxed, her smile sweet and naive. But her pool game was otherwise. Waving the rolls of second hand smoke from her face, she would aim the cue stick with cool composure, bringing her dark lashes over her blue eyes and letting her tongue rest behind her upper front teeth. She would make every bank shot. Jake kept his hands in his jeans pockets — his dark hair always covered with a smooth black cap. He laughed a lot, and his brown eyes always twinkled. He never drank more than two beers. I liked them. They appeared to have an air of confidence that could get them through an unpredictable winter. They had thought of everything: their cellar was full of cabbage, their wood pile was stout, and their doorway was armed with both skis and snowshoes. It was going to be nice to have new blood in the area.

After one of those cheery evenings at the bar, I left, defeated at pool once again, and stepped outside into the lonely dripping rain. The seat of my Schwinn was wet, sticking cold against my pants. Soggy brown leaves were crumpled in between my spokes. Squinting in order to prevent the stinging drops from poking my droopy eyes, I kept my headlight focused on the muddy trail in front of me. When I jumped from the watery seat to push the bike up the hill, since my bald tires could not grip the slippery leaves, I suddenly noticed the fresh three-wheeler tracks — tiny squares punched in the mud going up the road. New tracks! Axel was gone, the only other person who lived up this road was...Ella! Ella was back! She had been gone so long. I jumped eagerly back on the purple machine, high on my discovery, my early evening buzz crept back into my main bloodstream. I steered the bike wobbly on purpose and made figure eight tracks in the mud all the way to Ella's front door.

I did not know what time it was, but she was awake — unpacking her things from the summer. She was in a good mood too when she opened her door.

"Hi you drippy gloopy thing! Guess I can't sneak past you can I?" I threw off my saturated rain coat and pulled out a chair.

"Well but you did! I didn't notice you were home until now." She put the kettle on the stove and handed me a mug.

"Black currant tea all right?" I nodded. Her hair was untied and dangling straight and dark down her back. Her face still showed the very last remnants of a raccoon-eyed tan. Her lips were white from being chapped too often. The house smelled good, homey, even though she had just arrived.

Ella did not seem to be the slightest bit fatigued from her long drive through the rain and swirling leaves. Rather she appeared energized, glad to be home.

"I went to visit my mom for a couple of weeks" she said as she poured the boiling water into my cup.

"I was wondering why you weren't here yet," I said. She put the box of tea back in the cupboard and closed the door.

"Honey?"

"No thanks." She put a gob of the sweetener in her mug and joined me at the table.

"It sounds like I didn't need to be here."

"Oh." I shrugged. "Well, you just gotta ignore the bullshit."

"I praise you if you were able to do that," she answered. "My mom had saved all the articles for me about that spider crap. I couldn't believe how much of a write-up there's been. What's up with that?"

I laughed. "Who knows. But the summer's over. I figure everybody will forget about it after awhile and it will blow over."

"Well then you haven't been down south getting newspapers stuffed in your face."

I sipped my tea. "Guess not."

"It's still all over the news Heidi. It's so ridiculous. People want to close snowmachine traffic. But the only way they can get out here to see if they need to, is by snowmachine."

I laughed again, "Well I'm glad your mom's staying on top of it."

Ella smiled, "I know! Someone's got to I guess, and I don't give two beans about it!"

"You don't really? I thought you hated all those snowmachines driving around."

Ella played with the spoons on the table. "Well you know, they're awful, but its not really the government's place to get involved." She tilted her head and took a big long finishing gulp from her cup then set it down on the table definitively, "Besides, I'm not so sure I'll be around as much anyway."

My eyes popped from my head. "What do you mean?"

"Well, I just don't want to get stuck here the way everyone does. Just because this place is the end of the road doesn't mean it's the end of the world. Or the center of the world either. There's lots out there. I love my place, but geez Heidi, I'm only 34 and I've been here almost 12 years! At this rate, I'll be like Sue Bean!" Despite my shock and dismay at Ella's earlier words, I giggled.

"I don't mean anything bad about Sue Bean. I love her to death, but she's 48 and she's still hanging out single with her cranberries and alder carvings."

"Well she likes it," I said defensively. I hated the thought of Ella being around even less than she was now.

"Well I know. I shouldn't make it seem bad. But I have a lot of other things I want to know and do before I'm 50 years old."

I must have looked like I was pouting or sulking, for then Ella said' "Geez Heidi. It's not like you're sticking around forever! Ernie could be back anytime."

I did not answer her. The truth is, I had not heard from Ernie in a long while, and had kind of assumed he had forgotten about me and his dogs forever.

Ella got up abruptly. "Want some more tea? I do. I didn't drink enough on the drive in."

I sighed, "Yeah I probably should."

Ella laughed her warm laugh, "If you came here from the bar you should." She dipped a cup in her water bucket and poured more water into the kettle.

"Oh you know," she said, lighting the burner, "I met that kid who's staying here this winter."

"What kid?" I had not heard of any kid staying the winter.

Ella sifted through her cupboards for more kinds of tea. "You know, I forget his name. Some college kid. He's caretaking the Fallon's place this winter while they go outside. You haven't met him yet?"

"No uhuh." I frowned, trying to remember whether I had or not.

"Oh Heidi," Ella turned from the cupboards and looked straight at me. "You should."

His name was Francis. He had bright orange hair that erupted in a screwy tangle from every millimeter of his head. But his face was pale and youthful, and his skin was smooth and free of whiskers. He had wide open green eyes which stared intently into those of a speaker — sucking for information, anything to learn. His head was red, but he was green.

Truthfully, I have not mentioned the Fallons much for the simple reason that I did not know anything about them. All I knew was that they had a homestead on the other side of the river about five miles past the Kapps. They apparently owned quite a bit of land, but I had never been to their place. They occasionally came to town to get their mail and once in a while would show up at some occasion. But for the most part, they kept to themselves. Their caretaker Francis however, had no plans to follow in their reclusive footsteps — or lack there of I should say.

Francis arrived in Candle with a green and white mountain bike, fully equipped with front and rear head lights and cakes of Alaska mud in the spokes. Basically that was all he brought with him. It was all he needed. He did not know a thing about how to dress in cold weather, and had a lousy sense of direction, but he sure knew how to ride a bike.   The six or so miles between the Fallon's and Candle central did not hinder him from showing up in town at least once a day with his green and white companion — always eager to learn of any new happenings in town. Before he had been at the Fallons two weeks, he had already met almost every Candle resident, and knew where they had come from, and how long they had lived in Alaska. Two days after Ella told me about Francis, dribbling her tea as she laughed, he showed up in my yard as I was putting fresh hay in the dog houses.

He pulled up so quietly in his spiffy bike that he startled me. I pulled my head out of Nali's house, and there he was. His tall figure rested against the dog food can. His pale face was painted with a strangely huge grin amplified by large front buck teeth, his orange hair tossed like a fresh carrot salad. I jumped.

"Oh gee, I didn't mean to scare you. I'm Francis."

"Hi." I said, "My name's Heidi." Nali pushed her body against mine. I think she had been scared by Francis also.

"Hope you don't mind me stopping by. I heard your dogs barking

142

earlier. And someone said you ran a dog kennel. That's cool. I just really wanted to meet some sled dogs."

I smiled, "Well, here's 29 of them."

"Wow!" Francis's voice was encased in enthusiasm. "That's so cool. Are all these yours?"

What a thought. I laughed breezily. "No, no." It occurred to me that none of them were really mine. "Just these seven. Sort of. And then some of them belong to the Stevens. They should have been back a couple weeks ago. And the others belong to Fred Davison. Who knows when he'll be back."

"Wow, that's amazing. I mean it's just amazing to see this many dogs at once you know? And like, they all seem cool about being on a chain and stuff."

I laughed. "They're sled dogs."

"Wow, do you race?"

By then, I realized that I could tell this guy anything and he would believe me. But I resisted.

"Nope. Not with these dogs."

"Oh man. Do you think I could go dog sledding with you sometime? I mean, I wouldn't get in the way or anything. It's just so neat. I want to see how it works."

"Sure." I answered. "But we have to wait until we get snow."

Francis snorted a laugh. His nose folded up, withdrawing his lip and exposing his healthy gums above the buck teeth,

"Oh yeah. Thdudh. That makes sense. Um- do you need help with the dogs now or anything? I mean, I wouldn't want to get in the way or anything, but I'd love to help."

I didn't see why not. There was not that much to do, but the dogs always liked extra attention. "Sure, I'll show you around." I showed him the bitch pen for separating the bitches in heat, introduced him to every dog, and got out an extra poop scoop for him.

I could not believe how absorbed he became in the dogs. Marveling at the enormous pile, he shoveled spiritedly, asking me a ton of questions. He knew absolutely nothing. At least, that was how he came across. In a way, he was draining. But also a heck of a friendly guy and appearing to have only the best intentions. And somehow, his naivete was also empowering. It made me feel as if I had spent my life in Candle and knew everything there was to know about bush living. At the same time, Francis appeared too malleable. Able to be convinced of anything. It could be dangerous, really.

Chapter 12

Our first real snowfall did not arrive until the end of October. Even then, I was not ready for it. My yard remained a mess —filled with typical Alaska back yard trash that I had been too lazy to pick up: a few bent nails left over from a dog food shed project; various pieces of lumber lying here and there; and a couple of beer cans—remnants of a bonfire celebration I hosted with Ella, the Thompsons, Zach, Sam, and Beth. I watched the large flakes fall—hurriedly covering the evidence of my indolence. Blanketed in velvety white, my yard would don a graceful appearance that would last until breakup. But the mess and trash would always be there lying hidden under the clean snow.

Francis had become a frequent visitor to my dog lot. He was always eager to go mushing, but would almost as gladly lend a hand with the poop shovel. Saving food scraps became a regular part of his routine at the Fallons. He would carry a bag all the way over from the homestead to my house where the dogs (who had quickly overcome their fear of his screwy redheaded face) would heartily appreciate his fruitful visits. One or two times when I did not need help, I sent him over to Zach's. But Zach eventually used his very skilled diplomacy to tell Francis that his help was not needed. For some reason, he rubbed Zach the wrong way, but I started to become accustomed to Francis. His eager enthusiasm still amused me, but I also realized that he paid close attention to the hundreds of answers he sought. He was a very bright guy. His able management of the homestead and all its buildings, and of his well being living alone in bush conditions, showed he was a quick learner.

During my frequent dog lot visits with Francis, I also learned of the activities of Cassie and Jake, since Francis was spending quite a bit of time with them as well. Cherishing his new found idols, he was always eager to talk about them.

"I can't go mushing the next few days, " he told me one afternoon in his usual excited manner, "cause I told Cassie and Jake I'd help them frame up the arctic entrance they're putting on their house."

"That sounds good."

"Yeah, it's so cool — they're gonna beef up that house so it's a lot more energy efficient. I think they even got hold of a couple of solar panels! It would be cool if everyone did that. I think they want to try and help everyone in Candle make their places more energy efficient."

"Sounds good I guess," I said gently kicking Crocodile's mouth away from the stuff I was trying to shovel.

"Yeah, and also they hope the arctic entrance will shield off some of the noise. Uh, I think Willow just knocked over her water."

"That's okay. What noise?"

"From all the snowmachines," I flung a big shovel full toward the pile.

"Hmm."

"Yeah, they were telling me all about how horrible the snowmachines get. How noisy it is and stuff. And how they're impacting the tarn. It sounds really awful. I think we should do something about it."

"Well," I said scratching Fireweed's head, "Probably the best thing to do right now is to tolerate it." I do not know why I said that. Lord knows I had not been so tolerant of snowmachines myself the past winter. But how, I wondered, did Jake and Cassie know what it was like? I felt defensive I suppose. I was protective of our little community and did not want to see any more bad vibes being spread around.

Since the day of the fateful moose encounter at Ravens Creek, my relations with Herb and Louise had been good. No mention had been made of the Adele Hugston incident, or my aborted attempt to apologize. Since the dwindling of summer clientele, they had also had more time to hang out. I found myself going down there every couple of days to drink coffee with Louise or shoot the bull with Herb. A few times they even had me over for dinner with Fred Davison or Sue Bean. One evening in early November however, they gave me an exclusive personal invitation—not some offhand gesture while I happened to be sipping coffee. They actually called me on the CB and asked me to come down. I knew something was up.

Louise served moose meat lasagna and canned peas for dinner. I did not dare ask whether or not we were eating "Polly." I did not care to know the answer. Among the many things I learned during my two years in Candle, one of them was to try not to provide Herb with any fuel for crude jokes.

"Besides enjoying your company," Louise said to me while passing the of dish of lasagna, "We wanted to have you over for dinner tonight in order to ask you something."

I knew it. I raised my eyebrows and smiled. "Hope I'm not in trouble."

"You bet you are!" Herb blurted out with his mouth full of lasagna, "Louise wants to make you her slave!"

"Herbert!" Louise kicked him hard under the table and Herb started laughing.

"Ow! See how she treats me?!"

I chuckled and shook my head at Herbert.

Louise continued. "We plan on getting real busy in a few weeks. And naturally, it's difficult to find employees who are willing to live out here in the winter. We were wondering if we could ask you to help us out every now and then."

I did not answer. I was busy chewing.

"I know the dog kennel doesn't bring in that much money. Ernie usually would find some contracting or trail making to do to supplement his income."

I hated to admit Louise was right. Financial worries were something I had been denying. They just seemed so irrelevant in Candle. Sooner or later though, I would have to face the realities of a very viscous cash flow.

"We probably would only need you a couple days a week—for various chores. Anything from helping cook to making beds to shoveling snow. We'll pay you $5 an hour plus tips, meals, and you can do your laundry here anytime as well as have a shower."

"That's right. Indentured servancy!" Herb cried out, grinning.

"Herb!" Louise scowled at him. "Are you done eating? Go put some hot water on the stove."

Herb laughed obnoxiously as he picked up his plate and sauntered into the kitchen.

The laundry and shower privileges certainly sounded attractive. But still, I would have to think about giving up some of my free time. "Well, let me —"

"Oh master?"

Herb's dainty falsetto voice interrupted me from the kitchen. Louise picked up the two pot holders on the table and pitched them forcefully into the kitchen where I could hear Herb's mock cries.

"Ooh! Ow! You beast!"

I just could not imagine working around Herb. I was definitely impressed with Louise's ability to put up with him.

"I'll think about it".

"Sure, take your time—we have a few weeks until it gets busy again. Herb pranced out of the kitchen with a tray full of mugs and cookies, set it down gracefully in front of Louise, and gave her a kiss. I laughed and shook my head. Those two were a pair.

By mid-November, Francis had discovered that his green and white bicycle was no longer a suitable means of transportation and the frequency of his visits took a temporary plunge while he struggled on his own to learn how to ski. The first snowmachine tracks to be seen in the area were unexpectedly those of Jack Greely. With the revenue from a profitable season at the bunkhouse, he bought a brand new machine. I do not know much about snowmobiles, but I do know the engine was huge and fancy, capable of outrageous speeds. The handlebars were equipped with hand warmers, and the seat was soft and comfy. It was a powerful unit. And on it, Jack was not only a king, he was also a mischievous little boy. He tore all over the tarn. Up to the silver mine and back, to the Cohen's house, and around the Jensen's house a few times. Every little slope had a few half moons covering it, all the trails were set, and the airstrip packed. I could only hope that Jack would soon tire of his new toy. In any case, his demonic cowboy rides already sparked new fire into those hearts of his would-be enemies, and set a precedent for the snowmachine season to come.

While Tuesday mail days continued to be a good excuse for Ella and me to enjoy a weekly ski or mush together, it was no longer an occasion to inspire brushed hair, or clean clothes. I seldom met anyone there besides Zach and Ella, and occasionally Sam Hoina. All others did not feel like subjecting themselves to the anger and hatred of their neighbors. While I always looked forward to the fruits of the mail plane, Zach's empty house and the lack of dogs or other machines in front of it each week, only became a sorrowful reminder of the loss Candle had suffered. For me, this was a loss of flavor I loved—of old friendships, of neighborly care and love. While others fumed and whined, I mourned.

I found myself delivering mail to Cassie and Jake, and to Lou and Beth. Sam was bringing it to the Cohens since they no longer owned transportation. Jonathan, in thinking that his own use of snowmachines would be hypocrisy, had sold his machine to Sam. At the time, Esther was 9, and Sarah 7. Old enough to ski, Jonathan and Hazel figured. Unfortunately however, the fact remained that the Cohen's house was seven long miles from mail, or five if you skied directly across the tarn —too great a distance for a family to cover twice in one day.

I sort of assumed the summer tensions would ease in the peace of winter, and once again we as a community would come together joyfully in parties with squeaking dinosaurs, afternoon potlucks, or even usual gatherings at mail. Instead however, as winter progressed, the silence between neighbors only grew colder. I began to have dreams about seeing more than five people together in one room. More and more often, I found myself waking in the morning after having been shopping in a populated grocery store, attending a football game among hoards, or dancing in a crowded bar. Once I even dreamed I was trying to walk down the streets of Hong Kong. I kept brushing against the shirts of strangers as I navigated the city. The whole time I was apologizing to those I disturbed. "Sorry. Oh sorry." But they all ignored me.

Meanwhile in the day time I had been struggling with the decision of whether or not to work for the lodge. Louise really struck my sensitive chord with her remarks about my financial situation. Before our meeting, I had been content to count on my yearly permanent fund dividend to bail me out of any financial worries. Afterward, I could only think of all the things I could do with an added $80 a week to my bank account. Not to mention I absolutely hated—hated—doing my laundry. A washing machine would mean luxury beyond words. But

I could not escape my worries that getting involved with Louise and Herb and their exploitation of Candle's winters would mean eventual alienation from many of my other friends in Candle. Certainly $80 a week, or any monetary value for that matter, was not worth getting involved in the town's struggles.

I finally decided to confide in Ella during our weekly ski to mail. When I told her of my sensitive situation, she did not say anything at first. She just pressed her lips together, folding them up beneath her nose, and squinted her eyes in a far off look as if in deep thought. I skied beside her, nervously watching for changes in her expression and wondering what kind of harsh judgements she could be making — of course forgetting Ella's firm resolve never to judge. Finally she stopped and said, "You know Heidi. If you are thinking of not taking the job because you dislike that kind of work, or because you don't want the loss of freedom, then by all means forget about it. But if your only reason for saying 'no' is because you're afraid of what everybody will think, well then screw 'em. Take the job. Heck, you can always quit if you get sick of it and Herb and Louise'll understand".

Ella was smart. I just loved her. She was absolutely right about it not mattering what everybody thought. If people were petty enough to hate me because of my financial situation, then who really cared about them. I would not be hurting anybody. I decided to take the job. A couple of days a week would not be bad, and already I could feel the warm spray of a shower hitting my face.

At Thanksgiving, there is so little light that one always travels with a head lamp even, if all that is planned is a short excursion to haul water. A mellow dusky tinge sweeps evening light across the snow at 3 PM, and sunsets last so long ducking in and out behind the mountains, that one needs to have a bowl of popcorn in hand in order to watch the entire event. Nonetheless, helmet-clad thrill-seekers filled the Candle road with speedy machines on their way to the Lodge for the holidays. They were eager to learn what sort of attraction could compel Candle residents to so selfishly horde their wares. They were joy riders, eager to play in Candle. They knew it could very well be their last chance.

My entire Thanksgiving day was spent at the lodge. The entrance was lined with helmets. Heavy coats penetrated with fumes occupied the coat racks, and the dinner seats were brimming with happy adventurers. Louise sweated for days preparing for the event. At the last minute, she had been forced to buy cranberries from Sue Bean. I declined dinner invitations from both the Stevens and the Thompsons in order to help Louise and Herb. At least I got to smell and hear the comforting sizzle of turkey juices all day long. Jack came down for dinner as an invited guest, and we ate with the other guests. I sat at a table with a few large men, and Jack took the empty seat beside me.

My dinner companions, appearing heavy even before touching the fork, were the type that do not bother with slices of turkey, but go for a whole big leg at once. Between chomps, their faces yielded grins from fat rosy cheek to fat rosy cheek.

One guy patted the drool of gravy spilling down his chin with the cloth napkin, and asked, "So, you two live around here?" Chomp. I noticed Jack had removed his "Best in the West" cap and hung it on the back of his chair. His brown hair was still molded into the smooth shape of his hat.

"Yup, Just up the hill."

Chomp "That up by that mine?" Chomp

"No. Not that far. But it's real easy to get up there with a snowmachine."

Chomp. "I'd sure like to get up there and look around. And I bet my buddies would too."

"I could possibly take you up there."

I turned my head to stare at Jack. He must have felt my eyes piercing into his cheek, for then he winked at me.

Chomp. "Gee, that would be terrific." Chomp. "How much would you charge for something like that?" I could not believe Jack would just railroad Bernie's tour business without a thought.

"Well, why don't you take that up with the lodge. It will make things easier for you."

"Terrific!" Chomp. "We'll go up tomorrow morning."

I was angered by Jack's aloof attitude. I witnessed it all summer of course, but his selfishness was too blatant for me to stomach.

"How 'bout you lady? You gonna come up snowmachining with us?"

Absorbed in my shock at Jack, I was unprepared for the sudden turn of attention onto me. "I-"

"She don't snowmachine. She's what you call an environmental-ist!" Jack interrupted and laughed after swallowing a swig of wine.

151

The room was hot, and I felt the heat rise up my chest, and penetrate my neck and cheeks.

"Well, that doesn't mean you can't go ride on a snowmobile with us."

Grinning, Jack was quick with an answer.

"Oh yes it does! You might run over some goddamned spider or something!"

As much as I would have loved to, spilling Jack's dinner in his lap just did not seem quite appropriate at the time. I regret my hesitation now. But instead, I said, "Actually, I have to work tomorrow. And speaking of work. Better get back. Nice chatting with you all."

I picked up my plate and walked to the kitchen. I picked at the turkey on the counter as the dish water dripped into the resting suds. From my refuge, I could hear the din of happy chatting voices as big gulps of chardonnay were swigged. Despite being among a crowd of joyful diners, that Thanksgiving was the loneliest one I have ever had.

Herb and Louise were delighted with Jack's business proposition. With Jack as a guide, snowmachine migrations to the silver mine became a daily routine. Jack loved the opportunity to flaunt his snowmachining skills in front of an appreciative audience. And guests loved the ignorant lies they were told about all the buildings and their history. Meanwhile, frowns continued to be the prevalent expression on the faces of many locals that winter. Rumor had it that Jonathan was working on a new proposal to submit to congress. Jake and Cassie had been spending a good deal of time at the Cohen's house, and I assumed they were bringing in their outside expertise to make the proposal more legitimate. As usual, Francis always told me what was going on.

"They're organizing a statewide letter writing campaign! It's such a cool idea. You should make sure you get the stuff to write to the Governor and the President! And they're also going to make sure increased pressure gets put on the lodge! I hope it works! That place is evil! The snowmachines are horrible! I mean what if they ran me over or something? They wouldn't even care! All those people want is to go fast!"

I usually just let Francis go on when he started spewing. He did not know anything he was talking about, so I figured his prattling was harmless. I usually would listen to at least half of his words. If I strained out his excited blunderings, I could learn something.

"Oh, and you know what? Oh Heidi, you should do this. It's really a cool idea! Cassie and Jake are going to put up a big fence around their house so the horrible snowmachines can't get to their yard!" Now that idea seemed funny.

"Hah!" Larkspur jumped at my sudden outburst.

"No really. It's a good thing! At least they'll be able to save the environment and the air right in front of their house! I think everybody should get a fence!"

"Well, we'll see," was my only remark. I could not imagine that tall metal fences around everybody's yards would be much more beautiful than a speeding snowmachine.

After Thanksgiving, the influx of winter tourists on snowmachines thinned down a bit. The weekend had been quite profitable for me. Nonetheless, I was glad to have some fresh air. Francis reported he had seen a black cloud of pollution from the hills above the Cohen's one day, but I had chosen to include that with his list of other remarks to ignore. In any case, Cassie and Jake had asked their neighbor back in Minnesota to send out their video camera so they would be able to record all the snowmachine traffic and resulting damage, and if there was any smog forming, I am sure they would have recorded it on film for posterity.

I wish that either Jake or Cassie had been able to capture Bernie's accident on tape. That would have been an interesting encounter to have on film. I was not at the scene either, but I heard stories later from each Sue Bean, Bernie, and Jack. With their reports added to the bits and pieces of information I had heard from some of the lodge guests, I was able to put together a pretty good account.

Apparently a week or so after Thanksgiving, Bernie had been able to warm up his three-wheeler enough to get it started by placing a Coleman stove underneath the engine, and covering the whole vehicle with a tarp for an hour or so. The temperature was -10° Fahrenheit, and a little bit of sun managed to peer through the warm insulating clouds. The day was perfect for venturing down to the airstrip to pick up mail.

I guess Bernie had been planning on interviewing Cassie and Jake about the success of their fence and arctic entrance in blocking out the evils of snowmachines. Perhaps he thought their techniques were his solution. The prospect made him cheery and anxious to get to town. Most likely his anxiety had made him drive a little faster than usual down the steep packed trail. In any case, Bernie blamed ruts caused by reckless snowmachines for causing his three-wheeler to suddenly swing and flip head over wheels, flinging poor Bernie into the bank. While furiously cussing out Herb for being the source of the trail sabotaging machines, Bernie, then struggled to free himself from his powdery bath. His ears and nose had been stuffed with snow, and where his neck had been naked, it burned with icy surprise. The machine, lying on its side, suffered as well, with breathless coughs and spinning wheels in the fresh powder. Where it lay, the ground became an ugly blotch of dirty snow.

Bernie's ears were probably still plugged with snow when he stood back on the trail and leaned over to inspect his tumbled vehicle, for he says he did not hear the brigade of snowmachines led by Jack the tour guide buzzing up the trail at 25 miles-per-hour. When they rounded the bend behind which Bernie and his vehicle were standing, Bernie had only time to open his eyes wide and scream his most effective expletive before Jack's machine punched him in the side. Bernie tumbled to the snow clutching his ribs, and yelling I am sure, a most extensive display of vocabulary at Jack and his entourage. Jack was in shock, but the tourists jumped from their machines and tossing their helmets from their heads, ran to Bernie's aid. But Bernie would not let them touch him.

"Keep away from me you murderous polluting dirtbags!" He could barely move from the pain of broken ribs, but remained lying on his side, spitting his anger in a broken voice. "Get back on your friggin expensive monster machines and go tell Herbert Kramer what a wonderful guy he is for letting you drive up to my property and try to kill me! Let him know what a fantastic louse he is!" Bernie rested his head on the snow and tried to get more air in shallow breaths.

Jack revived from his nervy blow and finally said. "Okay you win Bernie. You're hurt. Just let us get you on our goddamned machines so we can get you out of here."

Bernie made an effort to get up, but in pain, his body plummeted back to the snow. His face was white and contorted with virulence.

"I'd rather stay here and die than get on any one of your stinkin' snowmachines!"

The tourists remained quiet. They were quite scared by the animosity, and worried about what sort of law suits the incident might involve, and how soon would it be before they would get to a phone to call their lawyers. Jack on the other hand, was another one never to hold his temper.

"Goddamn you Bernie. You <u>will</u> die if you stay here on this cold snow. You quit your frothing at the mouth and let us get your goddamned body out of here!"

"You keep your polluted hands off of me. I don't even want you touching me <u>after</u> I die. And neither you, nor that bastard Kramer is invited to my funeral!"

"Goddamn you Bernie!" Jack opened the box on the back of his machine and pulled out a rolled up wool blanket which he flung onto Bernie's chest. Then he got back on the machine and without even saying a word to his clients, plunged through the thick snow and willows and sped away back down the hill. The tourists, eager to retreat from the ugly scene themselves, made haste to turn their machines around and follow Jack's tracks.

Meanwhile, Jack, still enraged, sped his machine down the hill like a maniac. At the speed he was travelling, the -10° temperature would have transformed itself into a vicious wind chill upon his bare forehead. But the aching cold only made him urge the machine to go faster. When he reached his house at the end of the hill, he got on the CB radio to Sue Bean.

"Yo Sue Bean!...Yeah, Bernie's stuck up on the goddamned trail near your place. He wouldn't let me move his stubborn ass, so maybe you want to go look at him. He deserves to rot there though if you ask me."

By the time Sue Bean was able to reach Bernie, his body temperature was quite low—near ninety-two. He was shivering violently, which probably would have made any normal human being with broken ribs pass out with pain. The blanket which Jack had tossed upon departure still lay in an unrolled bundle upon Bernie's chest. Sue Bean covered him with a sleeping bag she brought, offered him some hot cranberry juice, and dragged him onto her sled which bounced and wiggled behind her four-wheeler as she drove back to her house. Then, that strong little red head dragged Bernie onto her couch over which she piled so many blankets that Bernie's ribs could not have moved even if they had wanted to. She threw another log in the fire and proceeded to cook some soup. She and Bernie both knew it would be a while before he would have the strength to do the necessary chores involved in living alone again.

I suppose if he had really wanted to, Bernie could have sued Jack or the Candle Lodge. But law suits are not the style of those who live without phones or newspapers. But I can also tell you that Bernie had no intentions of letting the matter die. No, most likely, Bernie had something completely different in mind in seeking his vengeance.

Chapter 13

As the holidays approached, the number of machine clad tourists spilling down the dark road toward Candle increased progressively. Ella and I struggled to understand why people would choose to drive hundreds of miles to visit our home when one could barely see it. It was like visiting Yosemite Valley during the night only. Although our loss of light was slowing to a welcomed halt as the solstice neared, there were scarcely four hours of daylight with which to examine the untamed magnificence of the Candle area. True, those few hours of December light are very special. The sun becomes an angel friend, appearing seldom, but creating the most magical blue jewels of light and shadows upon the sharp landscape. And too, the night is never a source of fear the way it sometimes is in other places. There is no oppressive inky blackness hiding cruel shapes, but rather a soft black, which pads the sharpness of shadows.

Nevertheless, I hardly think the scores of visitors were coming to Candle in order to appreciate the sweet darkness. Rather, I believe their visits were merely a blatant show of support for the snowmachine side of the spider battle. Many lodge guests were in fact registered as groups such as the Anchorage SnowMachine Association (ASMA), the Snowmobiler Outing Group (SMOG), and the SnowMachine Expedition League (SMEL).

The Thompson's fence that read "Snowmachine Free Zone" had already been knocked down, and there was sufficient tracks evidence to prove that the cause of the collapse had been a heavy snowmachine and not a wind storm. Of course, Cassie got the smashed fence recorded on film. Meanwhile, Sue Bean nursed Bernie almost all the way back to normal feisty condition. Needless to say though, the one-time-lovers of nearly 16 years earlier were not compatible roommates. As soon as Bernie was well enough to talk very much, she drove him back out to his upturned three wheeler on the trail and helped him get it started. That was when Bernie decided to move down to downtown Candle. Determined that snowmachines would kill him if he remained in his shack near the silver mine, Bernie sought safer residence. Fred Davison gave him the key to a little cabin at the bottom of his trail—just near Lou and Beth's house. Once Bernie's ribs were completely healed, he would have to go wood cutting, but in the mean time, the little shack had plenty of split wood with which to keep warm through the dark days of December and January. Zach, Cassie and I took turns hauling his water.

It was strange having Bernie live so much closer. With his new proximity, he was a much more visible character. Despite my known association with the lodge, he would call me to stop by his house for tea often—usually warning me to avoid near-death encounters with snowmobiles. He kept threatening to arm his house with some snowballs or rocks with which to hit dangerous machines as they passed by. Encouraged by the excitement of learning new words and philosophies from the crazy sourdough, it was Francis who became the most consistent visitor to Bernie's pad. Over a beer or a smoke, they would play chess and then Francis with his strong ribs, would help Bernie with a chore or two, all the while I am sure, sucking up Bernie's original doctrines.

I decided to spend Christmas day working at the lodge. But I did celebrate solstice at the Kissell's home. That afternoon Ella and I mushed the 4 and 1/2 miles into the hills behind her house to the Kissell's perch overlooking the tarn and the glacier. There had been silver mines in that area as well, although not as developed as the ones above Bernie's house. The Kissell's cabin was a cozy 12 foot by 16 foot log structure with a wonderfully homey aura. I felt instantly relaxed when I walked in even though I did not know the family very well. In contrast to their hyper seven-year-old son Zach, Lisa and Ralph were a fairly quiet pair. Lisa spoke in calm cool tones, but obviously had fervent views about the snowmachine/ spider situation. Both were ardently in support of Jonathan's activities to reform the area. They had always sought to remain out of conflicts Ralph explained, but the situation in Candle was becoming ridiculous, and they were willing to do anything to help change it.

Like the Stevens, the Kissells were a bit isolated, and heartily welcomed visitors with news. Ella let me entertain most of their questions. She remained out of the serious conversation by talking with little Zach. He was very excited about the prospect of new toys in four days. Ella was more interested in his old toys — especially his metal Tonka bulldozer.

After dinner Ralph asked me, "What do you think of that red headed kid?"

"Oh you mean Francis?"

"Yeah, that guy. He skied all the way up here one day. Scared little Zach half to death when he came into our yard without any sort of warning."

"It's not like he barged into our house, Ralph," Lisa interjected.

"A whistle would have been nice Li. He looks like the bogey man. Anyway, he was telling us about these folks — Cassie and Joe or something."

"Jake."

"Yeah, that's it. They're trying to get everybody to put up fences around their land to shut out snowmachiners."

"It's crazy" Lisa said.

"Well, don't be so quick to judge Li," Ralph's tone was smooth and mellow.

"Yeah, I can just see it. Big chain link fences surrounding everybody's property. We'll all get intercoms to let in visitors. Beautiful. Get real Ralph."

Zach interrupted, "Mama look!" He and Ella, who was sitting on the floor Indian style with her hands behind her and her head tilted back in hearty laughter, had put tape on the wheels of match box cars to make them into snowmachines. Zach was driving the bulldozer around the floor and scooping helpless snowmachines into his bucket then dumping them into the cat's water dish. Lisa laughed, "See, now that seems like a more effective solution."

"Oh, and you're telling me to be real."

"Well it's going to take something like that to get rid of the snowmachines."

"Mrs. Heyduke eh?"

"Well putting up fences is fine and dandy. But no one owns the tarn. Who's putting a fence around that? And sooner or later, they'll just get knocked down."

"I think one already did," Ella said without expression while pulling the defeated snowmobiles from the water dish.

"Well see?" Lisa stood up to clear the plates and make room for dessert. "It's going to take more than a fence."

Before Ella and I left for home with the dogs, the Kissell's joined us in bundling layers for the -25° night air, and we all stepped onto their front deck with a big bag of fireworks. Fireworks are much more worthwhile on solstice than midsummer. In celebration of the coming of more light, we all unleashed the wild colored rays. The sparks whizzed into the moonless sky, dancing whirring excitement—a fantastic flight of color. Whish! Crack! "Oooh!" Then fell as silent rain, disappearing into the wind.

The next morning I was flipping sheets in the lodge. I stuffed the pillows in their flowery covers, and carefully smoothed over the bed spread with my hands. Making beds was not so bad. The rooms were quiet, and I was warm. My hair was clean, and my laundry smelled fresh. Herb and Louise had been enjoyable to be around lately also. The stupid little slave joke had never disappeared, but now we managed to make a thing of it. I would show Herb scars where I had been whipped, he would sneak me a cookie from the master's larder.

I was folding up the foot blanket when I was startled by the booming voice of Herb coming down the hall way. "Heidi! Where are you Heidi?"

He burst into the room I was changing. I looked at his dirty boots and scowled at the tracks he was making on the rug.

"Nice joke Heidi, but it was not appreciated. You're looking to get yourself out of a job."

Herb and Louise could never afford to lose me now— three days before Christmas.

"What?" I stared at his angry lips.

"You know. Those two snowmachines belonged to a couple of high dollar guys. Guys without a sense of humor. Say goodbye to a nice tip!" Herb's face was wrinkled with agitation.

I could not understand what was causing his rage. A mere two or three hours ago we had been laughing while pretending to compare slave labor-induced calluses. "I'm sorry. I have no idea what you are talking about."

"Cut the crap Heidi. You're the only one around the lodge each day with dogs. And we both know Zachary Bishop has enough sense not to pull a stunt like that."

"What?"

"Yeah what. Maybe you thought putting a nice big pile of dog shit on someone's snowmachine seat was a funny joke. Well I don't. Because I don't laugh when angry customers storm out of my lodge." Herb then pulled his balaclava over his face and walked out the door.

I finished smoothing the wrinkles on the foot blanket. Despite Herb's fury, the corner of my mouth twitched with amusement. But did Herb really mean to fire me? I remembered the last time we had experienced a misunderstanding. I had been quite depressed at the loss of friendship.

I ran down the stairs and raced out the door without my hat or jacket. Herb was on his way to the generator shed. I caught up with his brisk pace. "Herb. What ever happened to innocent until proven guilty huh? Why do you assume right away that I did whatever you are talking about? Didn't you see me at breakfast? How am I supposed to mess with a bunch of snowmachines without you noticing huh?"

Herb stopped and looked at me. The cold air froze my nostrils when I breathed, and surrounded my upper body with chilling penetration.

"I don't know," he said. Then continued walking toward the shed. "But you're a female. They're sneaky."

"Herb!" I followed him into the generator shack. The generator roared its loud groaning voice. I yelled over the uncomfortable din. "Herb! You're my friend! I can't let you treat me irrationally!"

Herb grabbed a dirty rag from a shelf.

"Come on Herb. Is that how you want me to treat you? So I can say that you put that moose there in the middle of the trail to mess with me and my dogs huh? I should accuse you of that and that's okay huh?"

Herb picked up a five-gallon bucket of oil. "Okay Heidi. Drop it. Go finish those rooms." I turned and went back to the lodge. Friendship saved.

Soft white fluff densely floating from hidden clouds buried the trails. Lovely virgin dunes beckoned new streams of motorized metal to re-pattern the fresh layer. Zach said he had never seen so much snow fall in December before. Herb had me shovel walkways all around the lodge, to the generator shack and to the trash pile. We had not spoken of the poop-ridden machines again, although somehow news of the vandalism had spread all over town within 28 hours. Bernie was beaming when his ears received word of the induced exodus.

"I just wish I had thought of it!" He marveled to me over peppermint tea, "What a fantastic idea! I would have loved to see ol' Kramer's face when he caught wind of it!" He laughed and his face contorted itself in an odd mixture of mirth and pain as the giggles rumbled his injured ribs. "Too bad I'm in this rotten condition or I'd go gather a whole lot of it myself and smear it all over that friggin' place! I just wish I knew who the genius was so I could shake his hand!"

Of course I could not escape hearing about it from Francis either.

"Oh Heidi! Did you hear what happened at the lodge? Well I guess of course you did. How awesome! That's what they deserved if you ask me! Don't you think? I mean, if they almost killed Bernie! What if they had? They probably would have just run over him again! I can't believe the government hasn't done anything yet! But that was better anyway! Teach them to go strutting around our backyards!"

I must admit, I'd begun to get a little sick of Francis and his snide banterings. "Our backyards." Candle belonged to Francis just as much as it belonged to Santa Clause, or the tourists for that matter. I found myself not needing Francis' help quite so often. His buck teeth appeared to be becoming larger, his face more pale. He was letting his screwy tangled carrot crop grow. "I want to be able to wear it in a pony tail. The guys back at school probably won't understand my desire to express myself at first. But they'll eventually think it's really cool!"

The sight of the greasy curls dripping about his white face had begun to repulse me. But still, I could not bring myself to completely refuse his friendship. It was not like pickings were so fat around Candle. I did respect Zach's ability early on to tell Francis to get lost though.

On Christmas, the lodge was almost full. Louise cooked up three hams and two geese, four apple pies, five pumpkin, and two pecan. Herb cut down a spruce near the airstrip and brought it inside where we veiled it with popcorn chains and Christmas cookies. With several of the guests helping decorate, the final product turned out to be an interesting compilation of many different views of Christmas. This time I chose not to sit with the guests during dinner, but enjoyed the quiet solitude of a large dirty dish pile in the kitchen.

The following morning, after sleeping away the remnants of raucous late night festivities, there were many takers for a guided snowmachine romp to the silver mine. The dining room was buzzing with excited expedition members. Groggy, and dreary eyed, I helped stuff last minute sandwiches into plastic baggies for the eager tourists. Imagine everybody's shock and dismay when with snow suits zipped up, bunny boots laced, and face masks secured, three owners of shiny new machines stepped outside to discover three persons—Cassie, Jake, and Francis, chained together and around the expensive mobiles. Louise and I joined the group of tourists outside to investigate the reason for the shouting.

"We're protesting your negligent trespassing, lack of consideration of community members, and outright disregard for the sensitive environment of the endangered Kaifrie Blue-tipped Spider," Cassie said slowly, enunciating each word carefully. She rested limp on a bright red machine, both her arms outstretched behind her, and locked to the chain which encircled three parked vehicles.

"Goddamned idiot environmentalists!" Jack shouted, "Get the hell off of this 'privitte proppertee' before we drag your asses through the snow and show you what your goddamned environment is really about."

"Really, Mrs. Thompson," Louise was red with embarrassment, "This is very inappropriate behavior. Perhaps you need to learn a few more things about our community before you go chaining yourselves to things. We don't do that kind of thing here."

I found the situation rather hilarious myself. Quite a standoff. But seeing as how my amusement was not shared by others, I drew my turtleneck up around my mouth in mock suffering of the cold and covered the giggles spilling from my lips. Francis, who had positioned himself so he was lying face up on top of one of the vehicles, spat out his mouth, "We can't budge because we suffer like the spider. You're killing our town you jerky red necks!"

One of the larger members of the group stepped forward. "I'll show you suffering if you don't get the hell off-a my machine!"

But Francis continued to wail, "You evil riders have no respect! Your machines stink! And I can hear them and smell them all the way to —"

But his futile rampage was interrupted by Herb who suddenly appeared on the scene with a .44 magnum. "That stuff's not going to work around here!" he said, and motioned for the crowd to draw back.

"Herb what are you doing?!" Louise cried. But Herb ignored her concerns and shot the gun directly into the chain. I screamed, but Cassie and Jake only winced as the noise of the bang crashed through their skulls. Francis shrieked — his eyes popping open wide as the taut metal broke apart and collapsed to the snow. The machines were free, but the three protesters were still chained to each other.

"Next time you might not be so lucky!" Herb yelled to them. "So keep the hell away from my lodge!" Jack started his snowmobile, and took off. The tourists followed his example in a flock of groaning noise, spewing black clouds of foul exhaust into the faces of the would be heroes as they parted.

If anybody thought that the act of civil disobedience would discourage further snowmachine visitors to Candle, they were dead wrong. Where before, guests had merely been in tender support of the lodge and its battle, now they were wholeheartedly involved in the idiotic hatred that had been manifested. Hatred, like vile larvae that crawl into moist nostrils of caribou, seethe in fatal numbers, and take hold of helpless victims. The snowmachiners vowed to never back down. They would now make life miserable for those who had threatened to destroy their harmless recreation. There was no other direction in which to go now but to war.

Mail day had come to mean merely a weekly meeting between me, Ella, and Zach, and sometimes Sam Hoina. Occasionally the Kissell's would come down Tuesday mornings, and, once in a blue moon, the Stevens would make the long mush also. But for the most part, the event remained intimate. The influx of Christmas packages had slowed down. The week before, there had been so many boxes and bags of letters, that the three of us were hard pressed to unload the plane and sort the mail. Fortunately, Zach came up with the ingenious idea of harnessing Uncle Hickory up to a plastic sled, and making him our porter. Hick would wait by the plane until Dale loaded the pink carrier to its limit. (Dale had finally recovered from the terrible plane wreck which had cracked his pelvis and injured his spleen). Then Hick would haul the load over to Zach's house where we would empty it and send Hick back for more. A wonderful system. Only cost us a few milk bones.

While sorting the bundles of envelopes and cards that week following Christmas, I could not help noticing a letter for Jonathan Cohen with the insignia of the U.S. Department of the Interior on it. "Hey. I wonder what this is about!" I said, "Something for Jonathan from the government!"

Ella peered over my shoulder at the large manila envelope in my hand as she pulled the rubber bands from another bundle to sort. "Hmm. Department of Interior. Well, I could certainly speculate about its importance."

"Well, better just put it in his box," Zach said matter of fact. He was right. I popped the package into the Cohen's box. Examining the return address of another's personal mail is a federal crime. Still, it was difficult not to just see it.

The scores of first class letters addressed to the Candle Lodge had not passed by me unnoticed either. The unprecedented pile of correspondence was not of Christmas cards. I know that. Christmas cards come in box-shaped colored envelopes, filled with warm karma, usually addressed in fat round handwriting with a cutsie stamp. These envelopes were long, plain, and white — the address typed carefully in the center. Neither could they be lodge inquiries. Lodge inquiries are usually off hand letters stuffed into a spare envelope. The handwriting on the front — a work of curious naivete, and the address often mixed up or missing a few items. No, it was clear that this new onslaught of first class mail was of a unique sort. One that smelled distinctly of angry protest and futile pleas.

Herb did not approach me the next time his guests complained that they had found a pile of dog excrement on their machines. But I did not have to meet Herb's accusations in order to know that the poop phantom had struck again shortly after New Year's. I could tell by the way Herb stomped around the lodge. He poked around his tool shed and the pile of old metal and lumber he called his "bone pile" in a foul mood all day. Did not say a word to either me or Louise, but wore wrinkles so deep in his brow that critters could no doubt hide in the folds. We did not ask him what he was doing out there with his tools, just let him simmer alone. I also knew "the enemy" had attacked again by the pieces of conversation I picked up from the tourists.

"Those environmentalist types think they're pretty darn tricky."

"Dem tree huggers jist make my blood boil."

"This town has a real problem on their hands."

"Disgusting, deserve what they get."

After a few days, I determined what Herb had been up to out there in the bone pile grunting and muttering to himself about near sighted fools. He had been inventorying his lumber and equipment supply to see if he had enough on hand to build a garage. Herb was not going to feel happy again until he had built his guests a safe shelter for their snowmachines. He did not discuss his plans with anybody. He did not need to—he was driven by rage. He spent an entire day warming up the backhoe, steaming as he fiddled with the propane weed burner. He must have been crazy with anger to try to start that big of a machine at -20°. Eleven hours heating it, and only one hour driving the monster in the dark. He plowed it right through Louise's snow covered garden. Louise of course erupted red and purple when she realized her precious hard-to-come-by soil was to live under a snowmachine house. But there was no stopping Herb. The next day he started sawing and hammering away with no plans, help, or foundation, for that matter. All Herb did for days was saw and bang. You could not even see him working, for the constant cloud of sawdust that boiled from the construction site.

Snowflakes tumbled from the heavens while Herbert worked. Ceaseless snow fell thick. Every now and then, Louise would interrupt her indoor chores to go out with a broom to the site of her dear old garden. Silently biting her lip to suppress unleashed sorrow for the sacrificial soil—seeded with years of Louise Kramer sweat, she would sweep the rich white cover from the salvaged lumber, from the power tools, and from Herb's hat.

Herb worked like a fiend out there in the snow. Sweating at -32°, it is a wonder his power tools behaved beneath his tight sheathed fingers. I do not know if I would be able to use a speed square effectively with mittens on. In any case, the new structure was making headway fast. Herb eventually enlisted the help of Lou O'Connor who turned out to be more than eager to have a chance to show his support for snowmachines. I gather that for weeks the O'Connor's had watched the battle unfold, and had wondered when they should step in. From their house they could probably hear the daily rantings of Bernie shouting angry snowmachine sputterings to the Francis sponge.

Lou and Herb hammered and sawed as fast as they could during the next week. But as fast as they built walls, which were stood up one by one right next to the lodge in the old garden plot, they were not fast enough to prevent a third incident of snowmachine vandalism. This time, a Sunday morning, the sabotageur had been able to find some material that was fresh and soft—unlike the frozen hard little hot dogs that composed the majority of the pile. This savage smearing was the worst incident so far. The vandal had hit every machine that was parked in front of the lodge, covering both the seat and handlebars with the foul mess. Even Lou O'Connor's machine had been hit. Unfortunately Lou, terribly fatigued from a day of hammering, had returned to home in the dark oblivious. He did not smell the stink on the seat of his pants until he had sunk his exhausted buttocks deep into the antique cloth of their sofa from the silver mine and had heard Beth's loud screech of horror.

Sick with angry repulsion, every guest in the lodge that weekend had been forced to delay their weekend departure a day while the problem was cleaned up. Having missed important appointments, angered and worried wives, disappointed colleagues, most sensible tourists would have declared never to return to evil Candle. Some did, but many vowed also to return again and again, and again, until they could know that snowmachines had won once and for all.

I had been helping at the lodge that Sunday. But once the shit hit the fan, I scurried to finish my chores, decided against doing my laundry, and got out of there as fast as I could. Besides the fact that the place stank (literally), it was none too pleasant to witness seething, screeching tourists jostling about demanding hot water and rags, complaining of ruined snowmachine suits and savage residents. In addition, Louise had scarcely recovered from the ruthless murder of her beloved garden, and the new onslaught of nasty anguish was more than her temper or nerves could bear. The kitchen was subject to severe thrashing as pots were thrown about with noisy clanging, dishes broken, and soap suds left boiling on the floor.

I slipped out while she was vehemently sharpening knives, gathered Popik, Larkspur, and Kahtna, and headed for home. With the brief parting of snow clouds, the temperature had dropped to -38° and the wind chill upon my forehead furrowed itself into a burning headache. The sky was crystal clear beneath the thin stars. A waxing crescent guided my path—sneaking light between the long lines of silent trees. The thick layer of fresh snow muffled the contact of my metal runners gliding above the fluffy pack. How wonderful to have escaped.

After I had unharnessed the dogs and put the sled away, my steps toward the house were interrupted by the sudden dip in my head lamp beam upon the snow, revealing powdery poofs where the snow had been disturbed. I shone the beam carefully on the snowy ground and steered it up and down toward the spot where I had been dumping my shovels full of dog poop. The moon beams fluttered in and out behind my head lamp's vision. The layer of snow was not uniform. There were gentle dips and wiggles beneath the freshest layer. I studied the ground carefully. Tracks that had gone unnoticed in the white storms. I tromped through them, and all the way up to the mound of poop. Washed the glow of my light over the shadowy ground. Fresh tracks. Human footsteps up and down the hill from the lodge toward the pile. Back and forth to the pile. Tracks that were not mine.

My dogs began barking wildly. I jumped and turned. My headlamp beam met that of Herb Kramer who was standing in the yard.

"Watcha lookin at Heidi?" His voice was bitter, poisonous. "The new trail you've made between your pile of shit and my pile of shit?"

I stared at him. He was a different man again. Not funny, and not tender or caring.

"I gave you chances. I don't want to see you near my lodge again." He turned and walked away. The dogs continued to bark after him.

Chapter 14

I was relieved actually, when Herb fired me. With tensions growing steadily at the lodge, I knew sooner or later something was going to pop. It was just unfortunate that my friendship with Herb had to be included in the bang. At least now I had seven days a week free to myself again. I did not have to answer hundreds of questions regarding a spider (which for all I knew did not exist), I no longer had to pretend I did not hate snowmachines, and I no longer had to brush my hair. Unfortunately, I no longer got to wash it conveniently either.

Ella was angry when I told her how Herb had fired me. I was helping her fix and clean her stove pipe. We were both unpleasantly dotted with soot, and the floor was covered with black creosote.

"You know," she said between groans as she strained to fit the pipes together, "You'd think they'd at least come up with a reason. Like say the sheets were always wrinkly, or you never swept under the beds."

"But I always <u>did</u> do a really good job. Tell me when I can let go." I hated messing with the filthy material.

"Okay, not yet. Of course you did a good job. I bet you were the best employee they've ever had. But you're missing my point. I just hate seeing everybody here forget to treat each other with respect you know? That's bullshit, him getting mad and using you for a scapegoat. Okay that should be good. You can let go."

What a relief. "Yeah, I know. It's not like I was really happy with how he treated me. But, oh well. It's over with now."

Ella dipped her hands into a bucket of dish water. "I just wish that it <u>was</u> all over."

As with everything, the news of my termination at the lodge travelled through Candle like sizzling northern lights. No doubt, many found satisfaction in the conflict. Jake and Cassie were the first to make that clear to me.

They stopped over by my place a couple of days after my sinister meeting with Herb in the black and white shadows of the dog yard. I was relaxing in my house, playing the guitar, wearing my comfy black wool pants with the large hole. I had let my dishes pile up a bit—a sticky collection on the counter. My long brown braid hung over my shoulder in a tangle of homeless wisps. When my dogs barked a greeting, I continued playing. I hoped that if the visitor was Francis, that he would just stay in the dog yard and leave me alone. A stomp on the porch as boots were kicked free of snow—no such luck. Resigned, I put down my guitar and opened the door. I was surprised to meet the clean faces of Cassie and Jake.

"Oh! Come on in, Haven't seen you folks for a while. Want some tea?

"Please." Cassie pulled her hat from her head and her lively hair bounced out onto her shoulders. "You're welcome to come over to our house any time you know."

Jake pulled out my two chairs, and I put the kettle on the burner. For some reason since their futile chaining spree at the lodge, I had not felt like visiting the two. They were too intense for me.

"Yeah, I know. I've been pretty busy." I sat down next to them.

Cassie pulled up her chair and looked at me intently, blinking her long lashes as she spoke. "Well, we heard you're not working at the lodge anymore."

I ran my fingers over the design on my mug. "Yeah, well, it was getting to be sort of a hassle anyway. I'm actually sort of relieved."

"Well of course," Cassie smiled. "We're just glad now that you can be on our side."

"Our side." The phrase annoyed me. Were there always just two sides? And why should I have to be on any one side anyway? I got up to choose some tea, and without concealing my disgust, I said, "What do you mean <u>sides</u>?"

"Well," Cassie answered licking her lips, "Now of course you've realized what a crude jerk that Herb is. What a lousy way to treat you Heidi. But you should turn your anger into something constructive. You can help us put him out of business." Jake read the expression of sick confusion on my face, and spoke up before I had a chance to tell Cassie that she was full of beans.

"He's destroying Candle's environment. He needs to be stopped before its too late."

"You know," I brushed the slop of hair from my cluttered forehead. "I don't mean to be impolite, but I really don't think you guys know what you're talking about."

Cassie laughed. "Of course we do. We've read studies on the Kaifrie spider and how it has virtually disappeared. We can see for ourselves the damage that's being caused. But there's things we can do. We're ordering some sturdy fencing material. We think you should enclose your property with it. Hopefully others will do it also. Anything we can do will help. You can also send letters to Juneau, and also encourage writing to the lodge to tell them to stop. Can we put you down for a fence?"

I poured water into their cups. "No. This isn't my property, and I don't think Ernie would want a fence."

"Too bad." The tip of Cassie's tongue glided back and forth across her upper lip. "Well, you can at least help up discourage the snow - machine traffic."

"Hmm." I was noncommittal. I had viewed enough conflict and did not feel the urge to cause anymore. So far, I had not seen evidence that Cassie and Jake had really helped the situation. If anything, they were aggravating it, getting people stirred up and angry. And as much as I could figure, they really had no reason to. The whole thing annoyed me, and I also realized that I had no interest in spending any more of my time with Cassie. I let them finish most of their small serving of tea, and then reached for my jacket.

"I guess it's time to feed my dogs. I'll walk out with you." I led the couple outside. As is the custom when dinner buckets come into view,

171

my dogs voiced their enthusiasm wildly. They danced about their houses, yanking on the chain, some jumping up on top of their houses, and back down to the snow again. "Yay! Yay! Yay!" I dished the goo into their bowls, and each dog quieted as soon as they had been served, gulping down the slop like there was no tomorrow. Cassie and Jake walked away, and I returned indoors to let my dogs finish eating in peace. Usually after dinner, the dogs are happy and mellow. Often a happy howl follows the last gulp. But that evening dessert consisted of another round of anxious barking.

"Shut up!" I yelled from inside. But the chorus of commotion persisted. "What now?" I thought. There was obviously something else outside. I put my jacket back on, and went outside again. It was 3:30 PM, and the sun had already slipped away. A mellow orange glow emanated from beyond the mountains. "Shush!" Why were the dogs still barking? Their anxiety made my head ache. I looked at their faces, jaws snapping open and closed. Eager eyes, not watching me — but every one focused on the narrow trail which led to the pile of their waste. Following the direction of their noses, I walked toward the pile. There was my glory mountain. I usually tried not to look at the darn thing too closely. I only fed it. But I knew for sure that the mound of poop had been much bigger the day before. I peered over the stinky edge. There they were again. Fresh human tracks. Damn. How disgusting can people be?

Herb was ready when the poop phantom decided to strike again. All the snowmachines were parked neatly inside the finished new garage which abutted the east end of the lodge. Herb had scrounged up an old oil stove in his bone pile. It had a few rusty spots, but the old heater was plenty adequate to keep the garage at a reasonable temperature. A large door enabled one to close the new room, and to even lock it at night if the last user so remembered. Only the metal handle which was screwed into the outside of the wooden door remained vulnerable to vandalism. The broad handle was perfect for holding large chunks of frozen poop, which blended in perfectly with the dull brown color of the metal. The excrement was camouflaged so well in fact, that the unfortunate wife of the vice president of the SnowMachine Expedition League did not notice it before she attempted to tug the door open with her bare little hands. When Bernie told me the story later of how the woman had plunged her wedding band into a pile of dog poop, he said he could hear her horrified shriek clear up to his temporary abode at the bottom of Fred's hill.

I did most of my negative thinking while sitting in the outhouse. My throne of styrofoam which was encased by three walls, offered a peaceful view of the Talana ridge mountains peeking beyond the warm green of furry spruce trees. But the lofty vantage point provided no sound barrier, nor any distraction such as bobbing ears of seven excited canine pullers with which to block out the ugly nasal buzzing which droned constantly back and forth along the main road. "The freeway" I had come to call it. I would sit there and fume as the cheery peeps of chickadees were overshadowed by ugly destruction.

Herb recruited a fleet of snowmachiners to help him haul in 12 barrels of gasoline. More fuel than Candle had ever seen at once before. He parked the blue drums just outside the new snowmachine garage, and proceeded to pump out gas to his guests at the fantastic deal of $1.60 a gallon. This excellent new service enabled lodge guests to remain in Candle longer, and to reach a new height of snowmachine exploration. Recreation possibilities were limitless. Their noise would waft up to my bench, and then all I would be able to think about was how my world was changing, how little some people care. Why did humans so savor speed and pollution? And have so little respect for the land and people they trampled.

Polluting the fresh air above my head with a nasty black cloud was the extent of my stormy prowess however. Others were not quite so meek with their anger. The Thompsons had reerected a tall metal fence around their house. The new fortification was much more sturdy than its predecessor, and the accompanying sign painted in red temora **"Spider Protection Zone. Snowmachines Keep Out"** was far more provocative than the other.

The Cohens also surrounded themselves with a Thompson-provided fence. The metal beast circumscribed much of their five acres. Resigned, the Jensens had been convinced to protect their area with a fence as well, but Cal had not been able to stomach the idea of a tall metal one. When he strung a few wires about the trees that surrounded the property and hung Cassie's sign which read **"Snowmachine Free Zone"** behind a large spruce branch, you could tell that he was trying

173

to do what he was supposed to do to eliminate Axel Bend's competition, but was not wholeheartedly convinced that it was a good idea. The Jensens still owned two snowmachines and the three boys constantly fought over who got to ride them about the tarn, and who had to repair the engine damage.

I had not heard any banter flowing from the CB airwaves in a long while. My channel was quiet. I did not even know what channel everyone was on anymore—if any at all. I felt like there was some sort of secrecy going on—communications in the shadiest corners of the citizen band. I do not know why I even kept the thing on anymore. Perhaps it was part of the phenomenon of struggling to hold on with torn fingertips to the values and love we had shared as a community. I still hoped for happy conversation to bubble from the speaker—then everything would be okay.

Without the usual chatty meetings at mail, the Tuesday event began to be dull amusement. My personal mail—or lack there of—was completely devoid of stimulating material. So I came to seek amusement in other's mail. If by chance, Zach was not paying attention, I could sneak glances at the return addresses and guess the sources of the continual flood of letters swarming from the Lower-48 to the lodge. Hate mail. I was sure of it. Good things do not arrive with such abundance. A real waste of paper when you consider the reams of unread letters, quietly discounted and tossed into the firestarter box. If those environmental activists who sought to change Herb could only meet him, probably they would mourn the trees they futilely destroyed in their efforts.

I was so buried in the lodge's hate mail, and my illegal game of trying to decipher return addresses, that I barely noticed the thin airmail letter that arrived for me in the beginning of February. The envelope was one of those crinkly toilet paper kinds that only people who are lucky enough to travel very far away get to use.

Here was a return address I could not decipher. Jayapura. Where the heck was Jayapura? I needed to get out my world atlas. I clutched my solitary piece of mail. As thin as it was, it was worth more than 20 pieces of the lodge's hate mail.

"Where's Jayapura?"

"Who got a letter from Jaya-what did you say?" I looked at Zach's bearded face. He looked tired, sifting through his pile of personal junk mail.

"Jayapura. I did. What do you think, I go looking at other people's mail?"

"Hmmp." Zach was silent for a moment. Then he said, "Jayapura. Sounds Asian or something. But not Oriental. Sounds sort of South Asian or something."

Then it clicked. My eyes widened, and I instantly shoved the crinkly letter into my jacket pocket. I knew who the letter was from. I could feel the thin wispy envelope burning my curiosity muscles. But I could not open the letter at Zach's. I had to be alone.

The whole way home my heart pounded, adrenaline connecting the contents of my jacket pocket to my heart. What did I want the letter to say? Did I even know?

Before I ripped open the toilet-paper-envelope, I made myself a cup of coffee. Did I want coffee? Yes I did. No I did not need it. Should I have some tea? What kind of tea? Hmm. Maybe coffee? Yes coffee. Hurry, damn it, open the letter.

The thin blue paper that spilled out was covered with the thin scrawlings of chicken scratching—abrupt and hurried writing.

Dear Heidi. Thanks a lot for taking care of my dogs. I hope you liked them and had fun. Sorry I haven't written you earlier. Tomorrow I am flying to Point Moresby, and then I will fly to Sidney, spend a couple of weeks there, then to LA. I should be back in Alaska around the middle of March. Hopefully the dogs will recognize me when I get home. Don't worry about cleaning the place real well or anything. I'm sure you're much neater than I am. I apologize again for not writing you earlier but I'm just not a letter writer. But I've been having a great time. Hope you are too. Thanks a lot, Ernie.

P.S. Say hello to Herbert and Bernie, and tell Bernie I've found a wife for him here. EK.

The paper slipped from my fingers and I stared at the wall for a long time. The boiling water in my kettle rolled around in restless bubbles. I expected that a whole slew of emotions would pour out of me upon the decree of my fate. But the feelings train had not arrived yet. I stared at my wall, ignoring the impatient hiss of the kettle. Had I ever felt a sense of belonging in Candle? Was I glad that I was leaving? Was Candle my home? Was I now a tourist? Where would I go? Did I not despair at my loss? Would it be a singing relief to suddenly be free?

Maybe.

———————————

On February 7, the sun cleared its biggest obstacle behind my house. Instead of sneaking behind Talana ridge's high point at 2:45 PM, it soared happily over the mountain sending forth proud light and warmth as it sauntered westward. I must have gained 20 whole minutes of sunlight that day. The gentle windblown ripples on the snow glowed in the extra long bath of warmth. The ridges of swords surrounding the Kaluatna glacier were brilliant in the far off blue light. At 4 PM they were swallowed up by quiet rosy pink. They smiled in their limelight until dusk, when they became just lumpy shapes towering over the darkness.

Enclosed by danger, those high mountains were untouchable still. I wished that I could be so too. To be oblivious of the shiny black monsters that abraded the land with their mindless speed. If I only had a quarter for each time I had been forced to flee from a trail, or for each time I had been showered with exhaust. I could only laugh wistfully when I recalled the time Ella had gently coerced me to dance about amidst the white abyss of the Candle tarn with her one morning. Now it was the hub of snowmachine flight. Around and around, back and forth. The snowmachines loved the vastness as I had. Its starkness and silent views of danger however, they did not cherish.

On a sunny but -10° February day, I convinced Zach to let me borrow two dogs from his team to help me haul a load of firewood. Ella and I decided to brave the noisy scourge of snowmachines and venture up toward Talana Ridge a few miles where a bunch of dead standing spruce were known to exist. I do not know why I mentioned my plans to Francis that day. Perhaps to discourage him from my dog yard, for he was growing increasingly annoying with his constant talk and rantings about the snowmachine outrage. We were all aware of their existence, and I at least was trying my best to live with it and not feel exceedingly depressed or terrorized every time a flying ton of metal barely missed my skis, or when I heard the nauseous droning from my yard. I had in fact heard a few complaints from lodge guests, and even from a few locals throughout my two years about my dogs barking, and about the smear of their excrement on the road. I was trying to appreciate the two different types of noise and pollution and acknowledge that my self righteousness would not be a virtue. But every time I saw Francis, he had to bring up the problems.

"You should have seen it yesterday! I was hauling water for Bernie! So I'm coming up the road with a sled and two full buckets, and these assholes run me off the trail and make me spill the water I just hauled! I was so mad! I tried to throw snow at them! You know what I'm going to do next time?! I'm really going to throw something at them! That's what I'm going to do! Bernie'll help me. Those jerks! They have no right to exist!"

I usually tried to tone out Francis's naive ravings. They would only make me more upset. Anyway, I was not too pleased when I somehow mentioned to Francis that Ella and I were going logging for the day, and he volunteered to help. How should I have backed out of that one? I did not consider myself an especially mean person. However, my 20-20 hindsight did come up with quite a few phrases which I could have used to send him politely in another direction.

We did not leave my dog yard until after 11 AM. According to the radio, we were gaining nearly six minutes of day light each day. However, on Feb 11, it was still hard to get motivated at a decent hour of the dark morning.

Ella said nothing when I told her Francis was coming. Just shrugged her shoulders. I had not seen even too much of Ella lately either. One would think that since my termination at the lodge, I would have had plenty of time to visit her. But I was into mushing my dogs, and she had billions of little projects about the house. Somehow, our meetings were less frequent. I think the changes occurring in Candle had made hermits out of all of us.

No doubt Ella was a bit disappointed—as I was, that our day together was to be intruded upon by Francis. But at least it meant free help with hard work . One could not ignore that positive aspect. Ella merely smiled slowly at Francis when he skied up to my yard—ready with a harness about his waist for skijoring behind the team. Both Ella and Francis were to get a tow from me up to the wood lot, and then ski back on their own behind me and my (hopefully) full sled.

We headed up an old trail behind my house that Fred Davison had cut years before. Having never been there before, I shared my dogs' excitement in traveling new terrain. We bounded up the trail—Popik, of course, speeding up at each turn. With my mind concentrating on the fast corners and busy exploring the dense spruce forest, I did not worry about Ella and Francis skijoring behind me. I loved the suddenly secret world of trees dripping with fibrous black lichen.

Dead trees were bountiful. We would have no problem loading the sled up full of fuel. I threw in the snow hook and reached for my snowshoes. Francis was quick to kick off his skis and join me in picketing out the dogs.

"Wow! What a great way to travel!" He bared his large buck teeth in a wild grin. "Sure beats snow machining doesn't it? So quiet and no fumes! Man! Hopefully no snowmachines will come up this way!"

Ella and I refrained from commenting and instead proceeded with business. "There's a couple of good trees over here," Ella said, "I'll start snowshoeing a path over there while you turn your sled around."

I studied the hill we had just ascended. It was not extremely steep, but the grade was steady. With a heavy load, I anticipated that I would certainly become eventually out of control and bite it bad on one of those sharp turns. Better to chain up the sled. I pulled a couple of ropes out of my sled bag and began wrapping them around the runners. These "chains" would cause enough friction to keep me at a safe speed on the way home.

"Wow! Awesome!" Francis was all eyes and teeth. "I've never seen that before! Man! There's so much to dog sledding! You don't just sit on a machine and let your fat butt be raced around!"

"Hold the sled up, would ya Francis?" This would be a long day if I had to listen to Francis all the while.

"Oh sure thing! Man, could you imagine if everybody would have dogs instead of snowmachines? Could you imagine how quiet it would be around here?"

"Yeah, except for at feeding time, and when they got into fights, and when people started yelling about all the dog doo on the road." From the corner of my eye, I saw Ella, who was sizing up a few trees turn to look at me and smile with sympathetic amusement. I do not know why I felt compelled to antagonize Francis. I hated snowmachines. I loved dogs. But there was something about Francis that brought out the worst in me. He was so utterly annoying. I saw Ella put in her earplugs.

Francis continued as I finished wrapping up the runners. "Yeah but geez. At least the dogs are under control! But you know what I did to a snowmachine the other day? Ha, you'll love this, I put-" his voice drowned in the sound of Ella's chainsaw starting up, and I was glad. At that point, the buzzing voice of a chainsaw was more pleasant than the excited mutterings of Francis.

We cut and limbed eight stout trees that day—at least more than one dog sled load. I would return in the afternoon if there was time.

Certainly I was not going to bring Francis back with me on a return haul. His strong back was not worth his continual jabberings at snowmachines and talk of what he was going to do with them. It makes me exhausted just to recount Francis' banter. I kept changing the subject, or starting my chainsaw at opportune moments. He could not seem to get the point though, until late in the day when we were all swinging away with our axes, enjoying the sweet smell of freshly cut spruce needles as we freed the tall logs of their limbs. The conversation had been happily snowmachine free for sometime. Ella had entertained me with her fall plans to drive across the Lower-48 and visit her family. We had even had the opportunity to ease our sore muscles with laughter as Ella described her young nieces—painting a vivid picture of their affinity for covering their faces with spaghetti, when Francis all out of the blue says, "Did you know that snowmachines emit 10 times the particulates and pollution of an average car?"

At that point Ella put her axe down, and this is part of why I love Ella so much: looking earnestly at Francis' white face decorated with spruce bits and glistening naivete, she said, "Look Francis, we know you mean well, but frankly, we're all real sick of hearing you go off endlessly about how you hate snowmachines. We <u>know</u>. We're not maybe all so hyped about them all driving around like crazy either. But you're not helping by talking endlessly about it. You're just stressing us all out more. Maybe you need to close your mouth a little and listen to what your fellow neighbors have to say."

Right on Ella! It was that easy. Just tell him to shut up. How come I had not thought of it? Well, Francis did shut up. That is, he did not say anything more to us that day. I felt kind of bad. But not too bad. Francis did not appear to listen and open his mind anymore than before. No, through some sort of foggy mist, Francis saw clearly that it was his calling to forever free Candle of snowmachine tyranny.

As the days inched toward March, and the needle on my thermometer climbed out of its winter depression to find comfort resting between the 12 and the 24, the poop began to get really deep—if you get what I mean. Several snowmachines had been infected with an epidemic of the sleeping sickness. That is to say, they would not start. Many snowmachiners found themselves stranded out in the field and forced to hitchhike rides with any other passing mobiler, or walk long cold miles back to the lodge.

Being stranded is no joking matter. An explorer on a brand new machine capable of travelling 100 miles on one tank of gas could have found him or herself stranded somewhere up toward the Talana Glacier with no camping gear. Fortunately, the epidemic appeared to strike only locally — infecting mostly machines parked on the tarn area. Nonetheless, the many cases of stricken machines had visitors quite concerned.

At first the incidents were attributed to bad gas — that which was sold to visitors by Herbert. But when angry fingers wiggled at him, he quickly made public the fact that his gas was bought directly from Exxon, and that he himself filtered each liter two times to ensure that no extraneous sea otter whiskers made it past the pump. Then guests put their helmeted heads together and discovered that those machines which had been parked solely within the comfy oil heated lodge garage were never infected with the unfortunate condition. Only those vehicles which were left unattended for sometime outside the lodge were those that were forced to be abandoned. Ahaha! A violent attack of anti-snowmachine vandalism! Despicable. But true enough. A week into the glorious sunny days of March, the roads and tarn were littered with abandoned shiny new machines. The owners in haste to avoid penalties for arriving back to work late, had been forced to leave their cherished play-toys until they could return to Candle at a later date.

One Tuesday mail day, I and Zach were hastily sorting the bags full of first class letters addressed to the lodge, (so much hate mail you wondered what Louise and Herb were thinking), when we heard the nasal zoom of a high powered snowmachine and saw a flash of red from the corners of our eyes. By then, we were becoming accustomed to the sickening sound which constantly trespassed upon our peace and took no notice of it. We were then surprised when Uncle Hickory lifted himself from the very flat position upon Zach's floor he had taken to assuming lately and trotted toward the door wagging his tail.

"Come in!" yelled Zach, and in stepped Manny Kleinman.

Manny had been gone since October, supposedly down South visiting his kids. (Manny had kids? I know, strange). Hearsay had it that he spent the winter touring the country upon realizing that he was famous. Wherever he went, people pulled out news articles and asked the old man to sign his autograph. I also heard — and this could be a rumor — that Manny then started charging people one dollar each for performances of accordion music and his original two songs about Candle. Ella and I just about died when we tried to imagine Manny touring the nation with Ol' Griz and the accordion and selling his precious pieces of history.

I was glad to see Manny back. He looked terrific—his eyes were shiny, and his long white beard combed neatly. His bout with admiration and fame had done him good.

"Manny! Come on in. I'll get ya some orange juice!" Zach called to the little figure who stood in front of Hickory's madly wagging tail.

"Ah don't go botherin yerself Zach. Finish sortin my fan letters. I got plenty of time now that I got my own transportation!"

"Yeah I noticed! " Zach said in between pushes of the letters into the boxes. I never understood how Zach could sort while talking. Connecting the names to the proper boxes would take all my concentration.

"Where did you get the brand new snowmachine?"

"Isn't that great?" Manny was beaming. "Someone left it for me in front of my house!" Zach and I looked at each other. "Figure it was one of my wealthy admirers. Aren't those folks nice? Of course it wouldn't start right away. But I tinkered with it a bit. Pulled off the gas tank and drained it. And what do you know—ho, ho! Found a few little dog turds sitting in there. Jist mussing up all the gas and the fuel lines. Don't know how the little buggers found their way in there. But she sure purrs pretty now doesn't she?"

The piles of dog doo behind my house had become quite small considering the time of the year. But I had stopped worrying about it. What was I supposed to do? Lock up my dog shit? Right. Most people would be more than thankful to have it taken away. And I was actually. I could not feel a moral responsibility about my dog poop. Just as long as Herb and Louise did not think it was me who was dropping little frozen sausages into snowmachine gas tanks. And I am pretty sure they didn't. At least there were no more accounts of Herb storming up to my house ready to wring my neck. But I never saw him in a happy dandy mood again.

Whenever I saw Herb those two wrinkles between the brow were deeply ingrained several centimeters. I do not think Herb and Louise had ever envisioned the headache winter business would bring them. Most of their profits were eaten up by the costs of exporting stranded snowmachiners, and almost all of Herb's time was spent in the garage by the old oil heater draining gas tanks of bad gas. By the second week in March, he had over a barrel full of the poopy gas he did not know what to do with. And Lord knows, with all their hate mail, Louise and Herb already had plenty of firestarter on hand.

I did not tell anyone that I would be leaving soon. Not even Ella. For some reason, I figured it would be easier that way. We all had enough to think about already. Manny brought back the rumor from the Lower-48 that the Park Service was trying to acquire the area around Candle. Apparently a request had been made by the locals that the Federal or State government implement restrictions on motorized use in the area. This plot had many of my neighbors all stressed out. Lou worried that he would not be allowed to even run his chainsaw if such restrictions came to pass. The Stevens' did not care for snowmachines, but were worried about impediments on their way of life. Even Zach seemed to think it was a bad idea.

"This is Alaska. We should be allowed to do want we want to do, live the way we want," he said. Jack's comments were of course that "goddamned greenies were trying to run our lives." Ella would not say what she thought on the matter, but just pursed her lips and expressed once again the idea that maybe it was time for her to explore more of the world. Of course Jake and Cassie were delighted that the prospect had now become a rumor, and continued to work with Jonathan Cohen on planning possibilities.

Cal Jensen I think was uncomfortable about the whole idea, but just slunk into apathy and refused to comment on the subject—rather he always found something else to say like "So are you hosting the next town party?" or "Now this kind of canoe, now she's a beaut," or "Joan-where didya say you put that stash of Sue Bean's brandy?"

The outgoing mailbag did seem heavier than usual—filled with inquiries and comments to the legislature I suppose. Of course, we did not have phones, so none of us could for sure find out what was going on.

When the snowmachiners found out via the Candle Lodge (via Manny I suppose) exactly what sort of vandalism they had run up against, things began to get pretty ugly, or perhaps I should say, resumed being ugly. Aside from the white mountains, golden in the March sun, the blue blocks of ice cascading toward the Kaluatna

Glacier, and the red polls who had recently decided to frequent my feeder in flocks chatting aimlessly as they scattered birdseed all about my front yard, there was nothing pretty about the ongoings in Candle in those March days.

A cloud of pollution actually did hang over the valley, deposited there by hundreds of happy snowmachines; large unsightly chain link fences surrounded the property of several residents; piles of mostly frozen but yes sometimes fresh dog doo continued to be a sight along the seats and handlebars of snowmachines; abandoned hunks of metal littered the landscape; and Francis' huge white face continued to be a common sight within the area. And I say Francis was not pretty, not because of his ridiculously featured face and stringy red hair (well maybe partly), but because I somehow blame him for the stress that the area was undergoing. Certainly unjust of me, especially considering his final plight. I could have just as easily blamed Herb I suppose, or the Alaska Department of Tourism, or Jonathan Cohen for sparking up the debate, or Axel Bend for putting motorized boats on the tarn, or Bernie for making such a big deal out of nothing, or dear old Manny Kleinman for singing his stupid songs, or me I suppose. Yes me, for putting that very first piece of dog doo on that snowmachine in the first place. Honestly I only did it once—thought for some reason that it would be a good joke. I know now that it certainly was not, but never in the world expected all to come that did. Things just got out of hand. I am sorry for that.

Anyhow, as I said earlier, we all needed a scapegoat, and I certainly was not going to choose myself. No, unfair as it may have been, I maintained Francis as my scape goat because it seems to me that he was the one getting everybody all riled up and angry and stressed out. Did not keep quiet when he should have. I supposed he could not have come to Candle green and become riled up on his own. Now that I think about it, I guess Francis was a product of everyone, and it all rolled together in one ugly face.

Zach called me up on the CB a few days after mail and asked me if I had seen Hickory. No, I had not, I answered, and wondered to myself why Zach seemed anxious. Hick always roamed around wherever he wanted to. Then I wondered if Zach thought maybe something had happened to ol' Uncle Hick. What an awful thought.

Zach loved that sweet dog more than I had seen a father love a son. He talked to him constantly, as one would talk to their mate. Asked Hick where things were kept, what would be good for dinner, where to go that day. In the winter Hick always slept on Zach's bed, in the summer—on the floor right next to it, and on real, real cold nights—slept in Zach's bed, unless of course he (Hick) had worms. Zach never went anywhere without Uncle Hickory, and if visitors came, made sure they were promptly introduced to the dog before tea was prepared. I hated to think what Zach would be like without Hickory. I called him back on the CB.

"Hey Zach, did you find Hick yet?"

Zach laughed into the mike. Thank goodness. "Yup. I sure did. Not in time though. Takuma's in heat. Or was I should say. I gather things are pretty well taken care of by now." I pictured Takuma in my mind. She was a small, but beautiful dog. She had a black stripe that ran from her forehead to the tip of her nose, and a black tail. Besides that, she was frosty white—and a good strong puller.

"Well sounds like a mix you can't beat," I answered.

"Yeah well, I didn't really want any more dogs. But it shouldn't be so bad. Think about it if you want any puppies."

Oh I would have loved to have one of Hick's pups. I wish I had taken one. But I was leaving in a few days. Ernie could arrive any time. I had already started to think about how many showers per day I would have when I left, the friends I would see, all the plays and movies I would go to. And I could always come back if I wanted to. Of course I could. I had all the connections to find a place to live, and Sam Hoina would certainly hire me if I wanted a job. But at that time it was refreshing not to have to feel attached to Candle. It was not necessarily a place in which you really wanted to have ties.

The snowmachiners had had enough tyranny they decided, and had started plotting to put an end to snowmachine vandalism and the anti-snowmachine movement once and for all. On March 21—the first official day of spring (although if you ask me it marks the very middle), and the first day of spring break, ASMA and SMOG joined forces to do a little spring cleaning in Candle. The rumor had stretched to them that local residents were attempting to make the area motor proof. And if so, the snowmachiners wanted to show the world what and who mattered.

Fifty-nine of them drove into town at once. The noise was of 1,000 ruthless bumblebees. I could hear them 10 miles down the road. Lisa and Ralph could hear them way up at their house. Behind the seat of each machine, the driver sported a Jolly Roger Flag which flapped energetically in the wake of exhaust. They pulled into the lodge—not even one-third of them would fit into the garage—and told Louise who found herself exceedingly flustered to put them wherever she could. Feed them grits, stuff them together in one room. They did not care. They would pay full price, and they intended to help.

Zach called me on the CB shortly after the motorcade had arrived in town.

"Hey Heidi, Were you just up at my house?"

"No, I've been here writing letters."

"Hmm, somebody was here. The dogs just got all excited. I thought maybe you had just mushed by or something."

"Nope, wasn't me."

"Hmm. Okay, thanks."

"Yeah, check your poop pile."

"Check what?"

"Yeah, never mind Zach. Wasn't me."

"Okay, yeah, thanks."

Click, click.

I knew exactly why his dogs were barking. Only I still did not know who for sure the poop phantom was. I was not even sure that the night raider of my pile was just one person. In fact, by the number and different sizes of tracks, I was fairly confident that there were several phantoms. As for myself, I was not involved. I would like to reassert my innocence one more time. I have already confessed to my one whim.

In any case, the phantom—whoever he or she or they were, must have had a wheel barrow with them when they hit up Zach's yard, because 59 snowmachines is a lot of surface area. A plentiful amount of the stuff must be needed to sufficiently vandalize every machine. And whoever did the job sure did do an effective one. By the next morning, there was shit smeared all over every one of those Jolly Roger bearing snowmachines. What a chore that vandalism must have been in the dark frigid hours of the night. Obsessed. That is all I can say.

The pirate machiners—or whatever you want to call them had come prepared for enemy attack however. Almost all of them had secured their gas tanks with a lock. Those machines that had not been so equipped were casualties of course, but they were few. And what the phantoms had failed to notice in the dim wee night hours, was that almost all the machines had been covered with a thin film of plastic. Just rip it off in the morning, et voila, no poop! But ah yes, there was another advantage to this ingenious plastic idea of SMOG's: the poop may be collected and reused! What thoughtful conservationists! Reuse! One of the mighty three R's. Never throw away what you can reuse, unless you can throw it away and reuse it at the same time — which is exactly how these Jolly Rogers planned to take their revenge.

In all fairness, these snowmachines had full reason to seek revenge. They had initially come to Candle for pure harmless recreation, and if anything, to boost the economy. They had been met with sheer hostility, efforts to regulate them right out of existence, distasteful and altogether possibly murderous vandalism, and basic misunderstanding. You bet they felt they had a right to regain their hand. But what ensued!

The procession of snowmachines had come with extra flags, one of which they promptly offered to Jack, who very willingly attached it to his machine. (You would think he would have already thought of having one there). Then that morning, March 22, after poop-smeared plastic sheets had been collected, Jack led the expedition of vengeful motorists about town on a tour of all the supposed local offenders. You cannot imagine the noise! The din of that swarm of machines is beyond the scope of my pen. It made me nervy, scared. I felt as if something terrible were to happen. I put in a Joni Mitchell tape and turned it on full volume, did yoga, sewed, tried to think very relaxing thoughts, but still could not help wishing that Ernie had arrived before I had to witness this terrorism. What the procession did actually, was basic intimidation. Tactics learned in second grade from the school yard bully. They circled the Cohen's land, the Jensen's house, Bernie's hovel, Cassie and Jake's plot, drove past mine but did not circle it, and even went up to Lisa and Ralph's and frightened the wits out of poor little Zach. To this day I bet he trembles whenever he hears a snowmachine.

But that was not the extent of their bullying intimidation. No. Reusing their handy dog poop, the machiners hammered each house they passed with gobs of the stuff. Humiliating. They would circle the house as one beast, and then nail it. Slam Slam Slam. Remember now that the Cohens and the Thompsons had sufficient fences with which to block out such attacks. Nonetheless, as you might guess, those fences were well covered by the end of the day. The Jensen's fence had little effect in barring the hurling excrement. But the hurling excrement was a minor offense anyway since the Jensens were accustomed to having dog poop scattered about. My dogs were thrilled when the troop showered my yard with what my dogs would call last week's dinner. As the snowmachines passed, flinging their wares, the dogs barked and pounced on the gifts like kids who had just burst open a piñata full of candy.

The tactic had the most effect I am afraid, on poor Bernie. Trembling with anger so that his ribs ached upon hearing the overwhelming drone of machines circle his home, Bernie made the poor choice of letting his temper get the best of him. He grabbed his .357 magnum and opened his window a crack. He would show some genuine intimidation tactics! He pulled the trigger—planning to fire over the machiner's heads. Click. Nothing. When was the last time you cleaned your gun Bernie? Filthy as all get out. Can't expect anything to work right if you do not take proper care of it. Then again, Herb probably had kept Bernie's gun cleaning kit for the past six years. Swearing and sweating, Bernie then opened the window a bit more and stuck his head out just enough to offer appropriate remarks and finger gestures in perfect timing for a little hard turd to go WHACK on his forehead.

Did Bernie's disposition turn sour after that! Oh how much better Bernie's life could have been at that moment if he had known yoga. He slammed the window shut, ran his aching forehead under some painfully cold water, and then got on every channel of the CB ranting and raving at an oblivious Herb.

"You son of a horehound Kramer! I'll sue your butt cheeks off! I'll see the end of you!" He was not a happy soul. I did feel terrible for poor Bernie. But then, that was the extent of the snowmachiner army invasion. Deed done. Vengeance over. Most of the snowmobilers left that afternoon except for about a dozen of them. Town was calm. Hey that was not that bad. Yay! I felt relieved. Now we could all go on living normal lives. Things would be okay. Bernie would get over it. We could all get along. Couldn't we? Life would go on. Or would it?

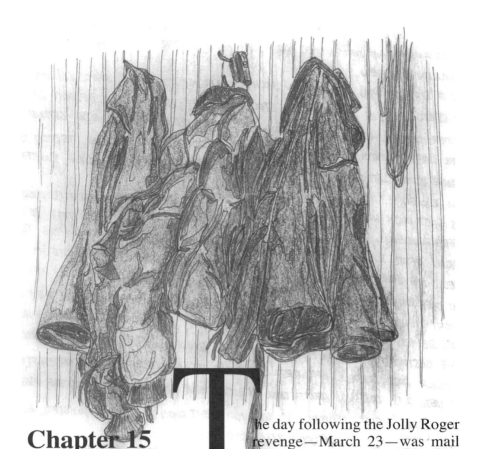

Chapter 15

The day following the Jolly Roger revenge—March 23—was mail day. I met Ella and we skied up to Zach's together. We did not talk of the preceding day's events. We did not talk too much at all actually. It was one of those warm windy March days: swirling dancing devils in the snow, and overcast. Too windy to chat. Smelled like snow would fall. Perhaps Dale would not make it in.

We were surprised to see another pair of skis leaning against Zach's porch. No one else ever skied to mail. When we pushed open the door and greeted Uncle Hickory who was busily wagging his tail, we were surprised to find Zach drinking tea with Jonathan Cohen. Jonathan must have left his home early in order to make it all the way over to Zach's by mail time. He said hello to us nervously, wide eyed and anxious looking—like a little boy on Christmas morning. He rubbed his hand along his knee as he spoke and tapped his foot.

"Didn't want to miss a great mail day!" He smiled at me and Ella and nodded his head up and down.

"I suppose," Ella answered as she pulled her hat from her head letting her brown pony tail swing about. "Looks kind of icky out though. Wouldn't you say? I wouldn't be surprised if Dale didn't come in today."

"Mm hmm." Zach nodded in agreement.

"Oh he will, he will!" Jonathan said quickly. "That is, I certainly hope he does. I'm, um, expecting something."

That was all he said, and we did not ask anymore. We waited 45 minutes for Dale. I took the occasion to give a little extra love to Uncle Hickory who had strolled over to me and put his paw on my knee.

"That boy's feeling proud of himself I suppose," Zach said grinning. "It's not everyday an old dog with a bad hip gets a chance at a young virgin."

Dale finally did make it in with our mail. He unloaded the plane in a hurry because clouds were descending as we worked. "Can't dilly dally today" he said, "Gather it will snow some big flakes soon. Chinook maybe." He gave Hick a pat on the head and was off.

Jonathan did not help us sort. He did not come to mail often enough in order to know the configuration of boxes. Instead, he sat in his chair tapping his foot, and watched us with tightly closed lips and wide eyes. As soon as he saw an official looking letter get sorted into his box, he sprang from his seat, grabbed the letter, and ripped it open. Zach, Ella, and I could not help but turn from our duties to watch Jonathan. He was so theatrical the way his anxious eyes scanned the typewritten letters—reacting with each word. Then he looked up at us. His face was beaming. "This is it! This is it! An order from the Governor himself: '**Snowmachine traffic in Candle shall be prohibited unconditionally for an indeterminate amount of time!**' Hee hee! I've got to show this to the lodge. Oh where's your CB. Can I use your CB?"

Zach took some time before moving his mouth. He, as well as Ella and I, was dumbfounded. None of us really understood what the implications of the letter were. "Sure. It's over there" Zach finally said, and then turned his attention back to the mail sorting as Jonathan called Cal.

"Hey Cal. I got it! It came! It came! We're in!"

Cal's voice did not exhibit nearly as much exuberance as that of Jonathan. No doubt he was flipping a suspender or two as he spoke. "Gee, that's good. Yeah, that's good."

"I'm going over to show this to Herb right now" Jonathan continued, "Want to join me over there so you can see Herb's face when he reads it?"

There was a pause. Jonathan tapped his foot and clicked his tongue. "Yo Cal, you copy?"

"Yeah okay Jonathan. I'll be right over. I'll just hop on my uh-. Yeah I'll get a couple of dogs and meet you in a few."

"Okay no hurry Cal. I'm on my skis you know."

"Roger, roger. See ya in a few." Jonathan started to reach for his coat. Then he stopped. "Oh. I have to call Jake and Cassie. They'll want to know. You don't mind me using your CB again do you Zach?"

"Go right ahead."

Cassie's reaction was entirely different than Cal's. She whooped with excitement into the mike. After a few congratulations and pats on her own back she said, "We want to go with you to the lodge. Why don't you drop by our house and we'll ski over there together."

After Jonathan left, we finished sorting in quiet—each thinking our own convoluted thoughts. As usual, my mailbox had nothing in it but a couple of clothing catalogues that did not even make good fire starter. When we had finished, Zach finally said "You know, this isn't right. I don't know if I feel so good about this. I know Francis is involved with Jake and Cassie, and well frankly, I am concerned that the issue may not be handled with a whole lot of tact."

"Are you saying you think we should go over there and act as mediators?" Ella asked him.

"Well," Zach pulled at his beard and folded his lips. "Maybe it would be a good idea. I'm not positive. But maybe it would be."

"All right then. Let's go on over," Ella said as she shoved her mail into her backpack.

We probably need not have worried about the issue being handled tactfully because the whole time that we had been merrily chatting and waiting for Dale, Bernie had been pacing back and forth in his little shack at the base of Fred Davison's hill, still steaming and brewing about the snowmachine attack upon his house. The whack on the head he had suffered had developed into a dandy marble sized lump, and the ensuing ache was no doubt contributing to Bernie's vehement disposition. By mid-afternoon, about the same time that Ella, Zach and I

191

were debating on the best methods of diplomacy, Bernie had worn an angry path into the plywood floor of his house.

No more injustice Bernie concluded. And tightening his back brace, set off toward the lodge to settle things with Herb face to face once and for all.

Zach and Ella and I were met on the trail by Lisa Kissell riding a beat up old snowmachine. She smiled and stopped when she saw us. "Now there's a fine trio. Where you three off to?"

Ella told her about Jonathan's letter from the Governor's office and about Jake and Cassie and Jonathan all trotting off to tell Herb. "Right," she said, "I heard something weird going on the CB when I was flipping through the channels to call you Zach. I wanted to ask you if I got any mail today."

"Ah, yup I think you did."

"So what's this about?" Lisa frowned. "Does that mean all snowmachines? I'm glad they're finally doing something. But how do they expect us to get around?"

"Well, you know about as much as we do" Zach answered. "Maybe we'll know more after this meeting."

"Right. Well, can you help me turn this thing around? I'll come with you and see what's up."

A warm wind was steadily picking up speed, and the boiling clouds gathering quite low by the time the four of us arrived at the lodge. I am still not certain who arrived on the scene first—Bernie, or Jonathan, Jake, and Cassie, but they were all there as well as Lou and Beth who had also apparently tuned into the airwaves banter and had driven down on their snowmachines to see what was going on.

Cal arrived shortly after with James driving the sled. Herb and Jack were in the garage surrounded by dead snowmachines devoid of gas tanks which were draining into 55-gallon drums. A handful of lodge guests were milling around Jack and Herb trying to help.

When Herb saw Bernie, or maybe it was Jonathan he saw first—whomever it was, Herb stopped what he was doing and told them to get out of his garage. He did not trust them around his guests' snowmachines.

"Kramer, I need to talk to you!" Bernie yelled to him in a very strained effort to control his rage."

"I've got better things to do than to talk to you Bernie" Herb started but was interrupted by Jonathan.

"Um, Herbert. I have a very important letter from the Governor's office I think you should see. Um. It mainly concerns you."

"Jesus." Jack muttered as Herb came out of the garage wiping his hands on his work pants and grumbling "What for god sakes?"

Now this was complicated, so forgive me if I do not have the next sequence of events completely straight. But this is how I think it happened. As large flakes of warm snow began to spatter the ground, Jonathan talked to Herb in his very civil and soft voice. "Um, Yes Herb. If you would take a few moments to read this letter I have here, you might in reading it notice that it has been decided by a few persons that — ."

He was interrupted by Cassie who yelled out, "Snowmachine use is now against the law!"

Who was interrupted by Bernie who stepped forward to Herb and yelled "Kramer! That's twice your people have tried to kill me!"

"Goddamned idiot greenies. Leave us the hell alone!" Jack stepped out of the garage.

"Really, Jonathan," Beth exclaimed, "What is all of this about?"

"I'll tell you what it's about!" Jack stormed. "It's about you folks trying to push us around!" and with his statement he pushed his index finger—not terribly forcefully, but aggressively into Bernie's chest.

"Don't you touch me!" Bernie yelled, and with his left hand took a hold of Jack's wrist. Jack formed a fist with his free hand, and as it headed toward Bernie's face, Herb grabbed Jack and held him. Herb's action surprised all of us, but not as much as did a flying piece of poop, which with the warm winds of a Chinook blowing, was softening. It shot out of nowhere and hit Cassie in the chest. Splat. White fluff came swirling down in globules, trying their best to maintain the condition of snow, but threatening to be rain. The great Candle Poop War had begun.

Cassie was shocked. But her reflexes were quick. With her mittens, she picked up what had not stuck to her coat. (She was obviously accustomed to handling the material) and flung it back toward Jack. She missed though, and instead, hit a Jolly Roger bearer square in the forehead.

Now do not ask me where they got it, but these lodge guests were fully equipped with poop ammunition. Reused again I suppose. Must commend them on that. Out came those remaining guests—hidden behind big clumps of falling snow, and they started hurling the stuff indiscriminately. After I saw a pellet hit Lisa, I ran for cover behind a snowmachine, and was soon joined by Ella. I was scared. I had never been involved in such a situation before. I felt as if I were in a huge scary snowball fight with lots of kids—but with no happy ending: a recess bell, or graham crackers staked in the immediate future.

Lisa, who also displayed keen familiarity with the substance, grabbed a handful, and in aiming for Herbert, hit Louise who had come outside in the blizzard to see for herself what all the screaming was about. The dogs were barking, and when I lifted my head up from behind my fort to see if they were okay, I got nailed in the cheek by Louise. Yuck. Then I could not help myself. Pure human nature took over. I wanted so badly to hit someone else with the disgusting stuff. Tension had peaked, and my only desire was to release it. I saw Jake in front of me. An excellent target. He and Cassie had started just as much trouble as anyone. I squinted my eyes to see through the blowing snow, aimed hard, and hit him good in the arm. What satisfaction.

Jake was surprised. I ducked back down behind the snowmachine. Ella was gone. I did not know where she went. But from my shelter, I saw others take cover as I had. Behind snowmachines, around corners, behind snow banks, even behind the dog sled as James Jensen and Lisa were doing. There was a choice spot, for with the dogs nervous, more ammunition was in the making. Then back and forth, the stinky brown blobs were being flung. Such anger, hatred, misunderstandings, it was all taking shape as pure shit. That is what it all boiled down to: shit.

I found out later where Ella had been. She was curled up behind Manny Kleinman's house crying. My strong Ella. How could she be crying? She, who I had seen brave the toughest, scariest terrain—this was nothing. I guess the poop war meant different things to each of us. For many, it was a release. For Ella, it meant the final breakdown of friendships, loves, and hopes she had been building for over a decade.

Bernie hit Herb square in the nose, and as the soft ick dribbled across Herb's face, Bernie yielded a loud cackle. He hooted and laughed. It was perhaps the most I had seen Bernie laugh since I met him. It must have ached his ribs something terrible, but he did not seem to care.

Herbert however, saw no humor in the situation, and started to lunge through the pelting excrement and tumbling snow toward Bernie. But just then, there was a deafening bang, which startled us all. Made me jump. It was Ol' Griz.

"What in the hell you kids all doing?" Manny held the gun which he had just shot into the air in the crook of his arm. "Ya got my poor gal all upset and dribbling tears over there, ya do."

The street was silent — our breaths muffled by the smooth whirling of heavy snow. Even the dogs were quiet.

Then, from up the street, came the flying hair of red — Francis, tearing toward us on a snowmachine screaming "YAH HOO!"

His speed was enthralling. He was heading straight for the snow-machine garage, and there was no way he would stop.

Louise screamed, and I must have also as the big white face of Francis yielded a satanic grimace and headed straight into the flimsy plywood door of the garage. Everybody ran out of the way, and the dogs resumed their anxious barking.

"YAHOO!" and Francis smashed right through the garage, splin-tering the ancient wood in his flight, and knocking over the old oil heater which faithfully pumped out blue flame to warm the room. The hot oil curled in with the gasoline on the garage floor dribbled from draining fuel tanks. As the flames from the heater approached the drums filled with bad gas, we heard the long agonizing screams of Francis. The sound was harrowing. An oscillating torment of cry which wound my stomach into knots. From the corner of my eye, I saw a flash of Uncle Hickory running heroically toward the scene of the accident.

"No Hick! No!" screamed Zach, terrified. But his calls were too late. The explosion knocked me flat, and when I opened my eyes, I saw through the blinding snow, towering hungry flames dancing evily as they devoured the garage. Zach's head fell to his chest, his lips and his eyes squinted together tight. He pressed his mittens to his face and did not move.

Roaring in the encroaching darkness, made milky by the falling snow, the shooting flames licked the garage area clean, and lurched hungrily toward the lodge. Louise shrieked and started to run inside to save her cherished belongings, but Herb held her tight and would not let her go. Wood splintered and tumbled into the hot crackle. Black clouds boiled from the mess as snow and fire battled against each other. Nature against nature.

We each stood motionless. Over 20 of us, watching the lodge break down into nothing. And we realized what we all — environmentalists, developers, mushers, snowmachiners, loners, family partners — all of us — what we all had done to each other.

Epilogue

Seven years have lapsed since I watched that fire eat away our hopes and fears, then skied home by myself to my howling dogs. I remember that ski well, wanting it to never end. Filling the tracks I made a hundred times before, happy and carefree. As the ground moved away from me, I wished my visions of the day would do the same.

I let Popik in that night, and let him sleep inside. I packaged my guitar securely and put it in the mail. Stuffed my backpack as full as it would get, and let my sweet smile get me on the back of a snowmachine waving a Jolly Roger flag and all. Left just the way I had arrived: ignorant of my future, and relying on my thumb.

Ella said that she would not mind taking care of the dogs for a week. Ernie was supposed to be in on the next mail plane, and then she thought she would be leaving soon as well. Was not quite sure where she would go after the next season of guiding. Probably New Zealand. We exchanged addresses of places where we thought we each might be, and then gave each other a warm and loving hug, tightly holding on to each other without speaking for as long as time allowed. I never wanted to let go. I can still feel her little arms wrapped around my broad back and smell the softness of her blue pile jacket.

Then we said goodbye. She could still be in New Zealand, I suppose. A couple of years ago I called the guiding outfit she had worked for. They said she had been gone a few years, took a new job.

I heard through some mutual friends in Cantwell that the Kissells left soon after I did. They went to their fish camp in Prince William Sound, and worked on the oil spill cleanup, and Lord knows where all that money took them afterward.

This flood of memories has suddenly swarmed my mind because of a letter I just received from my kid sister. Marika is eight and one-half years younger than me, and so it was very easy for a void in communication to develop between us the whole time she was in college, and I was in Alaska. I suppose she had no idea even of my time in Candle. But lately we have made attempts at getting to know each other once again.

This is her letter to me:

September 16, 1996

Hey there Heidi! Hope you're doing great down there in the Lower-48. I've been having a blast up here. I have so much to tell you! At the end of the fishing season, I met this great guy named Josh Hoina. You'd love him. He was flying for the sea food company. One day he said to me, "Hey my uncle's got this really cool place up near Cantwell. I haven't been there in a while, and would like to check it out. Do you want to come with?" So of course I was just thrilled when he asked me.

So that weekend, we get in his little plane (A 180 if you know what that is) and fly over the most outrageous scenery. Glaciers, and mountains. It was gorgeous. And we land within Candle Tarn National Monument. He said they used to land floats, but can't anymore because of it being a national monument and all. You can go in motor boats though, so we did that. His uncle has a place right on the lake way up toward the glacier—bought it from this family who went berserk and just wanted to leave one day. I guess they couldn't handle the lifestyle or something. So anyway, we boat all over the lake, or tarn, or what ever you want to call it. That was amazing. We zipped in and out of these icebergs coming off of the glacier. They're amazing. Some of them were blue—smooth and glassy. Some, all broken up, and filled with dirt. That was a really fun day. But it was pretty cold. The lake was beginning to freeze on the edges already.

Well so afterward we went to check out this old ghost town. There's really nothing there, kind of boring, but there was this old man hanging out in a rocking chair and he starts telling us all these weird stories and singing songs with his accordion. I tell you—this guy was loony senile. I do not know how he copes out there.

But anyway, so then we check out the beach, and skip some stones, and along comes this guy walking along the beach with his dog. Oh Heidi, you would <u>love</u> this dog! She's about seven years old, and her name is Chickory. She was so cute, was brown with a back splotch on back, a black mask, and a black tail, and her tail would never stop wagging. She would put her paw up on your knee, and look at you. She was so sweet! I wanted to take her with me!

The owner of the dog was really nice. He told us we should go up to the other end of the lake and check that out. He said there's an old mine up there, and this guy is buying it and is going to turn it into a ski resort. Can you believe that? That would drastically change that place which is so nice and quiet. Apparently some of the residents are bummed about it and want to stop it.

So we drive our boat to the other end of the lake, more near the mine, and there's a big lodge there, and a bunch of little gift stores and stuff like that—way tacky, it was weird. So then we hike up toward the mine. It was really pretty with the fall colors. Oh Heidi, you would have loved it!

So anyway, that guy has already started building the ski resort. It's going to be pretty wild. We met the guy. Josh knew him already I guess. And he was really nice, but really wacko. He starts off by telling me this sick joke about mosquitoes. I won't repeat it to you, you would probably be

199

offended, but ya know, isn't that a weird way to try and get to know somebody? Telling them a sick joke? I think so.

Well anyway, I'm back in Homer now, but I really like this Josh guy, and I might end up spending more time with him there. I'll keep you posted. This letter is long enough already.

Much love,

Marika.

So there is my story more or less. Me, I ended up leaving Cantwell and eventually going to Chapel Hill, North Carolina to finish school. Shortly afterward, I moved up here to Montana. It is not Alaska, nothing could ever be as wild or rambunctious. But I like it. There is a strong Alaska connection here. A lot of people know and remember its untamed beauty, and like to talk about it.

But for now, I am happy here with this being my home. It probably will be, until things change, as things always do.